SAM GAO

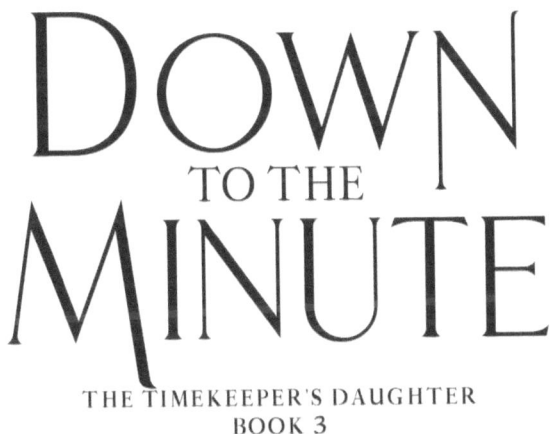

DOWN TO THE MINUTE

THE TIMEKEEPER'S DAUGHTER
BOOK 3

WHITE MOONLIGHT PRESS

E-book ISBN: 978-1-7376930-4-8
Paperback ISBN: 978-1-7376930-5-5

CHAPTER ONE
MARIA

C an I just say, I *hate* time travel?

Don't get me wrong. As far as superpowers go, it's cool as hell…until you sit down and actually think about it. You should recall from the previous two installments that intelligence isn't my strong suit. If you *haven't* read the first two books, then you're something of a time traveler, too! (That was a joke, though admittedly not a very funny one. Humor isn't my strong suit either.)

Unlike pyrokinesis or shapeshifting, time travel isn't very useful in a brawl. First off, I need some sort of blade to tear open a rift. I also need to concentrate on where I want to go, which is difficult when locked in combat. Not that I have a whole lot of experience dodging fists while trying to create a portal. I've only done it on my own once.

Despite its drawbacks, I would be remiss if I didn't add that time travel has its uses. If it didn't, I wouldn't have come back to the past in the first place.

I don't need to think of a specific year or date to travel to. I can find objects lost in time—for instance, an ancient sword with the ability to slay demons. Which, of course, is exactly what I end up doing—going back in time to find a magical sword that can solve all my problems faster than you can utter "that's way too convenient."

Yeah, *convenient*. If it were that easy, would I be lost in the past, completely unaware of what time period I've landed in? To top it off, I haven't seen the Divinities Sword. Not that I've had an opportunity to look for it. After landing in the past, nearly drowning in a lake, and running away from a group of naked men who went to bathe in said lake, I've been captured anyway by a group of elves. There, all caught up?

Oh, wait. No recap would be complete without mentioning my love life. Or lack thereof. I've had my ups and downs throughout the series (mostly downs), but the one bright spot in all this is that I'm finally experiencing being princess-carried in the arms of a super-hot guy, who just so happens to be a prince! And isn't that a prerequisite for these types of books? Something at the top of every checklist for YA romance novels? Well, y'all, I can finally cross this off my list!

But don't go cheering for me just yet. Not to be a total buzzkill, but wanna know something they don't tell you in romance novels? Being princess-carried sucks. It doesn't matter if the person carrying you is unnaturally gorgeous; it feels like lying down on two metal poles, one against my back and the other behind my knees. This can't be good for my spine. Note to self: make an appointment with the chiropractor when I get back home.

Part of the problem is being tied up. I've been taken prisoner, so of course the elves had to bind my arms and legs with rope. I don't know how masochists handle it; my skin is raw from all the rubbing and jostling. It's not like my body is in great condition anyway—as stated earlier, I literally *fell* into the past and landed in the middle of a lake. I'm drenched, cold, and tired. The elves only see me as a threat because they don't know just how physically weak I am yet. And I didn't exactly have a chance to explain myself.

Then again, even if I had been afforded the opportunity, I probably would have flubbed it due to pure shock. Because one of the first people I met here was a familiar face.

Just because the prince *looks* like Rhys doesn't mean he is. True, they are almost carbon copies of each other. I have a pretty good view from my vantage point, in his arms.

Doesn't that sound romantic? Tacking on "in his arms" to pretty much any sentence can be.

Eating peanut butter...in his arms.

Having an existential crisis...in his arms.

Questioning every interaction we've had...in his arms.

I'm getting sidetracked. My point is, the prince carrying me looks a whole lot like Rhys. Elongated elf ears poke out from a curtain of silky silver-blonde hair. He stares ahead with a stony gaze, his eyes caught somewhere between lavender and sky blue. Iridescent scales from his armor, presumably from the tail of a mermaid or a similar aquatic beast, dig into my skin. I've only known Rhys to wear button-downs and khakis, but armor adds bulk to his lean build.

Whether this is Rhys or not is the least of my concerns right now. Either way, he's captured me—not a difficult task, mind you—and I know for a fact that this isn't a sexy captive situation, since this series is *not* erotica. The best I can hope for at this point, based on how shitty the romance has been so far, are some fade-to-black sex scenes. Even at that, I highly doubt the elf prince is taking me back to his bedroom to ravish me. Don't get me wrong—in a few moments, I *will* be fucked. By life.

Yeah, I'm 80% sure he's going to torture information out of me. Doesn't that just figure? I don't think a "make love, not war" argument is going to sway him, either. I know I can't switch genres now—we've already come too far for that. But this is supposed to be a paranormal *romance* series. Where the hell is my romance? I meet all the requirements, don't I? I'm a plain-faced, mousy brunette who just discovered I have secret powers and a wealthy (albeit shitty) biological father. I grew up in foster care, for God's sake. Is a little bit of fawning too much to ask? Where the fuck is my meet-cute?

And no, walking in on Archer Kinsey naked does *not* count. That ship has sailed, anyway. I'm pretty sure he hates me, which is justified considering I lied to him about who I am. What other prospects do I have? Nic Woolridge is my cousin and he's repulsive to me as a human being. Ironic, since he's *not* human—he's half demon, a shadowborn like me. Marshall hit me in the face with a rock and threw me into a Nightmare cave. And Rhys is dead because of me.

So, yeah. Book three, and no romance for little ol' Mar. Fat chance I'll meet someone in the past, either. Can you imagine? That would be a *disaster*. I've already seen *Back to the Future*, all three movies. What if I accidentally change the future and erase myself?

Like I said, I don't know jack shit about time travel. Just that I can do it, barely. It's not my fault no one has heard of this kind of power before. Give me a pass, just this once.

Todd and Jenna haven't explained much to me, either. They're time travelers, too, and the least helpful, most cryptic people I'll ever meet. They told me that I'm "meant" to be in the past, or something along those lines, and they'll fix any mistakes I make. That would be much easier to believe if Todd and Jenna didn't need doors to travel. Unlike me, they can't just create a portal out of nowhere. But, looking around, I don't see any buildings or free-standing doors. I see trees, and dancing shadows, and the glow of a lantern in front of me.

Nights in the Veil are dark, and in the forest, no moonlight can sift between the canopy of foliage above. The prince, however, doesn't seem to have any trouble navigating. Every step he takes is calm but confident, and weirdly enough, I feel safe.

It could just be that my fight-or-flight instincts are malfunctioning, and I'm way too swayed by the fact that the prince looks like Rhys. That's probably it. Rhys always made me feel…not *safe*, per se, but calm.

But he's dead now because of me. The memory leaves a bitter taste in my mouth, but I try to shove it down. Unsurprisingly, it doesn't work. As Maria, as *myself*, I have a hard time letting go of the past. As if being a foster kid isn't bad enough, my brain tends to dwell on the negative aspects of my life to the point of obsession. That's why, for a while, I created characters—other versions of myself I pretended to be. But that's all gone out the window.

I never had to pretend in front of Rhys. I never *wanted* to, for some reason. A reason I'm afraid to explore. What can I do when he's already dead?

Anyway, I highly doubt this prince is Rhys. Sure, they look similar, but Rhys is—*was*—around my age, maybe a few years older. The prince looks to be about the same age. I don't know exactly how far back in the past I've come, but the Divinities Sword was lost hundreds of years ago. If I'm *that* far back, how could Rhys look the same? He's not a time traveler, and he wasn't a Time Agent. If I'm in the past and the prince looks the same as present-time Rhys, then how could they be the same person?

My head begins to hurt, but it could be from the blow I sustained last night. Faith slammed my head into that sink pretty hard.

But this is a new book. I refuse to get any more head injuries. I've had far too many over the span of just two books. That's enough, thank you kindly!

Glass-blown orbs of light hang in the distance, suspended in mid-air as if by magic. They illuminate the dirty path before us, revealing a clearing with an encampment of tents. The terracotta peaks of fabric pitch well over my head, at least ten feet in the air. The prince carries me down the main aisle of tents, which are arranged in neat rows, and stops at one of the larger ones. Drawing open the entrance with a gloved hand, he ducks inside with me still in his arms, my body pressed against his hard chest plate.

"Summon Kolvar," he orders, setting me down gently on a wooden table to the side.

Theodas, the elf who originally found me in the woods, hangs a lantern on what looks like a wooden coat rack above my head. He's still stark naked, though that doesn't seem to bother him at all.

The third elf, a burly man outfitted in metal armor, stands silently by the entrance. He doesn't have to say anything to send a message—*fuck with us and I'll kill you.*

"Night has fallen, and so has Kolvar. I'm certain he's

already gotten into the alcohol drums," Theodas answers, his brown plaited hair swinging behind him as he backs away. "Lyari is bathing with the rest of the group. Would you like me to summon him?"

"Lyari will do."

"Your Highness, with all due respect, this boy is not worth our efforts. We should interrogate him and kill him," the burly elf says, quickly becoming my least favorite of the bunch. *Boy*? Is he talking about me? "Slit the boy's throat and throw him in the woods. We do not need to bother Lyari with this."

Um, please someone go bother Lyari with this!

"The boy must be a fae spy," the burly elf continues. "How predictable. We just signed the treaty, and they already have their Summer Court assassins after us."

"I'm not," I interrupt in Elvish. Elves can detect lies — that's their inborn magic power — so I should use that to my advantage, right? If they know I'm not lying, maybe they'll let me go and I can continue my quest, getting as far away from the elf prince as humanly possible. Or should I say as *elvenly* possible? Get it? I'm using humor to deflect from this stressful situation. "I am not a fae spy. I am not a fairy. I have never even *met* a fairy before. I haven't ever spoken with one, and I don't plan to."

Maybe I sound too eager, but my life is on the line here. The prince studies my face, searching for something. Whatever it is, he doesn't seem to find it.

"He's telling the truth," Theodas, my nude savior, announces.

"Fae are deceitful," the burly elf argues.

"Fae are deceitful, but they cannot lie outright," Theodas explains, which is news to me. I'll just save that little nugget

9

of information for later. "They dance around the subject to avoid the truth. With these kinds of statements, it is clear the boy isn't fae. We should call a healer."

The prince nods decisively. "Theodas, summon Lyari and tell him to return at once."

Theodas gives a short bow and exits the tent, the wry smile never leaving his face.

"Your Highness—" the burly elf begins.

"Iacar, he has clearly stated he is not a fairy." The prince turns to me, his expression remaining stoic. I would expect nothing less from Rhys, if this is in fact him. "If you are not fae, who are you?"

"My name is Maria." I cringe as I say it aloud, but I'm afraid if I say something else, it will be misconstrued as a lie. If they sense even a single lie, I'm not sure how they'll treat me. Not well, probably. "I'm looking for a special sword. I got lost and fell into the lake. I didn't intend to come to your...place and harm you."

I choose my words carefully, struggling with Elvish vocabulary. I just started learning it a few months ago, and while I've improved considerably, it's still taking up a lot of brain power to communicate and understand. For the ease of this narrative, I'm filling in any missing vocabulary with guesses based on context clues.

"Maria," the prince repeats. My name sounds lyrical when he says it, and the moment I hear it, I want him to say it again. "Where is your home?"

"Georgia. It's far from here." That's a huge under-statement.

"Georgia? I have never heard of it."

"It's in the United States of America," I explain. "Through a portal to the mortal realm. Do you know of it?"

He shakes his head, confirming at least one thing for me: I'm *far* back in the past. Thank goodness I paid attention to Provost Mathers' lectures at school. Truebloods entered the first rift to the mortal realm in the 1800s, and by the 1880s, most truebloods in the Veil knew about the mortal realm. It's a big assumption, but I'm guessing if he's never heard of the mortal realm, I'm at least in the 1880s or earlier.

Which confirms that my time travel *did* work. I'm in the past, and I'm in the Veil. Now I just need the sword.

Spells require three things to work: magic, intention, and an anchor. To create the rift into the past, I used my blood as an anchor and focused hard on the Divinities Sword. I thought that meant I would land right next to the sword, but clearly I've been proven wrong. Look, it's not like I have much knowledge to go off. I'm doing my best.

If I'm this far back in time, then the prince and Rhys *have* to be different people, right? Even if truebloods age slowly, they wouldn't age slowly enough for Rhys to look the same here as he did in *my* time. That knowledge should put me at ease, but somehow it makes me…sad. Well, best not to focus on that now.

"It doesn't matter," I say quickly. "I'm far from my home and my family. I have no means of surviving on my own, and I have no intention of harming you."

"Your intentions are only to look for a sword?" the prince presses.

"Yes, I only want to look for the sword. If you release me, I won't bother you," I promise.

"It is dark and cold outside. If you have no supplies, you will die in the woods alone."

Probably true. Rhys packed me a backpack full of stuff before I left, but I doubt he could have predicted I'd need camping supplies. Even if I had the supplies, I've never been camping. I've slept outside before, but I don't think being locked out of the group home by Marissa Keystone and sleeping in my neighbor's shed counts as "camping."

"Your Highness," Iacar interrupts, "surely you cannot be suggesting—"

"Your Highness." Theodas enters the tent, along with another elf dressed in a green tunic and matching green trousers, very Peter Pan-esque. He's only a boy, a head shorter than me. His toffee-brown hair soaks his back with water, loose and long to his waist. Two silver hoops pierce his elongated ears. "Lyari is here."

"Your Highness," the new elf says, bowing his head toward the prince.

"Theodas found this boy in the woods. He is a lost traveler," the prince explains, cutting the binds on my wrists and ankles. "His head is injured."

Lyari steps before me, helping me sit and jerking my chin up with a small hand. "How old are you, child?"

Child? Funny, coming from a literal child. Lyari can't be more than thirteen, but he carries himself like an adult.

"Eighteen," I reply. I don't correct their pronouns—it's probably better that they assume I'm a man. I don't know that much about ancient elf society, but history hasn't been that gentle to women. Not to mention, I haven't seen a single woman in this encampment. That could make things dangerous for me, and without any means of protecting myself, I'm not too eager to reveal my gender.

"Eighteen?" Lyari's eyes widen in shock. "You look like a slip of a boy."

Hey, I'm bigger than *him*.

"He is older than His Highness," Theodas comments,

amused. That seems to be his default mood, not that I mind. At least one of us is having fun.

"By a year," the prince says dismissively. "His name is Maria."

Lyari examines my head. I'm afraid he'll want to see the rest of my body, but he doesn't ask. Instead, he says, "The boy needs a good wash and a change of clothes. We have clean spares. Your Highness, what do you plan on doing with him?"

"It is our obligation to care for him," the prince declares, much to Iacar's chagrin.

"It is *not*! He's a stranger!"

Theodas pipes in, "The boy is scrawny and weak."

I'd be insulted if it weren't true.

"He'll probably die on his own. We're passing through the Violet City anyway. Why not bring him along and drop him off there?"

"He's another mouth to feed," Iacar grits out. "If he gets lost in the Everwildes, it's his problem, not ours."

"We are not fae, Iacar. We are elves, and we have our honor," the prince says. "We will take the boy to the Violet City. We have the supplies to spare, and could use an extra set of hands."

"We *do* have our honor," Lyari agrees, "but Your Highness, with all due respect, this boy is not an elf. We owe him nothing."

"It is already decided. We will bring him with us."

Gee, thanks for asking *me* for my input. Though I guess I should be grateful they're not going to kill me. Quite the opposite, actually. If I can make it to the city, maybe I can find out more about the Divinities Sword. The alternative is sticking around in this area and looking for it without supplies or a way to get back home. Not that I can return empty-handed, lest another one of my family members get punished for my failures.

"At least let us search his bag for weapons," Iacar pleads. It's a reasonable request, I'll admit. "He could be an assassin."

"I'm not an assassin," I say, feeling the need to make that clear. "I have no intention of hurting anyone. I doubt I could, even if I wanted to."

I've made some progress in terms of physical strength and combat skills, but I can barely keep up with shadowborn, much less their more powerful trueblood counterparts. It's not fair that I *am* shadowborn with all the pitfalls and none of the perks. I'm weaker than my peers in more ways than one, and it's frustrating to say the least. But if life were fair, then I wouldn't be here in the first place.

I WON'T BORE YOU WITH A NIGHTMARE SEQUENCE. THAT'S my least favorite trope, you know—in books *and* movies. There's nothing out of the ordinary when it comes to what I dream about: failing my family, causing their deaths, being tortured by various bullies and foster siblings... That's already come to pass, yet the nightmares have only gotten worse, now with two additional cast members: Allegra and Rhys.

They say guilt eats at you, but for me, it's corrosive like acid. I'm not sure how much of my soul is left.

I bolt upright, my eyes stinging with tears. It's still dark out, and beside me, Lyari is fast asleep on his bedroll. The prince determined the physician's tent would be the best place to house me, giving me a change of clothes and a bedroll of my own. It's staved off the hypothermia, but my back is going to be messed up from the hard surface.

The prince kept my backpack to check its contents, which I had no desire to argue about. It's mostly clothes, anyway—nothing threatening or precious. Objects aren't meant to be held dear. They are fallible, and if they hold any meaning at all, someone will seek to destroy them. To covet something is a luxury.

I used to have a teddy bear, appropriately named Teddy. He was given to me for Christmas by one of the better foster families, and I mistook the gesture for love. Even after I left that home, I thought Teddy was proof someone loved me once, however briefly. He was my *friend*, if you can imagine how pathetic that is. And then he was thrown into the beach bonfire by that stupid bitch Alison Dolittle, one of my many enemies on the playground. Alison knew full well how much I loved that bear. She burned him anyway, teaching me a valuable lesson. Two lessons, actually.

First: if you ever get into a fight, don't wear earrings. They are very easy to tear off, even for a seven-year-old. Second: humans are cruel, and they learn how to be from a very young age. They will commit any act of evil as long as they can get away with it. And if it benefits them? Even *more* reason for them to do it. No matter who suffers.

Some people are genuinely good. Luke, for example. He didn't deserve to die, especially not like that. Shot in the head in front of his son. But Luke *did* die, because I loved him, and Neil knew that. Rhys died, too, saving me. Allegra lost her mother because of me.

The guilt spreads from my heart to my stomach, knotting my insides until I can barely breathe. These aren't things I can brush off or blame on my characters—it's because of *me*, Maria.

It's not my brightest idea, but I make my way out of the tent and into the cold night. The fresh air doesn't help me breathe better, but my tears have stopped now that I'm awake. Part of me wants to run, despite how impossible it may be. How can I run from myself? But another part of me wants to simmer in my negativity, as if to punish myself in the worst way I know how.

I try to calm my breathing, slapping my cheeks. No matter what I'm feeling now, there's no time to wallow. I can do that later. What's important is finding the Divinities Sword and getting the hell back to my own timeline. No matter what it takes.

CHAPTER TWO

"What is this?" Iacar demands. "Some sort of weapon?"

"Perhaps it's a bowl for mixing spells," Theodas suggests. "It is small and soft."

The contents of my backpack are spread out on a blanket in Lyari's tent, currently being examined by the elves. Rhys thought of everything when he packed this bag. Athleisure clothing sits folded neatly in a pile, joined by a series of brown sweatshirts, leggings, and T-shirts suitable for layering. The prince deemed the clothes safe, allowing me to change into a fresh T-shirt and a pair of sweatpants. I know I don't exactly blend in with the other elves, but I'm warm and comfortable.

My toiletries bag is currently under further investigation, however. The investigation is being carried out by Iacar, of all people, who I have learned lacks both tact and knowledge of feminine care products. If he did, I doubt he'd be shoving a menstrual cup in my face right now.

I don't even have the words to describe it in Elvish, so instead I say, "It's just a cup."

He snorts, throwing it back in my bag without much care. "And this?"

"I use it to wash myself." A 3-in-1 shampoo, conditioner, and body wash. Peach scented. It's travel size, but there are a few bottles—enough to last me at least a month. There's also toothpaste and a toothbrush, both of which the elves recognize. Apparently they have dental hygiene in this era. That, or the elves' straight, white teeth are a result of magic. I wouldn't be surprised.

"This is interesting." Theodas shakes the first aid kit like a kid shaking a present on Christmas morning. "What does it do?"

"It's for if I get injured." There are Band-Aids, disinfectants, painkillers, and unfortunately, a suture kit inside. I *really* hope I don't have to stitch myself back up. I can't even watch those types of scenes in action movies. I know they're fake, but it still creeps me out.

Lyari turns a manicure set over in his hands, crouching down. "Are these torture devices?"

Do these elves seriously think the worst of me? I guess they're being cautious, but still. I'm 5'4", on the scrawny side, and my chest is as flat as the day is long.

I shove the last of my breakfast, a roll stuffed with beef jerky, into my mouth. God only knows what animal it came from. But I'm hungry and by the time I see the granola bars in my backpack, I've already eaten half the roll. Beggars can't be choosers, and frankly it doesn't taste that bad.

Instead of explaining that nail clippers are *not*, in fact, used for torture—not normally, anyway—I have to demonstrate how they work. The elves are satisfied, or as satisfied as they *can* be, given the situation. It's not like I want to be here either, fellas.

"That seems to be everything," Theodas says with a triumphant smile. "I *knew* Maria wasn't a spy."

Yeah, because I literally *told* you that yesterday!

I can't be too frustrated with them. Their suspicion is warranted, but they still fed me and gave me a place to sleep last night. Theodas, in particular, has been nothing but friendly. Iacar and Lyari, on the other hand, aren't as easily won over.

"Pack your things," Iacar barks, glaring at me. "We leave soon. Lyari, go rouse Kolvar. He's sleeping in the cart again. Theodas, attend to His Majesty."

Lyari springs up, none too happy that Iacar is ordering him about. But he does as the older elf says, trudging his feet on his way out of the tent. Theodas follows close behind, stretching his arms over his head. Only Iacar and I are left in the tent, and an awkward silence falls between us.

In the daylight, his form seems even more massive. I always pictured elves as slender and lanky. Mostly because when I think of elves, I think of Elf on the Shelf. But Iacar is muscular, and his biceps are probably larger than my head. Theodas isn't quite at that level of muscle, but he's still jacked. I wouldn't want to receive a blow from him. I saw the definition of his muscles last night when he bared it all, without an ounce of decorum. But what the hell do *I* know about decorum?

Iacar surprises me by helping me pack my things, gentle with my belongings as he stuffs them into the backpack. It must have been waterproof, just another testament to Rhys' forward thinking, because none of my things were affected by the little dive I took in the lake yesterday.

"Ye look tired," Iacar says, his accent slightly rougher than before. A regional accent, I assume, and one he hides in proper company. "Did y'sleep alright?"

"I'm okay." After waking up in the middle of the night, I couldn't fall back asleep. "I wouldn't have survived the night if not for the elves' kindness."

Iacar grunts in response. "His Majesty abides by the old traditions. There was a time when we treated all foreigners as guests in our land. And then the fae took our 'ospitality too seriously."

"There's a treaty in place between elves and fae, isn't there?"

"For now. But it's only a matter of time before war breaks out again. The cycle will never end, because the fae want all of Eidera under their tyranny." He shakes his head. "Makes me wonder 'ow you arrived 'ere."

"What do you mean?"

"You 'ad to 'ave come on a ship," Iacar says impatiently. "But in the last few months, ships 'ave been blocked by fae. No one is allowed in unless they are 'elping the fae. You said you weren't, that you 'ad never even *met* one. So 'ow did you get to Eidera? And when?"

It's probably not what he wants to hear, but I have to ask anyway. "What is Eidera?"

Iacar looks at me incredulously, too shocked to even scowl. "Excuse me?"

"You keep talking about Eidera. Is that where we are now?"

Iacar grabs my arm immediately, dragging me to my feet. His grip is like iron, and I have to say, I'm getting tired of being grabbed by guys and dragged off somewhere. Use your words, people!

Even though I complain (in the safety of my own head), I hate to admit that I'm a little intimidated by Iacar's size and strength. He could crush my wrist if he wanted to right now, and damn is he getting close. He hauls me out of Lyari's tent and into another one across the path, surprising the elf prince with our sudden barging in.

"Iacar!" The prince jumps to his feet, shoving a letter into a book on his desk. "What are you doing? Unhand our guest at once."

"He doesn't know what Eidera is," Iacar says, his voice clipped and formal once again. "Ask him how he arrived. Where he's from. What he's even *doing* on our land."

"Iacar—"

"I don't know the word in Elvish, but I didn't come by ship. I arrived at the lake yesterday," I explain quickly. "I didn't know where I was going, and I didn't intend to come to Eidera. I used a spell of sorts to lead me to the Divinities Sword."

"A spell?" Iacar questions. "Some sort of teleportation magic?"

"Yes. It's hard to explain in another language. But I swear, my only intention is to look for the sword."

"But—"

"Iacar, enough," the prince commands. "You have seen her bag, and she carries no weapons. She also has not lied since arriving."

"*Her* bag?" Iacar turns to me. "You are a woman? So you *have* deceived us!"

"You thought I was a man in the first place!" I reply, throwing my hands up. "I don't know how you treat women here! I thought it would be safer for me!"

21

"Iacar, I will speak with her alone," the prince says wearily. "You will not say a word about this."

"My prince—"

"Go."

Iacar frowns but obeys. The elf prince, on the other hand, looks stressed as hell. Maybe he didn't get a good night's sleep either. Dark circles ring his eyes, and he's wearing the same armor from last night. If I had to wager a guess, he didn't sleep at all. Just like me.

"You aren't going to kill me, right?" I ask. "Because I'm a woman and all? I didn't lie about that. You just assumed, and I didn't correct you."

"You lied by omission, something the fae do often," the prince retorts. "Tell me about the sword you seek."

"It's called the Divinities Sword. It can defeat someone who uses blood in spells," I explain. "Do you understand?"

"A blood magic practitioner. They are more common in other parts of the realm."

"Where I'm from, there's an evil monster who can only be destroyed with the sword. If I don't get the sword and kill him, my family will die," I say, trying to appeal to his sensitive side. If he has one. Judging from his stony expression, he doesn't. "I was supposed to appear right beside the sword, take it, and leave. But I don't know where it is."

"You arrived in the lake?"

"Yes."

"Then we will look under the lake."

It doesn't take long to realize that once the prince makes a declaration, it's set in stone. If he says jump, I'm obviously supposed to ask how high. If he says we're looking for the Divinities Sword at the bottom of the lake, we're looking for the sword at the bottom of the lake.

I should probably be grateful he's helping me, though I suspect he just wants to get me out of his hair. His really nice hair.

Wait. No, Mar. Now is *not* the time to be ogling.

The way he says it so casually—"then we will look under the lake"—makes me think he's got some magic up his sleeve. We're in the Veil, after all. The benefit of being in a high-fantasy setting is writing away any plot holes with magic. But as soon as we reach the lake, the prince begins to strip.

"Oh my God!" I exclaim, spinning around.

"Excuse me?" the prince asks, unable to understand my English. I don't know the Elvish equivalent. Do they even believe in gods? Do I?

No, Mar! Not the time for a theological crisis, either.

"Why are you undressing?"

"I will drown if I wear such heavy armor."

Well, he has a point. But a little warning would've been nice. I hear a splash behind me and count to five before turning around again. The prince is still wearing an under-shirt at least, waist deep in the water.

"Don't you have a spell you can use to find the sword?" I ask dubiously. "Are you really going to swim under the lake and look for it?"

"I do not know of any spell or magic device to do that. Are you joining me or not?"

Fine. I take off my shoes and socks, leaving them in a safe, dry place on the shore. I strip to my underwear and bra, not wanting to get the rest of my clothes wet. At least the sun is shining, making the temperature bearable even when I'm half naked.

Whatever. It's not like I'm Mary Alice and I've gotta pretend to be demure. I'm Maria, like it or not.

Wading into the water, I swim toward the prince. "The lake is huge. And I didn't wait thirty minutes after eating breakfast."

"My men will not leave without us," the prince replies, definitely not grasping my limits as a human. Half human. Still not quite used to that. He dives under the water without warning, and not wanting to be left behind, I follow.

Opening my eyes, I push myself to swim to the sandy floor. Lake weeds grow sparsely, not thick enough to block my view of what lies below. There's no sword, for one. There's not much of anything. I thought I'd at least see some fish. Not that I even *like* fish. If the ones on Earth are creepy, and trust me they are, then the ones in the Veil are probably worse.

Since I don't see anything I kick back to the surface. The prince resurfaces a minute later, though he doesn't seem winded in the least. I guess he's better at holding his breath than I am.

"This is going to take a long time," I complain.

"Then we should hurry." He's completely unperturbed, diving back down.

He doesn't need to take as many breaks as I do, but even after thirty minutes, we've barely covered a fourth of the lake. I try to remember where I landed, further out toward the center, but still can't find anything.

"I appreciate your help," I begin, "but I'm cold, wet, and tired."

That seems to be a theme, nowadays.

To my shock, the prince takes the hint. "We should

return. I apologize — I thought finding your sword would be a simple matter."

"Is anything ever simple?"

"I suppose not."

We swim back toward the shore, walking on gravel and sand when the water reaches our necks. My teeth chatter, the cold air hitting my wet skin as I emerge. I wring my hair out, regretting not getting a blanket to dry off with before going in the water. I can't go back to camp in my underwear, but I don't want to ruin my clothes, either.

The prince is in worse condition than I am, but being a trueblood, it must not affect him as much. His clothes are sopping, and his long hair drips lake water down his back. This is merely an observation — no deeper meaning should be taken from it — but the water makes his white tunic transparent and leaves little to the imagination. Not that I'm staring or anything. As I said, it's an innocent(ish) observation and nothing more.

I know I joked around before about the prince ravishing me, but even if he didn't look exactly like Rhys, it would be a bad idea to get attached to someone in the past. For one, if I've taken anything from high school history classes, it's that condoms back in the olden days were made out of animal intestines. So are sausage casings. Gross! It's also a bad idea in general to get involved with people in the past, romantic or otherwise. But I don't have to explain that to you, do I?

I'm doing this because I don't see any other means of surviving on my own. The less I interact with the elves, the better. Though I imagine being cold and not forming emotional attachments should be easy for me. I'm the type of person who is only likable once you get to know me, and even then, it's debatable.

I mean, take what I just said for example. "Olden Days." I have a very vague idea of time periods from movies, but usually, time is split up in my mind as modern day, vintage, and old as time. Be it the 1800s or the 1300s, I know nothing. Why am I even a *time traveler*? Shouldn't a history buff have gotten this ability instead?

Not to mention that's *mortal* history. Forget any Veil history. I learned about it briefly at Southeastern, but everything we discussed was very general. It was a remedial class, after all.

"You are shivering. I will retrieve blankets," the prince says, avoiding looking at me. "Wait here."

Whatever you say. You're a prince, after all.

And possibly Rhys.

Look, I know it doesn't make sense. But does *any* of this make sense? I'm a time-traveling half demon in the middle of the Veil.

I didn't know Rhys for long, but spending so much time together, you pick up on things. It's hard for me to tell speech patterns in another language, but the way the prince carries himself is very reminiscent of Rhys. Then again, it could just be an elf thing. And my mind playing tricks on me, because they look exactly alike.

If the prince truly *is* Rhys, somehow…then what would I even say to him? I couldn't tell him the truth. Even being with him like this is changing the future. Unless we're working off the model of time travel where everything is already fixed, and whatever I change won't have an impact on the future. Or maybe it's a multiverse, and I'm in a *parallel* version of the past.

No, no. Too science fiction-y. This is strictly *paranormal* fantasy.

I sigh. Whether the prince is Rhys or not, I can't do anything about it. I didn't come to change the past, though I fear that might be an unintended consequence. I came here to get the sword, bring it back to the mortal realm, and defeat Astaroth once and for all. No matter what it takes.

There. *That* sounds like a chapter ender, doesn't it? Now, move along. Turn, or swipe, to the next—

The ground begins to shake, and for a second, I think it's an earthquake.

"Maria!" the prince shouts, galloping toward me on horseback. "We must go now. Do you know how to ride?"

"No! What's going on?" Isn't this chapter supposed to be over already?

He pulls me up onto the saddle, so I'm sitting squarely behind him. I have to wrap my arms around his body, mostly out of fear. Either this horse is much bigger than the ones in the mortal realm, or I've grossly underestimated how far off the ground horseback riders are.

The prince steers his horse forward, darting through the trees just as a giant begins to cross the lake. The giant in question is naked as a newborn and at least twenty feet tall. I wouldn't even reach its knee.

It lets out an animalistic roar and begins to run straight for us.

CHAPTER THREE

S ome little girls dream of a prince riding in on a white horse to come and save them. It figures I'd get a cheap knock-off version of that.

I cling to the prince as we dart through the trees, neither of us fully dressed. It's hard to care about modesty when you're galloping full speed away from a giant running toward you. The water barely slows it down, though by the time it crosses the lake, we're already halfway along the coast.

The prince tugs the reins, sending us flying deeper into the woods. We don't stop, even when we reach a dirt road. Eventually, the tremors from the giant's footsteps fade, and the horse begins to slow. It is only then that I realize how inappropriate the situation is.

Before you go clutching your pearls, or accuse *me* of clutching mine, I have to point out that I've been in much more compromising positions. But my past doesn't negate the fact that I'm now *in* the past, in my underwear, clinging to an elf prince. Despite the fact that we're both wearing clothes, they're so wet and thin we might as well be naked. I know time was of the essence and we didn't have a choice in the matter, but looking back, I probably should have grabbed my clothes from the beach before leaving. I don't even have shoes.

"We should be safe for now," the prince murmurs.

"There are creatures like that in this forest?" I ask, my voice high-pitched and squeaky.

"Of course. These are the Everwildes," he replies, as if I should know what that means.

"I know nothing about this land. The Everwildes?"

"We are in Eidera," the prince explains as the horse trots along. "Eidera is a continent originally belonging to the elves, but it is native to many kinds of creatures. Most elves and fae live in the north. The Everwildes stretch across the entire continent in the south. Due to the number of beasts in the forest, it is considered neutral territory."

"I thought you just signed a treaty with the fae. If this forest is so dangerous, why risk traveling through it?"

"There are two courts of fae—Winter and Summer. The Winter Court coerced Summer into signing the treaty; we've never had an issue with Winter fae, as we have no conflict of interest with them. The Summer fae are spiteful. If we traveled through their lands, we would only be met with malice and traps. My men are worn from war; we simply wish to return home. It is far safer to deal with the dangers of the Everwildes than continue navigating through the Summer Court's political schemes. They would invent any excuse to break the treaty, even plant false evidence and have us executed."

If that's true, then I guess they were right to be suspicious of me. "How long has this war been going on?"

"It is a constant cycle of wars and treaties," the prince admits. "I left home when I was thirteen."

"Thirteen?" I echo in shock. He's seventeen now. He's been at war for *four* years?

"Yes. I am eager to return home."

"So am I. Though I haven't been gone for four years," I add quickly. It's felt like years, but in reality, it's only been a few months. "Where are the others? Your men? Or, I guess, women?"

"Our unit consists only of men. And they are also escaping from the giant. We will meet with them at the ruins." When he sees my blank expression, he clarifies, "We'll follow the main road until nightfall, and camp out in the old Ayre ruins. They've been abandoned for years, but can provide shelter from the elements."

"You aren't afraid of...dead people?"

"Dead people?" He raises a brow. A single brow, like a magician or something. I'm instantly insatiably jealous. "What do you mean? Spirits?"

I nod vigorously. "Do you believe in, er, spirits?"

"Of course. But the ruins are not haunted. You are scared of them?"

"Yeah. You aren't?"

"No. Spirits cannot harm us," he says, wrinkling his nose. "You are quite...nonsensical at times, are you not?"

Ghosts can harm my peace of mind. It's too bad I don't have a portable DVD player in my backpack, otherwise I'd make the prince watch *The Grudge* and then we'd see who's "nonsensical."

"I'm not *nonsensical*," I reply evenly. "I'm just dumb."

"You are not dumb," the prince denies immediately.

"You simply do not know much about Eidera. I take it you have come from very far away."

"You could say that, yes." Try a whole *dimension* away. "Why are elves and fae fighting in the first place?"

"Land disputes, mostly. Elves are native to Eidera, while the fae came here by ship many years ago," he explains. "We lived peacefully and allowed them to populate uncharted areas in the east. But since now our borders touch, there have been many arguments over resources, and the fae are still looking to expand their territory. Add in political conflicts due to cultural differences and enormous egoists in power, and you have yourself a war."

That sounds like an oversimplification, but I'm grateful for the explanation all the same. It's much easier to follow when he puts it this way. Humans have waged war over less.

"Elves live a long time, right? So I guess it's easier to hold onto grudges and prejudices," I probe. "How long is an elf's life?"

"An elf's natural lifespan is long, but after so much war and strife, many have died young."

I want to ask how slowly they age, or any number of questions to discern if the prince is really Rhys without asking his name outright. But I don't know the words in Elvish, so I don't have many choices. Before I can ask him any further questions, we hear a shout from behind. Theodas rides with Lyari in his lap, and Iacar comes swiftly after on a large black stallion.

"Thank the gods," Iacar says roughly, pulling on the reins. He stops in front of us and dismounts to kneel. "My prince, the unit has scattered. We must make haste if we are to reach the ruins by nightfall. Where there is one giant, surely more roam."

"What are you wearing?" Lyari asks, squinting at me.

"Seductress! Temptress!" Iacar shouts, jumping to his feet. At least, something along those lines. He points a finger at me with a scowl. "Get away from the prince at once, wench!"

"I don't have shoes." I hold up a foot and wiggle my toes, not the most ladylike gesture. "I don't want to cut myself on rocks and branches."

"I will carry you, foul wench, if I must. Although it would dirty my hands," Iacar growls. "I will bear this burden for my prince."

"I'm not a wench and I don't want you to carry me."

"You don't have to make that sacrifice, Iacar," Theodas says seriously. "I'll do it."

Yeesh, you'd think they were talking about giving up a kidney or something. Dramatic much?

"We will find a place to rest, perhaps sand that would be more comfortable to walk on, and then we will eat," the prince suggests.

"My prince, we did not have a chance to prepare rations. My endless apologies," Iacar says. What an ass-kisser. "If we find a nice clearing, Theodas and I will hunt something for you while you rest."

"Let us continue on the road. We can discuss food later," the prince decides. "Theodas, scout ahead. Iacar will stay back."

"Yes, Your Highness," the elves say in unison.

Theodas and Iacar remain within earshot, so the prince and I continue the ride in silence. And let me tell you, riding a horse is *not* as comfortable as it looks in movies. By what I can only guess is noon, I'm afraid I've gone bow-legged.

The prince is, of course, perfectly fine. He helps me down, lifting me from the horse to a tree stump. And yes, I'm still acutely aware I'm only in my underwear. Iacar, ever the gentleman, finally gains enough sense to throw his cloak over my shoulders.

"Take it, temptress," he tells me, "and cover your vulgar body."

I'm not good at comebacks, especially not in another language, so I just accept it. At least I'm not half naked anymore, though I'm still barefoot.

"Thanks, I guess," I mutter.

"You are welcome, foul—"

"I'm not a temptress or a wench," I snap. "*Look* at me. Do I look that tempting to you?"

"Of course not. No woman can tempt me with her lustful gaze and—"

"Iacar prefers men," Lyari cuts in, toting a leather rucksack with him. "My Prince, will you be hunting?"

The prince nods. "You and Iacar should stay behind and build a fire. Tend to Maria; she is our guest."

Lyari is less argumentative than Iacar, at least to the prince's face. The boy gives a short bow, turning to me with a look of complete indifference. Suddenly, I get the feeling it's not my clothes (or lack thereof) he disapproves of. It's *me*. An outsider. To him and Theodas, and probably the rest of the elves, I'm a threat despite not being associated with the fae.

But all I can do is tell the truth—I have no identity here in the past, and nothing to make them trust me but my words. And who would believe the words of a stranger in the middle of an enchanted forest?

Well, I guess…me. I'm here with complete strangers, putting my life in their hands. And, more specifically, in the prince's hands. I tell myself I didn't have a choice, that even if I ran away, I would have no supplies and nowhere to go. But there *is* something about the prince that makes me want to trust him. His very presence makes it easy for me to be honest.

Just like Rhys.

It's an odd sort of feeling, something I've only felt with people I've known for a long time. But I don't think the prince will hurt me. He just risked his neck to help me escape the giant. Then again, my gut could be wrong. It has been before. Maybe it's best to always be on guard, to be prepared for betrayal at any point. Which I'm not. I have no backup plan, no ideas if things go south from here. I can't lie my way out of problems like I usually do, either. All I have is my own determination to survive. And my God, if that doesn't sound cheesy.

I'm not sure how the prince and Theodas are planning on hunting anything without weapons, but I'll just chalk it up to elf magic covering any plot holes here. That's the beauty of fantasy as a genre, right? The whole *deus ex machina* thing?

Lyari sits beside me while Theodas begins gathering firewood. He doesn't lift a finger to help, instead scanning me with eyes unbefitting of a tween. Lyari looks like he's seen shit, and frankly, he probably has. If he's traveling with the prince and his men now, then he probably served in the war. Growing up in an environment like that can't be good for one's mental health. Or social skills.

Exhibit A: "You are very plain," Lyari tells me. I'm not sure if he means to insult me or not, but if he does, it doesn't work.

"I know," I reply calmly. With makeup I look a lot better, but Rhys didn't pack any for me. Even if he did, it's not like I'd have the time or willpower to put some on. Who am I going to impress?

"Kolvar says that a woman must either be beautiful or talented. Rarely both. If you are not beautiful, what is your talent?"

"I'm good at lying." Though that's useless now.

Lyari squints at me. "That isn't a talent."

Trust me, kid, it is. But to be fair, I've gradually become worse at it. In my own defense, the characters were made for dealing with normal situations. Not magic ones.

"Then I guess I'm ugly and talentless," I say with a shrug.

"It's good to be honest about these things," Iacar interrupts. Somehow, when I wasn't paying attention, he actually set up a fire without matches. Did he rub two sticks together or something? I thought that only worked in movies.

Lyari doesn't feel like talking to me anymore, sprinting to the edge of the clearing to gather fallen branches and throwing them into the fire. Iacar, on the opposite end of the spectrum, watches me like a hawk.

"Ye were ill-prepared for this journey," he says finally, telling me something I already know. I'm half naked with a group of warrior elves in the middle of nowhere, with no way to protect myself, and no idea where I'm going. My period is also right around the corner, possibly coming *faster* since any sort of travel messes with my cycle. Rhys might have packed me a menstrual cup, but that's in my backpack, which is God knows where by now. Crushed under a giant's foot? Quite possibly. "'ow could yer parents 'ave let ya come 'ere alone?"

"It's hard to explain." Especially in another language. Though, even if we were both speaking English, I'd hardly want to talk about my situation with Iacar. He strikes me as the type to either be extremely sympathetic, or not at all, and I can't deal with either extreme right now.

Theodas and the prince return sometime later, dragging a deer behind them. I have no idea how they caught it or how they killed it, but after seeing them "prepare" the meat, I think I'll switch over to vegetarianism as soon as I return to my own time period. I've always seen meat wrapped in plastic at the grocery store, but that's a whole lot different from watching two elves skin, gut, and clean an animal in front of you. Worse, since I don't have shoes, I'm pretty much rooted to the tree stump I'm sitting on. The only thing I can do is spin around and try to tune out the elves talking about food.

But as soon as it's ready, my stomach betrays me by emitting a loud rumble.

"Someone is hungry," Theodas teases.

Physically, yes. Mentally, no.

On top of being a liar, weak, plain, and mentally unstable, I'm also a sell-out. Go figure. My hunger wins over my disgust, and I end up eating my serving of deer meat and then some. I don't even know what it tastes like; I just shovel it in my mouth, much to the disgust of the others.

"You eat like a savage," Iacar comments.

"This forest is dangerous. I could die at any time. I'd rather be full and dead than hungry and dead."

SAM GAO

"That doesn't make sense."

"I was hungry, leave me alone."

Theodas chuckles, while Lyari looks at me like I'm an insect. And the prince looks amused, almost. Hard to tell, given his chronic resting bitch face.

"We should continue moving. We've wasted enough time here, my prince," Iacar says. "If we're to arrive at the ruins by sundown, we must make haste."

"Yes. Theodas, put out the flames. Maria and I will ride ahead." The prince stands and lifts me into his arms again to help me onto the horse. I've gotta say, the more I'm princess carried, the more I'm growing to hate it. I need to get shoes and clothes as soon as possible so I don't have to rely on the prince. Relying on anyone for such basic things is just pathetic at this point. I know I'm not Wonder Woman, but I've spent the past few months training, getting stronger, getting…smarter? Kind of? Okay, maybe not *smarter*, but less ignorant.

The prince helps me onto the saddle before coming up, putting us in the same awkward position as before. At least I have a cloak on this time.

The ride isn't as bad as it was earlier. Or maybe it is, and I've just gotten used to being jostled around. We're not trying to escape a giant anymore, but my anxiety isn't exactly soothed. Anything could pop out at us in the Veil. Or, in this case, any*one*.

After a few hours, the prince's horse begins to slow. It isn't too long before it comes to a complete stop, looking around the trees. Nothing looks different to me, but the horse seems nervous. It backs up a few paces before going haywire, bucking the prince and I right off its back. We land ungracefully in a heap at the base of a tree, the ground not breaking our fall at all.

"Are you alright?" the prince asks immediately, sitting up.

I should be asking *him* that. He's got a nasty cut on his forehead. "I'm fine. But you're bleeding."

He ignores the blood dripping down his face and helps me up with a hand. "I am unsure what is happening, but please stay close."

"Your Highness!" Iacar rides up quickly behind us, but as soon as he draws near, his horse throws him off its back and sprints away, leaving Iacar befuddled on the ground.

"Iacar! Warn Theodas and Lyari not to—"

"Oh my. What do we have here?"

My head jerks up and I look around frantically, searching for the voice in the trees. A young man appears on horseback, wearing gilded golden armor and a wide smile.

"It has been a long time," the man says to the prince. "It looks like your horse has gone mad. Do you need help, Prince Vesryn?"

The elf prince stiffens beside me. "Prince Gwyn. What are you doing here?"

"I just happened to cross paths with you on the way back to the palace," the man says. I don't have to be an elf to know that he's spewing complete bullshit. "Do you need assistance?"

It takes a moment for me to register his question, though not directed at me. *Do you need assistance?*

He has a slight accent, yes. Vaguely European, a romance language, if I were to guess. Maybe I could pinpoint the region better if I knew more about other countries. Add that to the list of things I should study up on when I get home.

But it's not the man's voice that draws my attention, no matter how soothing and deep it is. It's his words, what he's saying, what he's *asking*. He's speaking English.

CHAPTER FOUR

I'm kind of disappointed the fae don't look like Tinkerbell. Prince Gwyn isn't so small I could step on him and run away, and he doesn't have colorful wings sprouting from his back. Unless they're hidden by his armor.

He *does* look like a Summer fae, though. I'll give him that. His brown hair is thick and curly, flowing over his shoulders with flowers strewn in the little braids. He looks at me with the most dazzling emerald-green eyes, alight with mischief. He isn't handsome like Rhys, but he has an almost boyish charm, despite his brutish bulk of muscles.

Gwyn's eyes sweep over me and I pull the cloak tighter around me. The elf prince steps in front of me as if to shield me from Gwyn's gaze.

"You always *did* have bad taste," Gwyn remarks. "Come along. I will gladly assist you, Prince Vesryn. We haven't had a chance to celebrate the treaty. Stay and have a drink with us at our camp."

"We should not. We are heading toward Ayre," the

prince explains. Or should I call him Vesryn now? Frankly, I'm a little bit surprised his name isn't Rhys. Does this mean that he and Rhys are two different people?

"You misunderstand. I was not asking." Gwyn smiles, dismounting his horse. "Iacar, good to see you again. Theodas, you as well. I see you've finally bedded a woman and created an heir. Good for you."

Theodas' face is wooden as Lyari trembles beside him, his eyes shut tight.

"I have no heirs," Theodas corrects, his voice placid.

"Ah. So you still have that nasty bout of erectile dysfunction."

"I am uninvolved by choice," he replies, maintaining an air of coldness. "It has little to do with what you suggest."

Prince Gwyn ignores him. "And you finally have a woman, too, Prince Vesryn. I thought you were too good for harlots."

Harlots? Is he talking about me?

"I will go with you, Prince Gwyn," the elf prince relents, "but the others should—"

"Nonsense. We have enough food for all five of you. Do you think I am poor, Prince Vesryn? Are you trying to say I do not have enough food for you all?" His voice drops low, dangerous. "You would dare insult me by refusing?"

"Of course not," Prince Vesryn says begrudgingly. "How far is your encampment?"

"Quite close on foot, Your Highness."

"Very well."

Gwyn raises a hand, summoning five more fae on horseback from behind us. We're surrounded now. "Let us escort our guests to the camp."

The fae encampment is not that different from the elves',

though their tents are green and blend better with the foliage around us. More fae await us when we arrive, all in thick golden armor with swords strapped to their waists. Could one of them be the Divinities Sword?

"Elaith, take our esteemed guests to a tent and give them fresh clothes and amenities," Gwyn orders. "Prepare them for dinner."

I don't think I'd taste very good.

A short bald man bows to the prince, his dark eyes trained on Prince Vesryn. "Of course, my lord. Please, *esteemed* guests, follow me to your quarters."

Barefoot, I follow the others carefully. Theodas and Iacar manage to remain completely emotionless, but Lyari isn't as good at concealing his true feelings. His hands shake, though he tries to hide it by clenching his fists so tight his knuckles turn white.

The fae Elaith takes us to a tent with a set of bedrolls tucked away on one side and a wooden bath behind a partition. He moves silently, bringing us each a set of clothes and a wet cloth to wipe our faces and hands with. I can't say I'm ungrateful, especially when Elaith gives me a pair of shoes. They're not glamorous by any means, but the sewn slippers are better than nothing at all.

"Thanks, Iacar." I shrug the cloak off my shoulders and hand it back to him. He takes it, staring at me, then Elaith, then me again.

"You tart!" he bellows. "Have you no shame?"

Elaith stares, his face flushing a deep red. I walk over, picking up the dress from him and holding it up. "Thanks."

Elaith says, "I will wait outside, my lady."

He stumbles out of the tent as quickly as he can, nearly tripping over his own two feet. Good riddance!

I slip the dress over my head, adjusting the ties on either side. It's a size too big and drags on the ground, and the style doesn't suit me at all. But the velvet is soft and warm against my skin, and it's better than being in my underwear. What's more, it smells clean.

"I have shame, by the way," I say casually, turning to Iacar. "If you want to know, I have it. But I can throw it away at any time. I guess that's a talent, too, Lyari."

The boy frowns. "You sound more coherent to me now. I understand your words clearly."

"The elves are using a Linguist's Orb, most likely. And Gwyn keeps one by his side at all times," Theodas explains. "It helps with the language barrier. Elves speak a common language, but there are many mutually unintelligible dialects in the fae language. They need the orbs to speak with their own kind."

I didn't know that kind of magic existed. That will be useful in the Veil; I should try to steal one.

"We must be careful," Prince Vesryn tells us. "We do not have the luxury of blaming our language on translation errors. It is best if we do not say or do anything offensive."

"That's not going to work," I reply immediately. "You said earlier that the fae are trying to use any excuse to take you down. Even earlier, Mr. Fairy Prince got his pants in a bunch because you tried to refuse his bogus invitation. We've gotta get out of here as soon as possible. Wait, they can't hear us, can they?"

"They are probably monitoring us," Theodas chimes in, moving behind the partition to change. "But I agree with you, Maria. Although I'm not sure what you mean by 'pants in a bunch' and 'bogus.' The translation is…imperfect."

I guess the Linguist's Orb thing doesn't do very well

with slang. "Regardless, I'm assuming we'll be forced to eat at dinner. And drink alcohol. You *do* have that here, right?"

"Yes. But Maria, what are you planning?" Theodas emerges from the partition, dressed in a black tunic and brown pants. "We must tread carefully. And you do not have any knowledge, it seems, on fae etiquette."

"I might not know about fae etiquette, but I know that this isn't a place where we can let our emotions run wild." I turn to Lyari. "You need to pull yourself together."

The boy looks at me, stunned. "Excuse me?"

"You look like you're going to rip out their throats. Not sure if you'd succeed, but that's what it looks like to me."

"You have no idea what they've done," Lyari replies in a low voice. "What kind of crap they put me through."

"I don't. But it doesn't matter right now. If you get angry, if you provoke them, we're all dead. None of us are armed, we're in a camp filled with fae, and unless you have any golden ideas, we're stuck here for now."

I know it's harsh, but I don't feel like dying because of some elf kid's angry outburst. I've made this mistake enough times myself to understand that venting your anger, even for a minute, is never worth the weighty consequences in situations like these.

You might be thinking, "Mar, you hypocritical bitch. You're lecturing a kid about losing control when you pushed Nic Woolridge off a balcony not too long ago?" Yeah. I am lecturing a kid about losing control of his emotions. The Nic thing was a mistake, and I was lucky nothing bad happened to my family afterward. But I'm not sure if this kid will be so lucky. What if they decide to kill him on the spot? I'm not going to watch a kid *die* because he mouthed off a little.

Besides, I'm only telling him what I wished someone had told *me* at his age.

"The rest of your people will be waiting for you at the Ayre ruins, right?" I ask, turning to Prince Vesryn. "If you don't show up, they're going to get worried. And then they're going to look for you and become fodder to the fae."

"Our people are not as weak as you think," Iacar interrupts.

"They don't even know the fae are here. But I'm guessing from the way the fairy prince approached us, he knew *we* were here. He probably knows about your warriors, too, which gives him the upper hand in a possible surprise attack." I lower my voice. "That's why Lyari is going to warn them."

"Pardon me?" Prince Vesryn looks at me sharply, as if seeing me for the first time. "He cannot possibly escape on his own. We are being watched, overheard—"

"The kid will know when the time comes. In the meantime, I'm going to stand behind the partition and close my eyes. Y'all should get changed. Dinner will probably be ready sooner than we expect."

THE FAE HAVE CREATED A MAKESHIFT TABLE OUT OF A tree, carved in half longways and laying perfectly on its side. Gwyn has us sit with him in the middle, packed in with fae warriors.

"This is fantastic," he calls, pouring us all drinks. I was right—they have a ton of alcohol. Even Lyari is served a glass, though I down my first one and his before anyone's the wiser. "No more war, only kinship. Isn't that right, Prince Vesryn?"

The prince nods stiffly, glancing at me.

"Oh, don't worry. Your woman doesn't interest me. I have a beautiful bride waiting for me when I return. She fetches thrice the price of your prostitute."

Hey. Are these truebloods blind? I'm *right* here. But maybe as a woman, my status doesn't matter. I'm sitting at the table, but only because Gwyn seems to think I belong to the prince. And he wants to use me as bait.

His wings are fully unfurled now. All the fae show off their wings, making it even more difficult to move or leave the table. Gwyn's, in particular, are a dazzling gold like the armor he wore earlier. They look too small in proportion to his body to be useful, but that's also what scientists say about bees. I shouldn't assume he can't fly.

"Have more, my dear," he says, leaning over to pour me a drink.

I accept it with a smile. I've already had two glasses, and while I don't feel buzzed yet, I have no idea how strong this stuff is. I shove some bread in my mouth in a feeble attempt to counteract the inevitable.

"Are you enjoying yourself?" Prince Gwyn asks me, leaning close. Not in a romantic way—I'm certain he means to intimidate me with a smile. "I had my chef prepare this feast just for you and your friends."

The food, a smorgasbord of meats, cheeses, pasta, and vegetable dishes, must have taken the whole day to prepare. There's no way it was prepared just for us, unless Prince Gwyn had his sights on the elves for a while.

"The food is divine," I reply, matching his smile with one of my own. "Your Highness, you are splendid."

"Oh, you think so?" His smile falters. "Are you, a lowly prostitute, propositioning me even though I have a bride waiting at home? You dare suggest I be unfaithful? Do you take me as a loose man?"

Vesryn opens his mouth to speak, but my reply comes faster. "Of course not. How could I, just a lowly woman, even *think* of propositioning a glorious prince such as yourself? Your Highness, it is an honor to sit at the same *table* as you. Forgive this humble servant for her crude behavior and manners. It is because of my lack of good breeding that I shame myself with my own commonness."

The elves stare at me, mouths agape.

Gwyn's mouth twists into a smile. "Well. As long as you know your place."

"Your Highness is gracious toward even the lowliest of beings," I say, laying it on thick. "I will remember this day for as long as I live. Thank you so much for having us here in your camp, at your table."

"You've found quite the submissive woman, Prince Vesryn," Gwyn comments. "She is of average face and body, but at least she understands great power when she basks in its presence."

"Your Highness, may I have the honor of serving you and your men as a display of my gratitude?"

"Why not? It is only natural that a servant such as yourself would cater to us." He waves his hand, allowing me to slip through the barrier of fairy wings and walk around the table to pour the fae warriors drinks and fetch food.

Thank God I stuffed my bra with a towel earlier. It's almost too easy. Push a little cleavage in their faces, do a little ass-kissing I learned from lewd novels, and these big, brawny warriors completely unravel. Amateurs.

Thirty minutes later, they're practically dancing on the tabletops from all the drinks I've poured. I've had quite a few myself, but unlike these guys, I know my limits.

Gwyn, meanwhile, is occupied speaking with Prince Vesryn. Neither seems drunk, but with the other fae being so rowdy, I imagine it's safe to speak to Lyari.

He's smushed between two fae, who heartily drink the wine I've poured. I made sure not to give Lyari any, but now, I think maybe I should have. He's still not very good at masking his anger or annoyance, but at least he hasn't had an outburst. Even if he does at this point, none of the fae seem to be paying him any attention.

"Get out of here, kid," I whisper, leaning over to shield him from Gwyn's view. "Find your way back to the ruins and tell them to meet us in the Violet City. You can get up from the table."

"What are you—"

"You don't have much time. Just go! I'll create a distraction." I stand with a smile, moving over to Gwyn and Prince Vesryn. While I have their attention, Lyari will hopefully be able to sprint into the forest unnoticed. "Your Highness, is everything to your liking this evening?"

"Perhaps it is the imbibements, but my dove, you seem slightly more radiant than before," Gwyn tells me.

Oh, *slightly* more radiant? Gee, thanks.

Still, I try to look flattered and smile. "Thank you, Your Highness."

"It is getting late, Prince Gwyn," Prince Vesryn says, but Gwyn doesn't even look at him. He's too busy focusing on me.

"Dove, please let me pour you a drink. You have worked hard tonight." Gwyn isn't asking. I know this well enough.

He hands me a small cup already filled with liquid, and while it's the same dark red as the other glasses, I have no idea what it contains.

Poison? Would he really poison me in front of Prince Vesryn? Gwyn thinks I'm his mistress. Then again, we're in the forest and I assume police and surveillance cameras don't exist here, let alone in this time period. I don't even know how they would do an autopsy or a toxicology report. There would be no witnesses if he were to kill me outright, and no consequences. But if I don't take the drink, couldn't he use that as an excuse to kill me anyway?

Damn it.

"She is not good with alcohol," Prince Vesryn interrupts. My gaze snaps to him, and it takes me all of two seconds to realize he's drunk as a skunk. Double damn it. I was so caught up in getting everyone else drunk, I didn't worry about intervening between the two princes. Though, to be fair, I thought the elf prince could handle himself. "I will drink it on her behalf."

"It matters not whether she is 'good' with alcohol. She cannot turn down my offer."

"Where I'm from, if one offers a drink, we must drink it in a special way. It is to show our gratitude," I explain. "May I show you, Your Highness? As a sign of my sincerity and worship?"

"You are no longer in your home country, I assume," Gwyn says, narrowing his eyes. "Just drink it, dove."

Oh, screw it. I drink it down in one gulp.

It tastes like crushed berries, but only for a moment before any sort of taste is burned away by heat and acid blazing down my throat.

Gwyn claps, a big smile on his face. "Most men cannot

handle that, let alone a weak woman such as yourself. You've earned my respect, dove. As much of it as I can give to a prostitute."

"Wow, thanks. You really know how to flatter a girl."

"Excuse me?"

"Oh fuck. Did I say that aloud? Am I speaking?"

Gwyn smiles. "You are, my dear. But it's alright. You are safe in my presence for now. So tell me. Who are you, and what are you filthy elves doing in the Everwildes?"

CHAPTER FIVE

A truth serum. Of course. I can't determine if that's better or worse than swallowing poison.

My entire body burns and my legs give way beneath me, sending me crashing to my hands and knees. Prince Vesryn leaves the table, rushing to my aide. He puts an arm around me and helps me sit, but my head is spinning so much, I can't keep myself upright without leaning against him.

"Who am I?" I repeat, the words coming out of my mouth like diarrhea. Ironic, since earlier I was spewing such shitty lies. Now I have no choice but to tell the truth. Whatever pops into my mind first. "Dude, *I* don't even know the answer to that question. I mean, my name's Mar Rochester. Like in *Jane Eyre*. When my dad abandoned me, he just *had* to choose the lamest name ever, didn't he?"

"Mar Rochester? What an unusual name," Gwyn muses. "I suppose I must ask one question at a time. I don't often have to use truth serum, but in this case, I'm glad I brought it. It doesn't work so well on elves, but you are weak."

"It's probably because I'm not a trueblood. I'm just...a

shadowborn. Not even a *strong* shadowborn. That's what they tell me, as if I don't already know. No matter how hard I train, I'm still basically human."

"I don't understand. Let us move on for now. Where are you from?"

"Douglas County, Georgia. I moved around a lot, so I don't really have a hometown."

Prince Vesryn's arms tighten around me. "Prince Gwyn, stop this at once. You have overdosed her."

"I gave her the proper amount. She simply lacks psychological resistance, her own personal failing," he replies. "I'm too interested in what she has to say. Tell me, Mar, why are you here?"

"No clue. I was supposed to land next to the Divinities Sword. I need to find it. I don't know where I am now, let alone what time I'm in."

"A sword?" Gwyn leans in closer. "What kind of sword?"

"The Divinities Sword. It's said to be able to kill blood magic practitioners. I need it to defeat Astaroth. Though to be honest, which I guess I *have* to be right now, I have no idea what a fucking sword is going to do. I'm terrible at fighting—could I even land a blow on that giant demon-man-thing? Probably not. But I've gotta get it because no other sword will be able to kill Astaroth." I sigh heavily.

Gwyn looks confused, and rightfully so. He stares at Prince Vesryn, then back at me, as if trying to figure something out. "Who is Astaroth?"

"A demon, I said. He's a giant demon who wants to... Well, I don't know what he wants. I don't know what *I* even want. But he's got a cult and he was imprisoned for something huge. Oh, and he practices blood magic. I told you that, didn't I? Hey, is the room spinning for anyone else? Anyway, he popped out of the ground like this giant, naked man-baby. Speaking of naked, he wasn't circ — "

"So, you are not looking to assist the elves?" Gwyn cuts me off, tired of my babbling.

"No. They're just bringing me to some city so I can find the sword. Actually, I need to get away from them as soon as possible. Not to be rude, but I don't want to spend more time with them than I already have."

He gives me an incredulous look, but since I've taken his truth serum thing, he's gotta trust me. Right?

"I think that should be enough questions," Prince Vesryn insists, his tone low. With my head against his chest, I can feel the rumble of his voice, and the rapid beating of his heart. Heat radiates from his body, which is kind of funny considering his cold attitude.

"I will determine when enough is enough, elf prince. Now, dove, tell me. Are you helping the elves in any way?"

"Help?" I laugh, though I'm not sure what's so funny. All of it, really. And none of it. "I'm more like a burden. Dead weight. They're the ones helping me. I...I can't help anyone. I just need to get away from here."

"You are eager to leave them, even if Prince Vesryn is your lover?"

"No, he isn't. I'm not a prostitute. I'm not a prostitute," I repeat, my words slurring. My vision blurs and I'm afraid I won't be staying conscious for much longer. Then again, maybe that's a good thing. If I'm asleep, I won't be able to answer his questions and continue making a fool of myself. "He looks like the guy who killed my dad. I have to get away from him."

Gwyn smiles, amused by my new revelation. "You think

Prince Vesryn is responsible for the death of your father? My, my. Now *that* is fascinating."

"No, no. You don't understand at all. He *looks* like Rhys. It's just…they have the same face," I babble. "And it wasn't Rhys' fault. He told Neil, but he's not the one who pulled the trigger. At the end of the day, can I really blame Rhys? Neil would've found out about everything if Rhys told him or not. But it's easier to blame Rhys than myself. That's what…I mean, that's who's really, who's fault… I'm the reason my dad died. I loved him, and everyone I love leaves me. When I was a kid, I used to think they left because I wasn't good enough. That's not true. I'm like a disease, and when people get close to me, I infect them. Or something like that. I'm not good with similes. Smileys? No, similes."

For a long moment, no one says anything. What's there to say?

I burst out laughing so hard my stomach hurts. "Fuck you. I hate talking about this shit. It's pathetic, and now I'm crying in front of a fairy prince. Or am I laughing? You know, I used to read stories about princes saving girls like me and giving them happily-ever-afters. But you're kind of a jerk since you drugged me and all. Am I going to remember this tomorrow?"

Prince Gwyn nods. "You will."

"Oh. Then double fuck you, fairy prince person. Your wings look like a butterfly's, but I hate butterflies. They're scary up close," I whisper. "Like, have you ever seen one *really* close? I have. There was one in *Spongebob* that… freaked me out. I was bugging out. Get it? Bug? You're like a bug. And you can't get mad at me for saying that 'cause you drugged me in the first place."

I can barely keep my eyelids open. They feel like they're

made of lead, and all I want to do is fall asleep. Or maybe I'm already sleeping and this is all some sort of long, hellish nightmare.

THE VOICES ABOVE ME ARE MUFFLED, AND WHEN I OPEN my eyes again, the clear night sky is covered by the roof of a tent. Peak of a tent? Whatever it's called.

Rhys sets me down on a bedroll, peering at my face with a worried expression. That makes me crack a smile, because Rhys has never really shown concern for me at all. Not when he forces me to run miles in the hot summer, or memorize vocab until I want to cry, or even when we're sparring and he mercilessly defeats me.

"I think you will be alright," he says quietly. "Just sleep."

"Thanks, Rhys. That's...that's awfully nice of you," I tell him. "I'm sorry about earlier. For telling the prince I blamed you for Luke's death."

"Maria, do I truly cause your father's death?"

"No. All you did was tell Neil that I breached our agreement. He would've found out either way. But when I watched him shoot Luke, it hurt so much. I thought what happened with Max was the lowest point in my life, but this was worse than anything I've ever felt. And just like with Max, I can't do anything about it. Even if I find the sword and kill Neil, nothing will fill the void Luke's death has left behind. I think when other people get hurt, someone teaches them how to clean the wound and apply a Band-Aid. But no one taught me how to do that, so my wounds just fester and grow. And now it's too late."

"Maria."

"I'm sorry, Rhys. I'm sorry. I didn't mean what I said to you. I wish I could go back and change things," I mutter. "I wish things could have been different. You were the only one in that hellhole I could be myself around. Even if you weren't my ally, it was a relief."

Rhys hesitates before asking me a very strange question. "What was our relationship?"

"I thought we were friends...but I was wrong. You worked for Neil. And now I'm..."

"Yes?"

"Tired," I say with a yawn. "I'm just really tired."

I WAKE UP WITH A POUNDING HEADACHE AND NOTHING but curses filling my mind. Seriously, what the fuck happened to me last night? Truth serum? Give me a fucking break. To top it off, I mistook Prince Vesryn for Rhys. How embarrassing! Where's the nearest hole? I need to bury myself *immediately*.

"Oh. You've awakened, wench."

I sit up to see Iacar and Theodas watching me from the corner, both already dressed and ready for the day. Well, isn't that just fine and dandy?

"What time is it?" I ask.

"Noontide."

Great. No idea what that means. Noon? Where's a sundial when you need one?

"Prince Gwyn has something planned for us today." Prince Vesryn's voice drifts over from behind the partition. He must be getting changed. Good—at least I can't see his face and psychoanalyze every micro-expression to cross it. "He specifically asked to wait until you rose, Maria."

That's not a good sign. Could he have discovered Lyari left?

I reluctantly get up and walk toward the tent opening, peeking outside. It's raining cats and dogs, the sky shrouded in dark storm clouds. It doesn't look like it's letting up anytime soon, but at least the tent is keeping us dry. Would the bad weather be a good chance to escape? The low visibility puts both the elves and fae at a disadvantage. I'm also not sure how well we'd do without horses.

"Was it you who orchestrated Lyari's escape?" Theodas appears behind me, so close I can practically feel his breath on the nape of my neck. I jump, nearly stumbling out into the rain until he loops his arm around my waist and pulls me back inside. "Tense, aren't we?"

"You snuck up behind me; that would startle anybody. And yes, I told Lyari to meet back with your men at the ruins and go to the Violet City without us. The fae can't hear us over the rain, can they?"

"No. We can speak freely," he assures me. "Do you have a plan to escape?"

"Oh, not a single one. I was hoping one of you did. Since y'all are warriors, don't you have experience coming up with battle strategies?"

"You were clever last night. Before I became inebriated, I heard what you were saying to Prince Gwyn." Theodas grins. "It takes a special kind of person to be able to throw away their pride, Maria. Where did you learn such a technique?"

"It's not all that special." I actually learned it from Katie Venderwahl, the biggest bitch in the ninth grade. She always twisted my words, but in front of others she'd play the victim. I ended up punching her right in the mouth. Unbeknownst to me, she was a black belt in Tae Kwon Do. Suffice to say, I lost the fight, and the bullying worsened. "Anyway, I doubt it'd work again after I called that fairy prince a bug."

"He let you survive the night, so he must have found you amusing." Prince Vesryn emerges in a plain tunic and pants, both of which look a size too small for him. I'm guessing this is another humiliation tactic from the fairy prince. What is he, thirteen?

"She has guts," Iacar admits. "For a boot-licking wench."

"I'll consider that a compliment."

"You should not."

"Too late. No takebacks."

"Iacar, Theodas. Leave us," Prince Vesryn cuts in, his gaze solely focused on me. This can't be good. "Maria and I must speak alone. Go find rations for yourselves and report back later."

And my intuition is right. Once Theodas and Iacar leave, there's no buffer between myself, the prince, and the awkwardness of the situation last night. God knows what he must think of me. All that blubbering crap about Luke, only to be followed by things about Rhys… God, and I thought I couldn't get any more pathetic. I've reached a new low.

"Do you have a plan?" I ask before he can say anything else. "Because staying here is clearly not a good idea. I told Lyari to escape and tell your men what happened, but I have no clue whether or not there's a protocol in place for this sort of thing."

"That is not what I want to discuss."

"Why not? It's the most pressing matter that comes to *my* mind. Unless…you don't trust me. That's fair," I babble. "I'm definitely not the most trustworthy person."

"No, it is not that at all. I think we should discuss last night, and what you meant about your father's death."

"I *really* can't discuss that. Like, ever. I was just drunk on Gwyn's potion, so I said all that stuff." I wave my hand. "It was all just nonsense."

"You took a truth serum. It was not nonsense."

"I don't want to talk about it." Especially not with him. With that face, exactly like Rhys'. I need to get away from him, because I am Maria, and I'm a coward. It's even harder now to shove down the guilt I feel toward him, entwined with the pain of Luke's death. And with it, shame. Always, always shame.

They say you can't run from your problems. And maybe you can't—but that won't stop me from trying.

Spinning on my heel, I dash out of the tent and into the pouring rain. My feet squelch in the mud as I race past the tents. No one is outside. It would be the perfect chance to escape. The fae aren't even after *me*—they just want the elves.

But as soon as I reach the edge of the camp, the elf prince catches up to me and puts a hand on my shoulder, pulling me back to face him. I can barely catch my breath, but the short sprint doesn't seem to have affected him at all.

The cold rain soaks us both, our clothes clinging to our skin, but the place where his hand rests on my body seems to burn right through the fabric of my dress.

"I apologize. I did not mean to…" He trails off, and for the first time since I've met him, he looks *vulnerable*. Pleading. Like he's going to get down on his knees before me and beg. But beg for what?

"What do you want from me?" My voice comes out softer than I intend over the roar of rain, but the prince has no trouble understanding.

The distance between us closes before I know it. His face hovers inches from my own, and I'm all too aware of his presence. His eyes, the same bluish-purple as Rhys'. His hair, like spun moonlight. The shape of his lips, the curve of his long ears...

There are some differences, too. Prince Vesryn is more muscular than Rhys, and his hair is longer. And while it doesn't prove anything, Rhys never looked at me the way the elf prince does.

I'm sure Rhys never saw me as more than a chore. Which is why the fact that he saved me from Faith is confusing. He told Neil about Luke, and then he turned around and died for me? Gave me a necklace that had been in his family for generations? Wrote me that letter? He signed it "Yours, Rhys." Does that mean something? Or is it how he signs all his letters?

Was it how he signed all his letters. Past tense. He's never going to write me, or anyone else, another letter.

While Rhys left so many mysteries behind—his actions seemed almost counterintuitive to the way he spoke to me—Prince Vesryn is different. They're both stone-faced, but Rhys was better at it than the prince is. The way the prince looks at me right now doesn't hide anything.

My cheeks blaze as he raises a hand, brushing wet strands of hair away from my face. My heart pounds and I swear he can hear it even over the rain. It's incredible how intimate this moment feels, with just his fingers grazing my skin.

All that matters right now is us, his face filling my vision, his hand cupping my cheek.

"My, my. Don't you two look cozy?" Gwyn's snide comment shatters the spell completely. I jump back, my mind spinning.

Was I just going to let Prince Vesryn kiss me?

I know I've kissed guys I just met before, at parties and stuff, but this isn't one of those times. I'm not sloppily drunk, I'm not Marilyn, and I'm not doing this as some sort of twisted manipulation tactic. I *wanted* to kiss him. Prince Vesryn, the elf prince. A total stranger. What's more, it felt natural. It felt *right*. Like there's something between us, some connection that isn't based on logic or shared experiences, something that can't be explained by mere words. It's electric and absolutely terrifying.

"I've come to a decision," the fae prince announces, smiling wide. He stretches a hand toward me, and I cautiously take it. The moment our palms touch, he jerks me toward him, forcing his lips onto the back of my hand. "My dove, I have decided. You will be spending the night with me."

Chapter Six

"This unscrupulous behavior should not be allowed. I forbid it," Prince Vesryn says forcefully, pacing the tent. "No, *never*. Not while I still draw breath."

"You can't *forbid* it," I point out, lounging on my bedroll. I'm a lot less worked up than before, thanks to eating breakfast. Or lunch. I still don't know what time it is, but my stomach is full and I'm staying hydrated. Isn't that what's important here?

"You are far too nonchalant about this, Maria."

"You *do* seem comfortable with this situation," Theodas chimes in. "Will you really attend to Prince Gwyn tonight?"

"I don't exactly have a choice. But look, it's not like I'm going to screw him. I'll think of something."

"Screw him?"

"You know." I motion with my fingers. "Have sex with him."

Theodas clicks his tongue. "You have a plan, then?"

"Yes." I plan to wing it.

"I do not care if you have a plan," Prince Vesryn grits

out. "If you fail, he will lay his hands on you. I will never allow that possibility."

"I must agree with my prince," Iacar says. To my utter shock, he actually looks *concerned* for me. "He would take you and ruin your prospects of marriage, sullying your name. Although he is a prince, relations out of wedlock are still frowned upon."

Oh, I almost forgot. Purity culture and sexism in the past. Well, what do I need a good reputation for? It's not like I plan on becoming a permanent resident here. "That doesn't matter. I'll think of something. But while I'm doing that, what will you three be up to?"

"It *does* matter," Prince Vesryn stresses. "I do not understand how you can be so calm about this, Maria."

"Wench, Prince Gwyn is rumored to have very specific tastes. He will beat you, to be blunt," Iacar says finally. "I don't mean to scare you, but you should not take this so lightly."

"Fine. And while he's beating me, you will be…? What? Guarded?" I sigh. "Look, here's how it is. We can't refuse his invitation, so let's turn it into an opportunity. The rain isn't going to stop anytime soon, which puts us at an advantage. You three should be getting the fae to lower their guard while I incapacitate Prince Gwyn. Get us horses we can use to escape, cut off *their* means of chasing us, and be prepared to leave at any moment."

"You? Weaken the fae prince?" Iacar scoffs. "You are but a mere slip of a girl. He is a highly trained warrior."

"Yeah. Which is why he won't see it coming. A little piece of advice for you all: most people let down their guard when they're in bed with someone. That's the perfect time to strike."

"I am still against this," Prince Vesryn announces. "I cannot guarantee your safety. Leaving you unattended with *him*... He has no sense of honor."

"I know it's a lot to ask, but I need you to trust me on this," I say firmly. "Prince Gwyn is only doing this to get under your skin. He's going to rub it in your face, make a big show of it. I'm not sure if he intends to kill me, but I'm going to approach the situation with that assumption. I'll be careful."

And Prince Vesryn shouldn't be worrying about me, anyway. He probably thinks he's responsible for me, but he isn't.

"If he hurts you..."

"He won't be the first, nor will he be the last. I'm not worked up about it, and you shouldn't be either. Now, I have to go make some preparations. You three should remember what I said."

I walk out of the tent before they can argue and make my way toward Gwyn's tent. He told me he'd have some of the servants prepare me a bath, but for a "prostitute" like myself, I don't expect much.

As soon as I draw open the tent flap, I see a large bathtub steaming in the center of the room. There's no partition for me to change and two servants stand on either side, waiting for me. What, do they want a show?

Whatever. In the group home there was no privacy. I learned to get over nudity real quick. Even before that, when I was younger, some homes would have us foster kids bathe together. Gender didn't matter, and neither did age. It was basically a communal bath.

I peel off my wet dress and undergarments, letting them fall to the ground in a soppy heap as I approach the tub. I expected a wooden basin, but instead, the material is white and smooth like porcelain. Red flower petals float to the surface and I test the water before sinking my entire body in. Sadly, this is the most comfortable I've felt during this entire trip. Beside the bath are lotions and oils and soaps that make me smell like a flower threw up on me, but not in a bad way.

The attendants pick up my clothes from the floor, not daring to look up. I take the opportunity to scrub myself down until the water cools. Who knows when the next opportunity like this will come? Might as well get squeaky clean while I have the chance.

After a thorough scrubbing, I change into a different dress—another velvet number with jewels sewn at the collar. I look like a proper medieval lady now, minus the fun headdresses. No underwear, though I assume Prince Gwyn doesn't think I'll need it. Asshole.

I talked a lot of shit earlier to Theodas, Iacar, and the prince, but in reality, I have no idea what I'm doing. One thing I know for sure is that there's not a chance in hell I'm sleeping with Mr. Fairy Prince. I might have an IUD, but I'm *not* getting some weird STD from the Veil. What would a magical STD even look like? Bees coming out of my—

You know what? I'm just *not* going to think about it.

When I'm "ready" for a "fun night" with Gwyn, the servants bring in a partition and a large bedroll, along with an assortment of pillows. As they come and go, I catch glimpses of the conditions outside. The rain isn't letting up, but it's gotten much darker out. It must be nighttime.

Gwyn enters, raindrops trailing down his face. He smiles at me, stretching a hand out. "My dove, you look...cleaner than before."

I force a smile and curtsy. "Your Highness, I have an idea. You've been working tirelessly. My people have a traditional massage method that might ease your troubles. Might I offer my services to you so that you can fully relax?"

"What do you require?"

"Fresh water, of course, Your Highness. Why don't the servants prepare that for you while I help you undress?"

He chuckles. "Eager, aren't we?"

Yeah, eager to get this the hell over with.

When I was Marilyn, I learned a lot about how to deal with guys. Of course, the way I dealt with them was extremely unhealthy and frankly I would never recommend teens to follow my example. But disclaimer aside, one of the major things I learned is that arrogant and misogynistic guys are the easiest type to manipulate. They think they're above you and they'll underestimate you. I'm positive Gwyn doesn't even see me as a human being.

Well, technically I'm not fully human. Neither is he. But you get my point.

Gwyn orders the attendants to clean and prepare the tub, while he changes behind the partition. Once the tub is filled with warm water, I rub scented oil on the sides.

"Oh? What are you doing, dove?" Gwyn asks, standing before me. I thought he would come out in a robe, since there are several sitting on a chair next to us, but instead he's fully nude. At this point, I'm not even fazed. His wings press flush against his back, folded neatly behind him. I guess this is how he fit them in his armor when we first met. They're stronger and more flexible than they appear.

"Your Highness, I just wanted everything to smell nice for you. This is part of the ritual," I explain, taking a towel from the table of toiletries. The servants leave at a wave of Gwyn's hand, standing outside the entrance of the tent in the rain. Poor bastards. "Please be careful once you get in."

He takes my hand and submerges himself in the warm water, settling to his shoulders. "I must say, I was surprised when Vesryn brought a lady of the night along on his travels. He has been quite adamantly against brothels in the past. Not much fun, you see."

I dip the towel in the water and drape it over Gwyn's neck and shoulders. Using the oil, I rub down his arms, feet, and shoulders. I've never given someone a massage, so I copy what I've seen on television and begin sliding my hands over his neck and back.

"I was going to kill you the first night we met, after giving you the truth serum. But what you said was interesting. Not a prostitute? Just a woman on a quest? And yet you sell your body to an elf."

I explicitly told him, and everyone else last night, the truth about myself and my situation. Still, the fae prince doesn't believe me. It seems that the truth interferes with his own beliefs, and rather than adjusting his beliefs, he twists the truth to suit him. How human.

"I understand why he keeps you by his side. Perhaps he sees himself in you—both 'cursed' to be alone," Gwyn muses. "Pure white doves are more to my taste. But every once in a while, I have an appetite for a singed raven. What do you think?"

"Your Highness, I am glad we understand each other. If not for your magic artifact, I would be unable to listen to your poetic metaphors."

"The Linguist's Orb. It is interesting how such a pocket-sized marble could be capable of such great magic."

"Your Highness, if it pleases you, close your eyes and relax," I soothe. "We're just getting to the good part."

I slip the wet towel over his face and pull it tight in one quick motion, shoving him down by the shoulders and holding him underwater. The element of surprise, combined with the oils I rubbed on him and the tub, is the only possible way to match his strength. I'm just shocked it works so well.

I read somewhere once that panicking while you're drowning makes the situation worse, so that's why I covered his face with the towel. I have to wait until his entire body goes limp before releasing him.

Killing Gwyn isn't my intention. I'm not sure how this whole time travel thing works yet, so what if killing someone drastically alters the future? I can't risk it.

I don't have much time. Thankfully the rain drowns out any sounds of struggle. Truebloods are more resilient than humans, so I doubt Gwyn will stay unconscious for long. I prop him up in the tub and make quick work of rummaging through his clothes. The Linguist's Orb falls out of his pocket, a blue marble thrumming with magic. I shove it in my pocket, along with several rings and coins I find on the table. They might be useful later. Scoping out my surroundings, I exit through the back of the tent, crawling in the mud on my elbows. So much for the bath.

But admittedly, that went better than I expected. The first plan I've come up with in the past actually worked out! It's too early to celebrate just yet, though. Returning to the tent with the other elves, I find only Theodas sitting alone. He leaps to his feet when he sees me, eyes wide in shock.

"Maria?"

"Shush. Where are the others?"

Theodas rushes to me, putting his hands on my shoulders. "Are you alright? What happened?"

"I'll tell you later. Gwyn is unconscious. We have to leave, *now*. There's no time to explain!"

"Alright. The prince is preparing horses, and Iacar is monitoring the guards. I was told to wait and make noise if anyone checks on us."

"Find Iacar and meet us by the horses," I say. "Also, where *are* the horses?"

"Turn right out of this tent and go past the trees and bushes. The horses are kept in a separate clearing," Theodas replies. "Hurry!"

We part without a goodbye, and I crawl once more out of the back of the tent and toward the horses. I imagine most of the fae are hidden in their tents due to the weather, but there are groups who patrol the main pathways. I hide in the bushes to avoid being seen, barely managing to sneak past two sets of guards and into the clearing.

There are at least a dozen horses with carriages, and to my surprise, the horses aren't tied to anything. There's no fence keeping them in, either. Are they just very well trained?

I search for Prince Vesryn amongst the horses, but it's difficult to see over them, or even under them. Wandering through the herd, finally I catch sight of his silvery head of hair and run toward him.

"Hey!" I grab his arm. "Iacar and Theodas are on their way. We need to be prepared to go."

"Maria?" he jerks back, shocked. "How did you—"

"No time," I remind him. "We need to go."

Prince Vesryn gives a sharp nod and mounts one of the horses, a jacked white stallion without a staddle. He offers me a hand, lifting me with impressive ease. As before, I'm clinging to his back.

Theodas and Iacar appear with no time to spare. They catch on quickly, mounting the closest horses they see and taking off. Prince Vesryn follows suit, the horse lurching to life beneath us. We take off at breakneck speed through the trees.

I'm not sure what the radius of the Linguist's Orb is, or if Gwyn has a spare, but I assume the fae will come after us once they realize they can't communicate with each other. Or when they find Gwyn's unconscious body. But for now, we've made our escape. If only every plan I made could go this smoothly.

The rain doesn't stop and neither do we. Not until we have to. The horses eventually grow tired from racing in the rain and I can barely keep myself upright. None of us have eaten or even gone to the bathroom since leaving the fae encampment.

Prince Vesryn finally begins to slow down when we reach a log cabin in the woods. It's at least two floors, and I can see the dim light of candles inside the windows.

"Your Highness, how shall we proceed?" Iacar asks. "Is this...an inn?"

"It appears so. The horses are worn and we must rest and regain our strength." The prince dismounts and gently lowers me down, placing me barefoot onto the muddy ground. My entire body feels numb from riding without a saddle for so long, and my teeth won't stop chattering. The elves are faring better than I am, though I have no doubt they're just as cold and tired.

"We have no coin. They will not take us in," Theodas says, his lips practically blue from the cold.

With a shaking hand, I reach into the pocket of my dress and pull out the jewelry I took from Gwyn earlier. I *knew* it would come in handy—I just didn't expect it to be useful so soon.

"You thieving wench!" Iacar grins wide, showing his teeth. "You took this from the fae bastard, didn't you?"

"And this," I croak, putting the Linguist's Orb in Theodas' hand. "Disable it for now. We don't want to draw attention to ourselves."

"You look frail," Theodas comments, peering into my face. "Come, let us go inside."

He doesn't have to tell me twice.

CHAPTER SEVEN

The exhaustion and stress of the day's events lead me to dream of Max.

It's a memory this time. I hate those the most. The ridiculous nightmares, like Max being a skyscraper-sized giant and crushing me, aren't nearly as scary. They're obviously fake. But the memories are real, and I can't just write them off as products of my overactive imagination or something that happened to one of my characters. Max only knew Maria. There's no buffer, no mental gymnastics I can perform to pretend otherwise.

I wake abruptly, a scream caught in my throat as I spring up in bed. My heart beats wildly and sweat pours down my face.

Just a dream, I tell myself. *It was just a dream.*

But God is that a horrible lie. It's never *just* a dream. Whenever I have these nightmares about Max, they're like intense echoes. I don't just remember how I felt, so helpless and alone and *angry* I wanted to explode. I feel it like a fresh and gaping wound, the twisted hatred and fear vibrating through my very bones.

It's been ten years since then. *Ten*. Why can't I just get over it already? Max isn't even dead and he's still found a way to haunt me. Ironically, I don't think I'd feel this horrible if he had actually died that day. The day I tried to kill him.

"Maria." Prince Vesryn calls my name, concern written all over his face. He reaches toward me, but I jerk away so violently that I slam my head against the wall.

"Please don't touch me right now," I rasp, tucking myself into the corner of the room. "I...I'm sorry."

He withdraws, dropping his hands into his lap. He sits in a wooden chair beside my bed, dressed in a fresh change of clothes. The room is small and bare, with just the bed, the chair, and a dresser. There's no mirror, which is probably a good thing since I must have fallen asleep with wet hair again.

But when I look down at myself, I'm in a dress. Different than the one I came here in. I'm even wearing underwear.

"One of the attendants here helped you disrobe," Prince Vesryn explains. "You must be hungry. I will have something arranged for you."

"How long have I been asleep?" I ask.

"It is lunchtime. You should rest more. We can leave tomorrow and reach the Violet City."

"No. We can leave today after I eat. We don't want to get caught by Gwyn and his soldiers."

"Do not concern yourself with Prince Gwyn. This inn is run by elves. Once we explained the situation, they agreed to help us. If any fae step foot near the property, I will know about it." He pauses. "He did not...hurt you, did he?"

"Gwyn? No, he didn't."

The prince nods. "I will bring you food. You can use the washroom in the hall if you would like."

A washroom? As in, an actual bathroom? Maybe all is not lost!

I've been leaving out the bathroom bits for your sake, dear readers, but I'll be honest with you: pooping in the woods is not comfortable. There's no toilet paper, only leaves. And I have to inspect each leaf to make sure there aren't bugs on them. You only make that mistake once.

I'll say it again: I *hate* time travel! All hail indoor plumbing!

The washroom has a bowl of water, a clean toothbrush, and toothpaste, but no toilet. There's a...bedpan instead. I'll leave it at that.

After cleaning myself up and taking care of business, I go back to my room and settle in bed. When the door opens again, Prince Vesryn arrives carrying a tray of stew and bread.

Theodas and Iacar trail after him, standing around my bed expectantly. With the three men around, the room suddenly feels small.

"We're safe for now, so I didn't disable the Linguist's Orb," Theodas tells me, sitting on the edge of the bed. Prince Vesryn shoots him a glare, and he abruptly stands. "I wanted to hear from you what happened yesterday. You were exhausted last night."

"Let Maria eat," the prince orders, setting the tray in my lap.

"The girl stole from the fae prince. That takes guts," Iacar says appreciatively. "How did you manage that?"

I take a bite of bread first. "I rubbed oil on him and shoved him underwater until he passed out."

"Excuse me?"

"Yeah. He had this big bathtub there, so I oiled it up, and then once he got in I rubbed oil on his body."

"His *naked* body?" Prince Vesryn presses.

"He thought he was going to take a bath, so he stripped down." I shrug and blow on a spoonful of soup. "One of the best times to surprise someone is when they're naked. Because of the oil, he had a hard time fighting me off. After he was unconscious, I stole stuff from his pockets and ran off to find you."

"Did he hurt you?" the prince demands. "Did he see *you* bare?"

"No, he didn't—but that doesn't matter. What's important is that we got out and we're safe for now. Though my legs still hurt from riding. I don't know how any of you are standing upright."

Iacar laughs, throwing his head back. Theodas joins him, nearly in tears. I don't know what's so funny. The prince isn't laughing; he's scowling.

"You mean to say that you left Prince Gwyn naked and vulnerable in the bath?" Iacar wheezes. "That little prig!"

"I didn't stare at it, so I'm not sure what size it was."

"Oh come now, my prince. It is quite humorous, is it not?" Theodas asks, clasping Prince Vesryn's shoulder. "This weak little woman bested the fae prince."

"She wounded his pride. He will come after her now, and next time he will not underestimate her," Prince Vesryn says tersely.

"Maria was brave. She should be commended for her troubles," Theodas says lightly, flashing a smile at me.

"Enough. Leave us." I've never heard the prince speak so harshly to Iacar and Theodas, but neither of them seems to mind much. They grin as they walk out, leaving the prince and me alone.

For a while, he doesn't speak, allowing me to eat in total silence. His stare is more than enough to put me on edge, not with *fear* but...

"Maria." His voice is softer now, and while he just says my name, I already know what he wants to ask.

"I'm fine," I assure him, finishing the last of the soup. "Don't worry about me, alright? I did what I had to do, and I survived. I'm good now."

"You are lying."

Rhys.

The way Prince Vesryn says it sounds *exactly* like Rhys. It catches me off guard. I don't know how, but those three words are all it takes for me to understand that this *is* Rhys. He might have a different name, and we might be in the distant past, but there's no mistaking it. The realization hits me like a ton of bricks.

"Maria," the prince says, now alarmed. He shoots to his feet. "Are you alright? Should I call someone?"

I want to be someone else right now. Anyone but myself.

Prince Vesryn is Rhys. I've been bogged down by "logic" and, frankly, hope that it wasn't him. Because if this is really Rhys, then I have to reevaluate every interaction I've had with him. Every tutoring session, every conversation over breakfast, and...

Rhys *knew* me in the past. Ever since we met, he knew

79

who I was. He even *helped* me. It doesn't make sense that he would tell Neil about Archer, does it?

I try to replay the memory in my head of when I confronted him. I assumed he was the one who told Neil, but Nic never said Rhys' name explicitly. And Rhys himself looked so surprised, he didn't immediately deny it, which I stupidly mistook as an admission of guilt. English isn't even his first language! He could have just been confused.

After the argument with Archer at the Halloween dance, I didn't see much of Allegra. It was as if she was avoiding me. And when I did see her, she looked haggard. She was with Rhys the day I confronted him. The day Nic pointed to Rhys *and* Allegra and suggested that one of them had told Neil about what happened.

Allegra must've confronted Neil. She probably asked him if we were truly half sisters, not out of malice but out of curiosity. I can't even get mad at her for that—she didn't know what was at stake for me. Oh my God. I blamed Rhys. I yelled at him, told him I never wanted to see him again. And then he died for me.

I begin to hyperventilate. Yet again, the only person I can blame here is myself. Not Faith or Neil, or even Nic. It's me, always fucking things up and making the people around me miserable.

But I'm in the past right now. I can *change* things, right? I can fix it. If I can't, then what the hell kind of use is this power anyway?

But how do I even go about fixing it? The easiest method would be making him dislike me. I don't know how Prince Vesryn turns into Rhys, or how he gets to the future, so that's out of my control. But I can definitely make him not want to help me. If he hates me, he might try to sabotage me. It's better if he's indifferent toward me.

I can't lie to him, though. He'll see right through that. Maybe it would just be best to leave him right now, while he doesn't feel anything for me aside from obligation.

"I need some time alone," I finally manage.

Prince Vesryn hesitates. "I am concerned for you. I was hoping we could speak."

"I'm really tired right now." Not technically a lie. All this thinking has me drained. "Please let me rest."

"Very well. Call on me if you require anything."

As soon as he leaves, I curl up in the bed under the covers. I can't ride a horse by myself, but maybe I can just leave in the dead of night. I think I still have some of Gwyn's jewelry left, but it's in Theodas' possession. I can take it and go, make my way to the Violet City myself. Or, better yet, return to my own time period and try to travel again.

This inn *does* have doors. I wonder if I can reach the Infinity Hallway.

I'll need something sharp to draw blood. If worse comes to worst, I'll just bite myself. Anything to get out of this situation. Away from Rhys.

My stomach turns, and I wonder if it's only *guilt* I feel toward him. Or something more.

But I shut that train of thought down right away. For me, there *is* nothing "more." Even if there was, it doesn't matter. Rhys is dead unless I can figure out a way to prevent it.

I roll out of bed and look around the room. Prince Vesryn took the food tray. The prince—I mean, Rhys—is probably worried about me based on my erratic behavior. Acting now would only draw his attention.

Then again, would he care? He only views me as someone he is obliged to help. If I just got up and told him I needed to leave, would he really stop me?

Maybe I'm being too rash. I don't have my backpack yet, and the only way I'll get it is if we meet Lyari and the other elves in the Violet City. Until that point, I can just act normal. Cold, even.

Making up my mind, I head out of the room and downstairs. Rhys is there, sitting by the fire with Iacar. They're speaking in hushed tones, and immediately stop when they see me. They couldn't have been discussing *me*, right?

No way. Probably some elf thing I'm not supposed to be privy to. Rhys might have some weird attachment toward me right now, some sense of duty to help me, but Iacar is different. Aside from finding my antics with Gwyn amusing, Iacar doesn't seem to like me very much. Why should he? We're strangers.

"Maria," Rhys greets cautiously, standing. Now that I look at him, *really* drink him in, I don't know how I could have possibly thought they were different people. Maybe I knew it in my heart but didn't want to admit it. Seeing him now almost makes me want to cry.

"I'm sorry about earlier," I begin, casting my eyes to the floor. "Can we, um, talk? In private?"

Rhys doesn't hesitate like I do. "Of course. The horses need feeding. Perhaps you can assist me."

"Yeah, sure."

I follow Rhys through the back door of the inn. In the yard, there's red-painted wooden housing for at least ten horses. Only five are being used, three of which are for our horses. The horses we stole from the fae.

It's not quite sunny, but at least it's not raining anymore. The ground is still damp and slippery, and the air is frigid. Rhys takes a bag of carrots from a bin on the side of the stable and begins to give one to the first horse, who obediently nibbles on it.

"Are you feeling alright, Maria?"

"Yes. I wanted to thank you for everything," I say, standing awkwardly by his side. "I'm sure I caused trouble with the fae. After all you said about Gwyn trying to find an excuse to punish you, I went and attacked him."

"No need to worry. I doubt he will be spreading the story of a woman overpowering him. Fae are quite…old-fashioned in that regard," Rhys replies. "But you seemed upset this morning. Did you have a nightmare?"

I hesitate before nodding. "I did. No matter how many times I have the same nightmare, it still scares me."

"It must have been severe to affect you so."

"I haven't been totally honest with you. I mean, you can tell when I outright lie, but I've kept things from you. Important things."

"Such as?"

"I think I've been misrepresenting myself. You should know that I'm not a great person, and I don't really think I deserve your help. Now or ever," I say, my voice more desperate than I intend. But he needs to hear this, no matter how difficult it is to admit. "Once we reach the Violet City, and I get my things from your men, we should part ways. I'm grateful for your protection, but it's clear to me now that this is a journey I need to take alone."

Receiving his help will only put him in danger. He's been

away from home for so long, he *deserves* to make it back safely. I've taken so much from Rhys already.

I can speculate as much as I want, but I don't truly know Rhys' motives in my own time period. I have no idea how he felt about me, or if he had any goodwill toward me at all. But I *do* know he took care of me, even if it was just on an order from Neil. And that one night, after the Nightmare attacked me, he helped me get revenge on Marshall and Lilly. He didn't have to do that, but he did anyway.

"Maria, I do not understand."

"I'm trying to say that when we part, I'll be fine. You'll have fulfilled whatever sense of duty you feel toward me and you won't have to worry anymore," I tell him.

"You believe I am helping you simply because I feel a responsibility toward you?" He takes a step closer to me, and I have to crane my neck to get a good look at his expression. His brow furrows, and it's like he's both confused and angry.

"Why else would you be bringing me to the Violet City?" I ask. "Not to mention, you could have just left me in the fae camp and escaped by yourself. It's not exactly honorable, but it would have bought you time."

But Rhys wouldn't have done that, not even to some weirdo he met in the woods less than a week ago. I know it even before I say it.

"After seeing you use such interesting methods to help us escape the fae camp, I believed you to be more intelligent than I had originally given you credit for. Perhaps I was mistaken," he says, which nearly makes me smile despite the ridiculousness of this situation. That's something Rhys definitely would have told me—a gentlemanly roast. "Do you truly not understand me?"

He leans forward, his hand resting on my shoulder. My stupid heart races at his proximity.

"Maria." The way he says my name feels intimate, intense. "Look at me."

I do, staring into those lavender-blue eyes, searching for the answer to a question I'm terrified to ask.

Fear grips me, and I know that whatever is happening right now needs to stop immediately. Before I do something stupid again.

"I'm not someone worthy of your protection," I whisper, stepping away from him. "Hear my words and know they are not lies."

"You are not lying. But that only means you *believe* it to be true."

"I've hurt people without remorse. Killed people—or tried to," I blurt, in a desperate attempt to convince him. But his gaze is steadfast, like he *trusts* me or something. That only makes it worse. When people put their faith in me, I always let them down. "Those weren't accidents. They're not things I can blame on others. I've hurt people, not because I had to, but because I *wanted* to. And I don't feel any guilt about it. That's the type of person I am. I need you to understand that."

"Why?"

"So you can cut ties with me before it's too late."

CHAPTER EIGHT

Kenia is the resident innkeeper. She's so tall she has to duck through the doorways, lowering her chin subtly as she sweeps into each room. She's not as muscular as Iacar, but she could easily pass for a bodybuilder. And it looks like she puts them to good use; I saw her outside earlier. She came at just the right time, interrupting my painful conversation with Rhys to chop firewood. Her skin is warm, sun-kissed from a hard day's work.

Lensa, her daughter, helps run the inn. She's everything I pictured an elf lady would be, with flowing golden curls to her waist and bright blue eyes clearer than a cloudless sky. She serves us dinner in the dining room on the first floor, bringing out tray after tray of various meats, breads, and vegetables. At first I'm concerned it's too much. And then Iacar starts eating. I guess those muscles don't just come out of thin air.

Kenia doesn't seem to mind at all, clapping him on the back with a hearty laugh. "It is an honor to serve the prince and his companions!"

Lensa nods excitedly, leaning over to fill Rhys' plate with food. She goes as far as cutting up his venison into tiny chunks, despite his polite protests. At least, I *assume* that's what he's doing by the shake of his head and that awkward look on his face. I can hardly hear them from my end of the table.

The first step to emotional distance is physical distance, right?

"She's trying to express interest," Theodas whispers, leaning toward me. While Rhys sits at the head of the table, I'm stationed at the other end in a pathetic attempt to put as much distance between us as possible. It hasn't gone unnoticed. He keeps looking at me, like he wants to say something but doesn't know what.

I don't blame him. For once, I'm at a loss for words, too. My body feels wooden just sitting here, trying to pretend like everything is fine when I know it's not. Or, it *won't* be. Not to get too nihilistic on you. But in the back of my mind, there's a seed of fear that nothing I do will matter in the end. That Rhys will still end up dying because of me. Normally I would shove this fear aside, become another character and gloss over it. But I can't bring myself to pretend — not because I don't want to. There's something keeping me *stuck* in Maria-mode. It's frustrating, to say the least.

But Theodas is either oblivious to my inner turmoil, or he's choosing to ignore it. Either way, I'm grateful for his company.

"Elves used to be taught never to express romantic interest in a partner unless they were married, and even then, never in public. Nowadays it has changed considerably, but old courting rituals like this persist outside of the capital and cities. Village girls are less forward," Theodas explains. "Lensa can't directly state her intentions, so she serves him food as a sign of affection and care. I believe she hopes to earn his favor, and perhaps bed him tonight."

If he's trying to test me, it isn't working. I break off a piece of bread, fresh from the oven. It's still steaming as I dip it in my tomato stew. "Good for her."

"You are not concerned?"

"Um, no? Why would I be? They're both available, right? And adults?" I shrug. "Well, I guess the prince is only seventeen. Is he considered an adult?"

"Twenty is considered 'adult' and is the traditional age of marriage. But affairs before that are common."

"Then what's the problem? Jealous?"

"Oh, my gods no," Theodas says with a laugh. "I have no interest in that sort of thing. Never have, actually. My parents think I have a mental condition. Word has spread throughout the country, even among the fae, that I am eternally unattached."

"Eternally unattached? Seems dramatic, if you ask me. How old are you?"

"Old enough. But my lack of interest isn't medical, despite any else's insistence." His eyes have a certain shine to them, and I get the feeling it isn't easy to talk about this. "Well, I have been told I am a bit meddlesome when it comes to matters of the heart. Do not take my words seriously; I only wish to tease you. Now, what are you doing with your food?"

"Uh, making a sandwich?" I cut the bread open and fill the inside with slices of cheese. It's kind of like a makeshift grilled cheese and tomato soup combo, but fresher and honestly *way* better. Like some artisan shit you'd get at a fancy café.

SAM GAO

"I am unfamiliar with the term," Theodas says.

"It's a type of food. You cut the bread open and put stuff between the slices. And then you eat it. Here, let me help you." I make one for him from a roll, letting the cheese melt between both sides of the warm rye. "Don't burn your mouth."

Theodas takes the sandwich from me and imitates me by dipping it in his soup. Cautiously, he takes a small bite. His eyes light up immediately and a smile stretches across his face. "Exquisite! And this is called a *sandwich*? What is the origin of the word?"

"No idea. But they're pretty common where I'm from."

"What a mysterious place. Please, tell me more." Theodas continues to eat, pushing his braid over his shoulder.

"There's not much to tell." So many inventions in my time don't seem to have been invented here yet. I don't even know how I'd go about explaining the internet to him, when the only light in this inn is provided by candles.

Still, I try my best to entertain him by giving him movie recaps of all the classics. Maybe it's the wine in his cup or the discovery of sandwiches, which are bound to make anyone giddy, but Theodas is captivated by the plot of *Footloose*.

"A town forbidden to dance. How *archaic*," he comments in horror. "What other stories do you know?"

"Um, a lot. Hey, there's this one called *The Lake House*. It's weird in a good way," I suggest. And, appropriately, it's about time travel. I begin to tell Theodas a plot summary, but I can only explain the concept of the time-traveling mailbox to him before Rhys interrupts. I didn't even hear him come up behind us.

90

"You seem to be enjoying yourselves," he says, squeezing beside me. "Care to share?"

Lensa follows him, though the only seat she can take is across from us. She smiles at me and says, "You two get along well."

Which two? Me and Theodas? Or me and the prince?

Of course she means me and Theodas, I chide myself. She wants to "bed the prince," according to Theodas. Why would she make a remark about how the prince is close with me? Rhys hasn't spoken to me since sitting down at the table!

Stupid Mar.

"Maria was simply telling me a thrilling tale about a mailbox that can transport love letters through time. It's rather touching," Theodas says, pouring himself another glass of wine.

"Love letters through time?" Rhys scoffs.

"Hey, love letters are romantic. I *liked* this movie. I mean, uh, story." Plus it has Keanu Reeves in it. An insult to Keanu is an insult to me.

"Have you ever received a love letter, Your Highness?" Lensa asks innocently. I don't think she's acting, either, like some girls do. She's been nothing but kind and welcoming since we arrived.

"Such things would be inappropriate," he denies immediately.

"So that's a no, then," I say.

Rhys shakes his head. "I have received many letters from young ladies wishing to accompany me."

"When's the last time you were in elf court? When you were thirteen, right? That doesn't count. A love letter has to be sent by someone who *loves* you. It's in the title." Not that

I would know firsthand. But I've watched a lot of romance movies. And that equates to real-life experience. "Anyway, it's just a story."

"Maria is very good at telling stories," Theodas adds. "Tell them about *Footloose*."

"I just told you about *Footloose*."

"I would like to hear it again."

"You sound like a little kid."

Lensa giggles. "One would think you two suit. Do you not agree, my prince?"

I make the mistake of turning to Rhys for an answer. Judging by his face, he does not agree at all. And then he outright says it.

"Maria and Theodas would be a poor match. For one, Theodas is too old for her," Rhys declares.

Theodas' jaw drops. "Your Highness, I am but two years older."

"Theodas is also uninterested in romantic relationships," Rhys continues. "Even if he were, their personalities would surely clash."

"You sound jealous, my prince." Only Iacar would lack the social skills to point that out. I didn't think he was listening, still chowing down on Kenia's food.

For a moment, no one knows what to say. Rhys himself looks shell-shocked.

I try to smooth things over with a laugh, waving the thought away with my hand. "You're mistaken, Iacar. Theodas and the prince do not seem interested in each other, and they certainly aren't in me. Not everything is about love and romance. There *is* a story I know, a very exciting one, that is not about romance at all. It's called *Beetlejuice*."

After I begin telling them all about *Beetlejuice*, *E.T.*, and

Howl's Moving Castle (which Theodas agrees is his favorite), the wine begins to take its toll. One by one the elves retreat to their bedrooms until only Rhys and I are left. Just what I wanted to avoid.

We find ourselves by the fireplace, and I make sure the distance between us is maintained. I sit in a chair while he stands, leaning against the mantel. The fire casts a warm glow on his face, making him appear even more dazzling than normal.

"I believe we should finish our conversation," he says quietly. "From earlier."

"Well, if you insist. I *do* have another story in me," I reply.

"I do not want another *story*, Maria. I want—"

"The truth, I know. But this story is important. It seems like one you need to hear."

Rhys crosses his arms. "Fine, then."

"Once upon a time, there was a girl who didn't have parents. In her country, children without parents are sent to temporary homes where the children are taken care of. The girl was passed around like a used tissue, hoping that one day, the temporary home situation would become permanent. She waited and she tried her best to be good. Love is something earned and everything she did was in pursuit of that.

"One day, the girl was moved into a new house and she immediately loved the family. They were kind to her, generous. They treated her better than any other. She felt loved and she wanted it to last forever. But nothing lasts forever. In this family, there was only room for three people: a mother, a father, and a son. The girl didn't know at the time, but there was never a place for a daughter.

"Things were incredible in the beginning. One day, when she and her brother were playing, she fell down the stairs and hurt herself. She thought it was an accident. She *told* everyone it was an accident. And then it kept happening —these sorts of 'accidents' around her brother. By the time she realized they were not accidents, it was too late. No one believed her, and those who did turned a blind eye.

"Because it didn't matter if something happened to her. No one cared if she died. There wouldn't be any consequences, and certainly no rewards for saving her. And if there is nothing to gain, people will not act in the defense of others. It goes against their very nature to put someone else's life above their own, especially that of a stranger.

"The girl was afraid of her brother. She began failing in school and pushing what few friends she had away. She lashed out at the only person who cared about her, nearly destroying their friendship. Time passed, and one day by chance, she saw her brother with his friends. They were laughing, smiling, and having a great time. And something inside the girl, something twisted and evil, woke up.

"She never considered fighting back against her brother, because she was so terrified of what would happen if she failed. But after seeing him smile, anger replaced her fear. Because why did he get to be happy, to have friends, to be totally unaffected while he was ruining her life? She never knew how much hate was truly in her heart. And she couldn't stop thinking about it; it was always at the back of her mind, eating at her.

"The girl didn't want him to *die*, per se. But she wanted him to disappear. To not exist anymore, to not be able to feel happiness. He took that from *her*. She wanted to take it from him, too. So when the opportunity present itself, she tried to kill him. She pushed him down a flight of stairs and he broke his leg. He survived and healed completely. He even got a scar removal treatment. In the end, he walked away. And she was branded a problem child.

"That household changed everything for her. The girl walked out a completely different person. Adversity has the power to make one stronger, but for the girl, this was not the case. Now, the girl is selfish. She is a liar and she hurts people, whether she intends to or not. She can't forgive anyone even if they sincerely apologize. And she will never change no matter how hard she tries. She knows that she's a lost cause. She only hopes others will understand, too, even without knowing her story, that she doesn't really deserve compassion and love anymore. And she doesn't deserve help, either. She doesn't *want* help, because everyone who helps her ends up getting hurt."

"Maria." Rhys says my name like it's the end of the world, and suddenly I can't bear to look at him anymore.

It takes everything in me not to run from him again out of shame. But he needs to know what I've done, so he can understand why he needs to stay away from me.

"Tomorrow we should leave," I whisper. "Let's go to the Violet City, I'll get my backpack, and we can part ways amicably. And then you won't have to deal with me again. I am grateful for your help—that's why I'm warning you now that nothing good will happen if we continue to travel together. This was always the plan, anyway."

After a long pause, Rhys relents. "If that is what you wish for, Maria, I can hardly refuse you."

It isn't what I *wish* for. But it has to happen—for both our sakes.

CHAPTER NINE

The Violet City isn't as far as I initially thought and we arrive by midday on horseback.

Theodas takes my hand in his, helping me off the horse. I chose to ride with him instead this morning, in a feeble attempt to evade awkward interactions with Rhys.

"It will be easier to travel through the city on foot," Theodas explains in Elvish. We've disabled the Linguist's Orb for the time being—we don't want the others around us to notice us using it. Here in the city, there's a greater chance of a fae attack. The city is still in neutral territory, which means the fae could have spies here. Rhys, in particular, needs to stay under the radar.

I thought that having a cloak with a hood drawn over his head would draw *more* attention, but apparently that's the fashion here. The streets swell with people in black cloaks and it's apparent not everyone is an elf.

When I pictured a magic city, I expected it to be more foresty and natural. And, because of the name, I thought there'd be more purple. There *is* purple, by the way—the flags hanging from the streetlamps all have violet flowers embroidered on them. But the buildings are all Tudor-style, built with a mixture of bricks and stucco framed by decorative timbering. Flower boxes line the windows, overflowing with plants. It's picturesque, almost like I'm in a fairytale.

Except I'm not. In a fairytale, I mean. Sure, there's a prince, a monster, and a magical sword. But I'm not a hero, I'm certainly not a princess, and I'm not some damsel in distress, either.

Now, you might be thinking, "But Mar, you kind of *are* a damsel in distress. You're helpless and constantly relying on others to protect you." Yeah, that's true. I'm weak. But I believe I've mentioned already that I'm not beautiful enough to count, and while I have to rely on others, it's not like they swoop in to save me because they *want* to. Archer did nothing while I got hit in the face by Marshall with a rock. Todd saved me, but only from himself, and that doesn't really count. So in conclusion, I'm not a damsel in distress. I'm just in distress. A...time traveler in distress?

Huh. That doesn't sound as good, but we'll go with it.

"How will we find Lyari?" I ask Theodas. "I need that backpack."

I'm pretty sure my period is due soon, and I want to be prepared when it comes. God only knows what women use for period products here. Do you know what they had instead of toilet paper at the inn? A stick with a sponge on it.

Again, time travel sucks.

"The royal family purchased a permanent room in one of the inns," Rhys cuts in, his voice low. "There is a supply of money there, and discreet servants. We will wait and put a code in the newspaper. Lyari and the others will know where to look."

Oh, so I'm stuck with the prince until Lyari figures out a secret code in the paper? That's fantastic!

At least we'll have a place to sleep. And while we're here, I can explore the city and find information about the sword with my poor Elvish language skills.

Iacar leads the way to the inn, which is off the main road, down several winding side streets, and up a flight of stone steps. I'm panting like crazy when we finally arrive. The inn is tucked away in a corner of the city with a gorgeous view of the town center below.

Rhys speaks with the innkeeper at the front desk, an older gentleman elf, while Iacar and I hang back by the entrance. His hand rests on a new sword he procured from Kenia, though he doesn't really need one. He looks like he could kill with his bare hands.

"What were ye talking about with the prince last night?" Iacar asks me bluntly.

"I don't know what you mean," I reply, playing dumb. First Theodas, now Iacar?

"'is 'ighness didn't seem too 'appy when 'e returned last night. Did ye fight?"

"No." Not technically. "Why are you so interested in that, anyway?"

"Protecting the prince is my sworn duty as a guard. I promised 'is sister I'd protect 'im, too."

"Protect him? You mean from me?"

"Yes," Iacar answers seriously. "I do. Last night, when ye sat with Theodas, 'is 'ighness appeared jealous."

"Jealous?" Don't make me laugh. "He clearly—"

"He clearly what?" Rhys asks, appearing behind us. He

crosses his arms and raises his brows, challenging me to finish my sentence.

I look him dead in the eyes and say, "Then he clearly can't read the room."

Rhys is quick to reply, "One reads novels and newspapers, not rooms."

Oh. I guess that saying doesn't translate well in Elvish. But *you* get my point, don't you?

"Iacar. Do you care to explain?"

Iacar shrinks back, laughing nervously. "Your Highness, I was simply telling the wench that you are, er, very—"

"He thinks you're interested in me," I say, "because he thinks you were jealous that I was telling Theodas stories last night. But I think he's wrong."

"Oh? And what if he is correct?"

I'm positive Rhys is testing me, trying to probe how I react and nothing more.

I'm not *blind*, though. There is some interest on his part, but it doesn't feel romantic. It can't. He's probably just curious about where I come from, and maybe my horrible accent in Elvish. I know for a fact he's not interested in my plain face, and certainly not my body. My personality isn't much of a winner either. Especially not after what I told him last night about Max.

Even if we weren't in a time period that I can only assume is a bit misogynistic, my admission was pretty horrible. Anyone would go running for the hills after hearing that.

"Well, if you were jealous, you don't have to be. Theodas isn't interested in me. He's all yours," I reply. "Did you settle the matter of the room?"

Rhys stares at me for a beat before nodding, letting the

whole "jealousy" question go. Thank God. "Yes, it is done. The rooms are being prepared now. You are welcome to rest, if you so choose, Maria."

"I have some business to take care of."

"Excuse me? What business?"

"None of yours," I quip. I know it's cold, especially since he's been helping me, but we're to part as soon as Lyari reunites with us. Rhys shouldn't interfere any more than he already has. "I'll be off."

"Wait! I will accompany you."

"That's not a good idea."

"Why not?" Rhys demands.

"I'll be back tonight. Don't worry about me. I'm fine." I take off before he can argue further, walking back down the steps we came from. Only, now that I'm in the city, my horrible sense of direction has kicked in and I don't know how to get out of the maze of backstreets. I pass the same stray cat licking itself six times before finally reaching the town square, and by then, the sun is about to set.

Seriously? My stomach rumbles and I make my way through the bustle of people toward a tavern packed with patrons. Luckily, I still have a ring from Gwyn in my pocket and a few coins from Lensa. She gave them to me this morning when we departed—sweet girl. She also gave me a piece of paper and a feather, which I used to roughly sketch out the Divinities Sword. It's not the best drawing, mind you, but it's distinct enough.

I'm not an avid gamer, but I've played a few open-world fantasy games. Inns and taverns are where players get information, so I figure I'll start there for anything I can find out about the Divinities Sword. Is this a foolproof method? You take a guess—I got the idea from a video game. But hey, it can't hurt to try, right?

The tavern smells like freshly baked bread and roasted fish. The patrons are mostly men, filling the air with laughter and clinking glasses. In the warm glow of the candlelight, the interior feels cozy.

I shimmy toward the bar counter, getting a coin out of my pocket. "One drink."

The bartender, a middle-aged elf woman with wild dark curls, grins at me. "What'll you have, dear?"

It's difficult to understand her regional accent, especially over all the noise, but I manage to comprehend the gist of what she's saying. "Wine. Whatever you recommend."

"Change, sweetheart? Or should I open a tab for you?"

"A tab," I say. "I'm looking for something. Anyone here know anything?"

"What do you mean, dear?"

"Is anyone here particularly good at...finding things?" I clarify, hoping my Elvish skills don't fail me now.

"Ah, I see. That gentleman over there is who you're lookin' for." The bartender points to a heavy-set bearded ginger elf wearing a pointy velvet hat and a gold chain around his neck. He's got a ring on every finger, and a huge smile on his face. "He's not cheap, though, honey."

"That's fine." I pause. "Say, am I able to request a specific waitress to serve me?"

IT'S BEEN A FEW MONTHS SINCE I STARTED QUESTIONING my faith. I'd been raised Christian, obviously—I'm from Georgia—and while I was never devout, I believed. This whole shadowborn business has me doubting, but tonight, I pray to God. I'm not even sure if He can hear me, and even if He does exist, can He hear prayers from the Veil?

Whatever. Worth a shot.

God. Or gods. Whoever. Please, please do not let this fruit drop out of my dress. I know it's wrong to stuff your bra to trick someone into giving you information, but it's for the greater good. You get it, don't you?

Silence.

Well, here goes nothing.

I exit the powder room with two small melons, sliced in half, stuffed under my dress. The juice runs down my stomach, making me smell sweet and filling the front of my chest. It's seduction time, baby. And if he's not interested...well, this was all for nothing.

My target is Selnar Jodan, a wealthy merchant in the Violet City who sells more than just shitty pottery (which I learned from the bartender after giving her nearly all my coins). Selnar is a regular at this tavern, and an expensive information broker. I guess video games didn't lie to me after all. But unlike in games, these NPCs aren't just going to help me for free.

I walk over to Selnar's table with a smile, wedging myself across from him. "Lord Selnar Jodan?"

He looks at me, his eyes traveling to my chest appreciatively. I guess the melons were a good idea after all. "Hello, dear. What can I do for you?"

"I've heard many great things about you," I purr, leaning over the table. I *really* hope this sounds seductive and not painfully awkward in Elvish. Second languages are hard. "I was hoping to meet you tonight."

"Pray tell, what brings you to me?" He smiles knowingly. "Do you seek information? A man you are interested in, perhaps?"

I channel Marilyn as I say, "Oh, there is a man I'm interested in. I'm talking to him right now."

"Tell me more."

"I've heard you can outdrink any man in this city," I continue. "Is that true?"

"You seek a challenge?" He barks a laugh. "And why would I entertain that, my dear? What would the terms be?"

"If you win, I'll pay for your tab. If I win, you pay for mine. It's just a harmless little game." I touch his forearm, stroking his sleeve with a finger. "You'll play with me, won't you?"

"Only because you asked so nicely. But I believe we should up the stakes," Selnar adds, maintaining his smile. He's no spring chicken—that makes this even more fun. "Why don't we trade information? For every additional drink I consume, I get to ask you a question."

"Alright. And if I drink more than you?"

"You're quite presumptuous, little lady. But I don't mind. Elyon will judge us," he says, resting a hand on the shoulder of the woman beside him. "She is the owner of this fine establishment. She is impartial."

I doubt that. But I have little choice in the matter. Elyon sits beside Selnar, nearly as tall as he is. She could be a model in my time, with her long legs and luscious blonde hair. Well, I suppose the elf ears might stop her.

"It's a deal then," I decide, raising a hand toward the bar. An older waitress scurries over, her face wrinkled and worn. "Two of your strongest wines, please."

She nods quickly, not wasting any time on meaningless

chatter. As she returns to get our drinks, Selnar doesn't take his eyes off me.

"You are not as simple as you appear," he announces, though he seems pleased about that. I'm fairly certain it's an insult, but I take it in stride.

"I am just a girl, sir."

"Hm. Sure. I look forward to uncovering your secrets."

Go ahead and try.

The first drink goes down smooth, just as I thought. Selnar drinks it in one gulp, wiping his mouth with the back of his hand. Elyon doesn't allow him to order a second glass until she makes sure I've finished mine. I was worried she would be partial to Selnar, seeing as he's a regular here and I'm a total stranger, but the woman has a calm, collected demeanor about her. She doesn't even let Selnar take food from the table while we drink.

It's difficult to believe *this* is the strongest wine the tavern has, because by drink seven Selnar isn't even swaying yet.

I blink rapidly, my movements slowing.

"Had enough, girl?" Selnar teases. We've drawn a small crowd, and the other patrons laugh at his question. Of course they would bet on Selnar over me. Status aside, he's twice my size.

"Hardly," I slur. "Another drink, please."

The waitress complies faithfully, handing us both another glass.

"Perhaps you should admit defeat," Elyon suggests. At first I think she's being kind, but then she adds, "If you get sick here, I *will* have you clean it up yourself."

"I'm...I'm fine," I reply, downing another glass. "How many is that?"

"Eight, miss," Elyon says.

Selnar doesn't begin to sway until drink ten, leaning on the table with his head drooping. I think all the drinks are starting to hit him at once.

I down my eleventh drink. "Are you finished, sir?"

Selnar looks at me, but his eyes aren't focused. *Finally.* Eleven drinks to take this monster down?

Elyon seems to be thinking the same thing. She shakes her head. "Most customers can only tolerate two glasses. We don't keep a large supply; we're going to run out of this wine soon."

"That's enough for me, Elyon. This little lady has a steel stomach," Selnar says appreciatively. "I —"

"Maria!" I turn my head. Rhys barges into the tavern. He storms toward me, anger clear as day on his face. Jeez, what's got his panties in a twist? He grabs my chin, jerking it up so he can see my face clearly. "What are you doing?"

"Unhand her, sir," Elyon says sharply. "Miss, do you know this man?"

"Yes. It's fine, Elyon," I assure her, giving Rhys a big smile. "How did you find me?"

"One of the workers at the inn came in to tell his friends of a silly little girl who had challenged Selnar the Great to a drinking competition."

"How did you know he was talking about me?"

"He said the girl was not an elf," Rhys says, getting even angrier. "You are *drunk*."

"I am winning."

"Maria, we will go now. Lord Selnar, whatever she has promised you —"

"No, sir. The little lady has won this match," Selnar explains, a big, dopey smile on his face. Yeah, he's definitely feeling those drinks now. But I honestly didn't take him for a graceful loser. I have new respect for him. "She has also earned the right to ask a question."

Rhys looks at me incredulously. "*You* defeated Selnar the Great?"

I ignore him and address Selnar directly, my hands trembling as I take the picture of the Divinities Sword out of my pocket. "I am looking for this sword. It is a magical artifact with the ability to banish evil. Do you know how I might find it?"

Selnar examines my drawing with a frown. "I apologize, I haven't seen a thing like this before. Not through *my* channels. But you might find out more in the Red Light District. Most traveling merchants pass through there. The Sleeping Fox is the most famous brothel; if anyone knows something, a courtesan there would."

"Many thanks." I tuck the drawing into my pocket and rise, clutching Rhys for support. "It was a great honor, Lord Selnar."

"Goodbye, miss. I believe we will meet again." He takes my hand and kisses it.

Rhys nearly drags me out of the tavern to the street, angrier than I've ever seen him.

"Why did you look for me?" I ask. "I told you not to."

He replies by scooping me up. Ugh, not the stupid princess carry again! He lifts me as if I weigh nothing and walks so quickly through the cobblestone streets that I have to really hold on or else I'll fall straight to the ground.

"What are you doing? Put me down!" My complaint is futile. He begins heading back to the inn through the series of alleyways, navigating them with ease.

Is that...also some kind of magic? It's so dark; I don't know how he can tell where we're going.

"Why aren't you listening to me?"

"You are more foolish than I thought," he grits out, carrying me up the set of stairs leading to the inn. Hey, how did we get here so fast? Don't tell me the inn was this close to the tavern, when it took me hours to find my way there earlier. "Iacar and Theodas advised me to leave you to your own devices. 'How much trouble can one woman get into?' they asked. And then I heard that you challenged Selnar to a drinking competition, for *what*? For information? Even if he *is* a gentleman, anyone could have taken advantage of you tonight. You are in a foreign city alone, where you do not even speak the language fluently."

"I'm understanding *you* just fine," I snap. "Can you put me down now? All this jostling really makes me need to pee."

"No. You are intoxicated."

"I think you mean, *intoxicating*," I joke. He doesn't laugh. Ouch. "Look, if you put me down, I can explain everything, okay?"

"What is there to explain?"

"First of all, I'm *not* drunk. If I drank eleven drinks, I wouldn't even be alive right now. Probably."

"Then how did you—"

"I *cheated*," I say, lowering my voice. "Now are you going to put me down?"

Rhys blinks at me, bewildered. Slowly, he sets me on my feet. We stand together in front of the inn. I glance beyond the edge of the overlook at the town below, the lights twinkling like stars in the sky. It's a clear night, and the full moon casts a brilliant light on Rhys, making his hair even paler than usual.

"I paid off the server," I explain before he has a chance to ask. "She was giving me juice, not wine. I gave her a ring I stole from Gwyn in exchange. After speaking to the bartender in the tavern, I figured that would be cheaper than giving the ring to Selnar directly. I also didn't want him asking where I got it. The waitress didn't care if it was stolen — she has kids to feed. She gladly agreed to the deal."

"You cheated," Rhys repeats. "You cheated an elf. An elf who can tell whether or not you are lying."

"You shouldn't be too reliant on that power," I warn. "Besides, I didn't technically lie to him. I just spoke in a way that would lead him to believe I was drunk. There's a big difference."

I brace myself for another lecture, but instead, Rhys begins *laughing*. I've never heard him do that before. What's worse, he's smiling. Rhys. *Smiling*.

Lord help me.

I turn away quickly, my face as red as a tomato. "Stop that!"

"What?" He chuckles. What the hell is he so giddy about? Does he think I'm joking or something?

I hold a hand up. "Do *not* come any closer."

"Maria—"

"No. You are just...you're too handsome!" I blurt. "You're good-looking all the time, but when you smile like that, it does weird things to me!"

I can barely express the feeling in English, let alone Elvish. Of course, this only makes Rhys smile wider. I try not to look at him, but he steps closer to me. This is dangerous.

"You think I am handsome?" His tone completely changes, becoming gentler than I've ever heard it.

Oh boy. This was *not* the time to say something stupid. But now that it's out there, I guess there's no denying it.

"Anyone with *eyes* would think that," I huff. I sneak a peek at his face, which is a mistake. Not only is he still smiling, but he's smiling directly at me. It's too bright! I'm melting!

"Then I suppose I should only smile for you."

Holy hell. What the fuck did he just say?

My heart begins to go into overdrive, and my brain is currently on the fritz. So naturally, the only response I can think of is the absolute dumbest thing anyone could possibly say at this moment.

"I really *do* need to pee."

Can I just...throw myself down the set of stairs right next to me?

I run, full speed, into the inn. Thank God Rhys doesn't follow, since I don't actually know where the bathroom is. I ask a worker, sweating profusely and barely managing to get the words out in Elvish. I must look high or something. The worker kindly points me in the right direction, so I can happily lock myself inside and freak out.

But, may I remind you, I am in the past. So the "bathroom" is a bucket and a stick with a sponge tied to it. And after I do my business, eventually I will have to go back and share a room with Rhys, Theodas, and Iacar. I won't even be able to escape my embarrassment by sleeping.

It's going to be a long night.

CHAPTER TEN

I really do *need to pee.*
 I really do *need to pee.*
I really do *need to pee.*

All night long, those stupid words have been playing on repeat in my head. Thankfully Rhys asked the innkeepers to give me a private room for the length of our stay, so I didn't have to sleep in the same room as him last night. Can you imagine? The awkwardness would've been ten times worse, if that's even possible.

What on earth would possess me to say something like that? Am I just so socially inept that I can't come up with a better reply to...whatever it was Rhys was doing yesterday?

It *felt* like flirting, but it couldn't have been. Looks aside, I've done absolutely nothing to make him desire me in any sort of capacity. It's not like I have a winning personality or any talent whatsoever. If anything, all I've shown him is that I'm a useless, bland bitch!

So if he's not interested in me, then did I misread the

entire situation? My Elvish isn't that great, and learning nuance in a foreign language is difficult.

He threw me off with that smile, though. And the sound of his laughter.

Oh, how old am I, *twelve*? I need to get my act together here! I've dealt with good-looking guys before! Archer is hot, too, albeit in a different way. But when he kissed me, I was never this shaken.

How does Rhys have this effect on me? It's not like I'm in love with him, in the future *or* the past. Is it the guilt? That's still pretty intense, and if my long history of self-hatred has anything to show for itself, the regret I feel over Rhys' death will never go away, even if I *do* end up saving him. But there's a fat chance of that, by the looks of things now.

Rhys waltzes into the dining room the next morning with a radiant smile on his face. At least one of us slept well. It almost pisses me off how happy he is, while I'm here toiling over my inner demons like some emotionally stunted middle schooler.

"Good morning, Maria." He sits beside me, so close I can smell the lavender bath oils on him. Damn it!

"Good morning," I mutter into my eggs, unable to summon up the same cheery exposition. I tried to stuff down my feelings with food this morning, making myself scrambled eggs and toast in the kitchen, but it does little to ease my humiliation and stress. Why is it that negative emotions are always plural, never singular?

"What are you eating?" Rhys asks, an innocent enough question. But his proximity is just making me angry, on top of the confusing concoction of emotions I already feel for him. Where does he get off being so calm about this?

"Eggs and pepper sauce with toast." I don't know what animal these eggs came from, but they don't look much different from eggs in the mortal realm. The pepper sauce smothers the taste anyway, leaving my mouth scorching. In a good way, I assure you.

"Did you sleep well?"

What does it look like, Romeo? God, can he just stop being so charming? It's really starting to piss me off!

I cautiously raise my head and immediately regret it. Sunlight pours in from the windows, perfectly shining across his face and making his entire being glow. I almost forget to swallow my food, looking at him.

Thankfully, Theodas arrives just in time to save me from another mortifying slip-of-the-tongue. Iacar trails behind him, rocking the bench when he sits beside me.

"What's wrong, wench?" he asks, not a trace of concern in his voice. "Are you constipated?"

Yeah, emotionally. "Good morning."

"I heard you bested Lord Selnar in a drinking competition last night," Theodas says. "Perhaps we can visit a dress shop and get you something more suitable for your frame and color palette."

"That sounds exciting," I say, "but I have plans."

"Oh? A secret rendezvous with someone?" Theodas jokes.

"No. I've got to go to the Red Light District and check out a brothel. Do you think they're open right now?" It's still pretty early.

Rhys chokes on air. "A brothel?"

"Yeah. I need some information. You don't happen to have a map so I can find the Red Light District, do you? I got lost yesterday trying to find the tavern."

"You do not have money to get into a brothel," he grits out. Man, there's no trace of a smile on his face now. Maybe I just imagined the whole thing.

"I can provide you coin," Theodas offers. Rhys shoots him a glare, but he ignores it completely. "I can escort you this evening, Maria. It will not be safe for you to go on your own."

"The Red Light District is dangerous," Rhys agrees quickly.

I shrug. "Then it's settled. I'll go with Theodas."

"No, I will go with you," Rhys insists. "Theodas can wait here for Lyari and the others."

"My prince, forgive me, but you should not be roaming around so freely without guards," Iacar interrupts. "We do not know what lurks in the city. It is a dangerous place, and showing your face last night at the tavern was unwise. You should remain hidden for the time being."

"But—"

"I agree, Your Highness. Besides, I can take care of Maria myself." Theodas pats my head. "Why do you smell like fruit?"

"I cut up a melon to make my chest look bigger last night."

"Ah. I see. Well, there is a public bathhouse for women not too far away. Shall I guide you there?"

"That sounds like an excellent idea." Really—I could use the bath. And the chance to get away from Rhys.

The weird thing is, despite the turmoil in my heart, I still want to be around him. What's wrong with me?

Lyari will bring my backpack eventually. And when that happens, I'll leave and never look back. Hopefully that will be enough to prevent his death in my own timeline.

Except…what if it doesn't? And if Rhys doesn't die, does that mean I will? He saved me from Faith. Without him, I had no chance of fighting back. Even though she was just supposed to be a normal human.

No, I'm getting distracted. What I really need to focus on is getting the sword. There's no point in overthinking when I can't possibly know the answers right now, and I'll drive myself crazy trying to figure it out. At the end of the day, whatever happens, I still need to kill Astaroth. And to do that, I need to retrieve the Divinities Sword.

"I'll wash these, and then we can leave," I tell Theodas, taking my empty dishes to the sink. I can't bear to look at Rhys' face anymore, at the risk of doing or saying something I'll regret. But his silence tells me all I need to know.

The public bathhouse is nicer than I expect, and frankly, cleaner. Patrons wash themselves off completely before stepping inside the tubs for a soak.

You'd think I'd feel weird about being naked around a bunch of elves, but it's surprisingly less nerve-wracking than I thought. I know public bathhouses exist in other parts of the world—even in the U.S., there are those fancy Korean spas—but I've never tried one until now.

I wish I could say that I'm so relaxed, being nude doesn't bother me. But I'm not relaxed. Quite the opposite, actually. My brain defaults to my Rhys problems, and when I try to ignore those, all my other skeletons come crawling out of the closet. Finally, when I can't take any more of the silence, I dry off and leave.

To kill time, Theodas takes me to a bunch of stores in the

city, but he's more interested in shopping than I am. At the end of the day, I have to help carry his bags from the various bookstores and craft shops back to the inn. We don't run into Iacar and Rhys, thankfully. After unloading Theodas' things, we make our way to the Red Light District.

The Sleeping Fox is the largest building on the street. Glass spheres of glowing light float suspended around the cobblestone path, leading us through a garden overflowing with wildflowers. Inside the lobby are gilded statues of headless nude bodies, which squeal as they move to change poses. I guess it's some sort of magic, but to me, it's creepy as hell.

The madam of the brothel, thankfully, has a head. She's dressed more modestly in a gown similar to mine, with a square neck and a long skirt. She doesn't have elf ears, I notice, nor does she have visible wings.

"How may I help you?" she asks, her English perfect. They must have a Linguist's Orb here, too. Makes sense, given the fact that travelers from all different places come here for...services? In any case, it will make the information seeking a whole lot easier.

"We want a special night," Theodas says smoothly. "Who are your most popular employees?"

"Depends on if you have enough coin," she replies.

Theodas, unperturbed, hands her a drawstring coin purse. I have no concept of money in the Veil, or in this time period, but she looks pleased as punch by his offering.

"Right this way." She drops into a deep curtsy and escorts us to another room, which leads outside. The building is shaped like a square with a garden in the center, all arranged around a weeping willow tree with glowing flower buds. As soon as the madam steps outside, her skin begins to glow the same pale pink as the flowers of the tree, shimmering the closer she gets to it. Her hair, too, shifts from plain brown to iridescent opal.

"Tree nymph," Theodas explains, pointing to her back.

She takes us through another set of doors, back inside, and past a hallway of doors until we reach a banquet room with food already spread out on the table. Four women stand in the corners of the room in sheer gowns.

"Please enjoy. I will have Dirue and Gaelith prepared and sent to you," the madam says. She exits the room, closing the double doors behind her as Theodas and I take our places at the table. The four female attendants immediately begin to fill our plates, one massaging my shoulders.

Theodas, however, refuses the shoulder massage.

"Is this uncomfortable for you?" I ask him.

He shakes his head. "Not particularly. I am indifferent to it. But I would prefer not to be touched, especially by strangers."

That last part is pointed, but the female attendants take the hint and focus more of their attention on me. Well, that suits me just fine. One of them actually begins cutting up my food and feeding me, kind of like Lensa had done with Rhys. Except, in this case, I think the attendants are just doing their jobs and *not* expressing interest in me.

Well, it's not like I'm ever going to have this experience in my own timeline. I might as well enjoy it.

"Is everyone here a tree nymph?" I ask the room.

The attendant massaging my shoulders giggles. "Many of us are."

"Tree nymphs are born asexually through their parent tree. It's something I appreciate about them," Theodas says. "When a tree absorbs enough magic, it can become a parent tree. The nymphs it births have a duty to feed it more magic. Their life is tied to the tree's."

"And they feed it more magic through sex?"

"No," another nymph laughs. "We simply care for it and pour elixirs on its roots."

"Elixirs *do* cost money, and so do land taxes. That is why we have this business here."

Another couple enter the room before I can ask more questions. They're both dressed in similar sheer clothing as the attendants, but with so many layers, it's a bit more difficult to see their privates underneath. Not that I'm trying to get a glimpse or anything.

These must be the courtesans the madam sent. They're both elves, judging by their ears, and they're at least ten years older than me. The woman smiles as she enters, much less stunning than I expected her to be. No offense, but she almost looks *normal*. Prettier than me, of course, but nothing like the other elves I've seen. Even the nymphs in the room are more plain than other truebloods and shadowborn I've encountered.

But then, the female courtesan opens her mouth and begins to speak. "Hello. I am Dirue."

Her voice is like honey, and even though she's just speaking a simple introduction, it almost sounds like a poem or a song. She dips her head politely, her long neck glistening with moisture.

"I am Gaelith." The male courtesan approaches with a smile, his scent an overwhelming cinnamon and apple mixture that immediately makes me feel at ease. He sits beside me, the cut of his tunic giving me a peek of his smooth chest as he moves his arm. Underneath the tunic he wears a billowing skirt in multiple sheer layers, like the female courtesan. He has androgenous features, which he pulls off well. "May I pour you a drink, my lady?"

My reply comes out automatically. "Yes."

"I have never seen you before, my lady," Gaelith says, pouring me a glass of wine. He leans in close, his wheat-blonde hair brushing my shoulder. "What brings you to the Violet City?"

"Information," I reply, cutting to the chase. I pull out the drawing I have of the Divinities Sword from my pocket and flatten it on the table. "Have you ever seen this sword?"

Gaelith studies the drawing, tracing my messy ink strokes with his long fingertips. "I'm afraid I am unfamiliar with this type of accessory hanging off the sword, my lady. Perhaps you can tell us of its attributes?"

"It's a blessed sword. It can kill blood magic practitioners," I explain. "I think it has a spell inscribed on the side."

Dirue also takes a look at the sword, but shakes her head. "I do not know of a sword such as this one. You are sure it is inscribed? Not many blacksmiths will do that nowadays."

"It's a magical artifact," I explain.

"Perhaps you should visit the Night Market, then. There will be an auction in two nights," Gaelith suggests. "There are always oddities for sale, though it *is* by invite only."

"The invite being coin," Dirue says with a snort. "If you are wearing fancy enough clothing, they shall let you pass."

"Thank you for the tip." That makes things easier. Ish.

In truth, I was kind of hoping they'd know exactly where the sword is and how to find it, but I guess this lead is better than nothing.

Theodas rises to his feet, already finished with his meal. Maybe he's not totally comfortable with being here, after all. "Thank you for the information. Maria, let us return."

"You are leaving so soon? You paid the fare for the night already," Gaelith says, his head tilting to the side. "Are you sure you must leave?"

"Thanks for the information," I say. "If something else comes up, we'll pay you another visit."

Gaelith doesn't argue further, instead taking my hand and kissing the back of it. "If you need any aid, my lady, please ask for me directly. I would be happy to assist you again."

Of course he would—for Theodas' money. But hey, Gaelith has to make a living somehow, right? And even though it's part of his job to flatter patrons, I'm *glad* Gaelith kissed my hand. The emptiness of the gesture puts things into perspective for me when it comes to Rhys. There were a few times I was delusional enough to think he was going to kiss me, and now, I finally understand why it felt so weird.

Most of the guys I've been with before were just flings. I knew they were empty and meaningless—I *craved* that, because a no-strings-attached policy meant that there was nothing at stake. When I kissed Ethan Kinsey, which feels like it happened a lifetime ago, it was just because he was doing me a favor. And with Archer, yes we kissed, but we were still getting to know each other.

It's not that Rhys' relationship with me was ever intimate, physically or emotionally. I didn't know him that well —I certainly didn't know he was a prince before coming to the past. There's something different about him, though. Maybe I really *do* have some sort of feelings for him. The intensity of those feelings remains a mystery—one that can never, ever be solved.

CHAPTER ELEVEN

"I feel as though we are in *Miss Congeniality* and you are Sandra Bullock," Theodas exclaims. "Except, of course, you do not have even half the fighting prowess Lady Bullock does."

Be careful, Theodas. Your Sandra Bullock bias is showing. Even though he's never seen the woman before, apparently Theodas thinks she's the bee's knees. Her, and anything Studio Ghibli. He hasn't even seen the animations; my rudimentary descriptions don't do it justice, especially not in Elvish.

We're stationed in a sitting room at the inn, and true to its name, there are a ton of places to sit. None of the sofas and chairs match, but I imagine this used to be a storage room before the prince requested to use it for his own purposes. And by *his* own purposes, I mean Theodas'.

"She's still unimpressive," Iacar grumbles, helping himself to another cookie on the coffee table. He lounges on an orange velvet upholstered couch, taking up most of the space by sitting with his legs spread and his arms hanging off the wooden back. "A wench will always be a wench."

The seamstress' brow twitches, and I swear she's going to jump across the room and rip him to shreds. She walked all the way up to the inn at Theodas' request to show me new dresses, but every single one I've tried on so far has been rejected by the elves. Not that they should even have a *say* in the matter, mind you. Iacar is already difficult to please, but add in Theodas and Rhys? Total nightmare.

Theodas has strong opinions when it comes to fashion, even when the clothes are meant for someone else. For every dress I try on, he asks if it can be made a different color before tomorrow night. I guess it's possible with magic, but the seamstress explained twice already that the spell needs to "cook" and won't be ready in time. By her third explanation, I suspect all she wants to do is pack up and leave on the spot. That's not to mention Theodas' other asinine requests, Iacar's insults (mostly aimed at me), and my own disinterest. Yet the seamstress is still here, forcing herself to smile for the sake of her coin. Having worked at a fast-food chain in the past, I can relate.

"This dress is the best we've seen so far," Theodas comments, twirling me around by the hand. "What do you think?"

"It is no different than the one before," Rhys replies coolly. He's been oddly quiet since I returned from the brothel last night, only speaking when spoken to. But I can't tell if that's because he's trying to keep a low profile in front of the seamstress, or if there's something more to it.

"The sleeves are tight," I comment. They're actually cutting off my circulation. Is it from all the workouts and training I did with Rhys? Or is it all the bread and cheese I've been eating? The latter is more likely.

"The sleeves are supposed to be tight, my lady," the seamstress explains politely, tucking a golden strand of hair behind her elongated ear. "It is the fashion nowadays."

Yes, but how am I going to punch someone's lights out when I can barely lift my arms?

Oh, who am I kidding? I'm not going to be able to land a hit on any trueblood. The thing with Gwyn was a total fluke, and I can't count on getting lucky like that again.

"I like the style, but the color is off," Theodas decides. "Are you certain you will not wear a corset, Maria?"

"I'm positive." I don't need to pass out in the middle of a task.

"Ah, well I suppose after what happened to Elizabeth Swann in *Pirates of the Caribbean*, you would be correct in your apprehension." Theodas sure has a good memory for someone who hasn't even seen these movies with his own eyes.

The seamstress takes me behind a partition and dresses me in yet another gown from her seemingly endless supply. The gold embellishments on green silk make the outfit look more modern for sure, and the sleeves are a bit looser, but I don't exactly scream "belle of the ball."

"Can't I just wear a tunic and pants?" Rhys, Iacar, and Theodas initially mistook me for a guy anyway.

"Absolutely not!" Theodas exclaims. "You have to look rich. Polished. *Sophisticated.*"

He says another group of adjectives in Elvish, and while I'm not sure what they mean, I'm certain they're other synonyms of "rich."

"Well, I'm finished for the day." I take off the dress and put my normal one back on, which is comfortable and doesn't drag on the floor. At least I can run away in it!

Which is exactly what I do.

"Thank you," I say to the seamstress quickly, flattening out my skirt.

"Wait, Maria! Where are you going?" Theodas shouts.

"I need some air!"

"There's perfectly good air in here—oi!"

I'm already out the door.

It's a sunny day, but the early spring weather makes the temperature perfect for training outside. I should probably get back to that routine, though I'm not sure who I could ask for help. Iacar seems like he'd be way too harsh, and Theodas gets distracted easily. Rhys could be an option, if not for the whole "avoiding him" thing. Then again, I'm doing a pretty shit job on that front. It's hard to avoid someone you live in close quarters with, especially when they're your only means of shelter and food. And when they don't want to be ignored.

Rhys follows me outside to the front of the inn, the wooden door creaking open behind me.

"Oh? Did you come outside for fresh air, too?" I ask, trying to remain casual.

He strides over and leans his arms on the stone wall, overlooking the town. "It *was* getting a bit stuffy inside."

"Unbearably so."

"Are you truly planning to attend this auction tomorrow night with Theodas?"

"I don't have much choice; I need to find the sword. I'm not sure what will happen if I return home empty-handed. Nothing good, probably." Not if Neil has anything to say about it, and I trust he will. He's already proven how serious he is about forcing me to comply with his plans. "Why do you ask? Are you worried about me?"

"Attending an underground auction at night is dangerous on its own, and I imagine most of the items for sale are illicit based on the details of the event. Do you know where it will be held?"

"Yeah. Gaelith sent over more details this morning." Along with a bouquet of roses. But I'll leave that part out.

"I suppose you have proven yourself quite capable, but that does not prevent me from worrying."

"You don't owe me anything. I have a hard time believing you're helping me because of some honor code or elven tradition, or even purely out of the goodness of your heart." People just...aren't like that. Follow the rule, not the exception. Though, if I'm being completely honest with myself, my gut tells me Rhys *is* the exception—the type of person who helps others without expecting anything. That makes my refusal and rejection all the more important.

"That *is* how most are," Rhys agrees. "They will only help if they gain something in return."

At least he understands. "And what are you getting from me?"

"If I told you, would you believe me? You cannot lie to me, but I can lie to you. I wonder if anything I say holds weight in your heart."

I answer without thinking. "Of course it does."

"Is that so?" he muses.

Rhys might be mysterious and indirect at times, and sure, I don't know him *that* well. Even when he was tutoring me, he never really talked about himself. But weirdly enough, I trust him. Both in the past and the present.

Don't get me wrong—I know this Rhys and that Rhys are different, but they feel the same to me. What's strange is, *Prince* Rhys is so much warmer to me, while *my* Rhys was cold as ice. Most of the time. It makes me wonder what happens between us. Am I going to do something bad to him? Make him resent me? The possibility shouldn't bother me, but it does.

"The other elves have not yet reached the inn," Rhys says, changing the subject. "If they do not bring your backpack to you, how will you continue your journey?"

"With difficulty." The supplies will make things easier for me, but it's not a dealbreaker. "If I find the sword at the auction, then I won't need the backpack."

Not that I anticipate obtaining the sword will be easy. Even if it *is* in fact at the auction, I'm broke as a joke. I'm likely going to have to bargain for it or steal it. Considering I have no grounds on which to bargain, the latter option seems more likely.

"Tomorrow night, if you permit it, I would like to accompany you to the auction," Rhys tells me finally. "I will wear a mask to conceal my identity."

"No. It's too dangerous." In all sorts of ways.

"That is precisely why I would prefer to escort you. But I will not force my company upon you. Of course, it is entirely your choice."

I falter. "I don't want to see you hurt. Not because of me."

Not again.

"I will not be," he replies, and perhaps his confidence is not unfounded. "But I speak multiple languages fluently and will be able to assist you should you require it."

He has a point.

"I'm not your friend. I'm not your *anything*. Why are you concerned about me?" I blurt. It's a stupid question to ask, I realize. Then again, I've been acting like a dumbass this entire chapter. I know it; I own it. Does it make the fact that, instead of pushing him away, I'm doing the opposite? No. No, it does not.

Never ask questions you don't want the answers to.

Rhys takes a moment before answering, staring deeply into my eyes. "I believe you already know, Maria."

I do. But if neither of us admits to it aloud, or even in our heads, we'll be able to ignore it. At least for now.

"You are certain this is where we are supposed to be?"

"Pretty certain."

"You are lying."

"Thanks for pointing that out."

And here I am, thinking this night couldn't get worse.

Rhys, true to his word, wears a white mask to conceal his identity. I thought that covering half his face would reduce the strange feeling I get when I look at him. I was very wrong. He kind of resembles the Phantom of the Opera, the Gerard Butler movie version. Except Rhys is an elf and his hair is pale blonde, and he's not wearing a suit. But I bet he would look great in —

Shut up, Mar!

The seamstress ended up leaving me with a dress yesterday, a purple floor-length gown that's surprisingly lightweight once I get it over my head. It's not very flattering, and Theodas doesn't pull any punches in telling me so, but it will serve its purpose.

That is, if we even make it to the auction house.

Gaelith was kind enough to send over a map and mark the entrance to the venue, but I still can't find it, even with Rhys' help. It's validating, at least, that Rhys is having just as much trouble reading the map as I am.

"I'm sure it's over here," I whisper, pointing to a small shop squished between two larger buildings.

"Perhaps this is a secret entrance. Let us try."

We approach the shop with caution and use the metal knocker on the door, but no one answers. Instead, the door opens on its own.

Rhys and I exchange a glance as if to ask, *Should we go inside?*

The answer is: we don't have a choice.

A curtain of shadows hangs over the entrance, preventing any light outside from spilling in. The darkness is so unnatural, I'm guessing it's a spell of sorts to keep intruders away. Makes sense, given this is supposed to be a *secret* auction. I just thought there'd be some sort of bouncer at the door. That's one less complication, I guess.

Feeling around with my hands, I clutch a handrail by my hip and descend a steep stone staircase. When we reach the bottom, there's still no light, and no doorway either. Instead, all I feel is a wall in front of my face. And cobwebs. Oh God, get me out of here!

I reach above my head, pressing the stones like buttons until the ground begins to shake. Rhys grabs my arm in the darkness to steady me. The wall blocking our path pops open a crack, revealing another room on the other side.

Now that's what I call dumb luck! Rhys and I pry the wall open wider until we're both able to fit through the passage.

Paintings lean against one wall, while a maze of metal racks filled with artifacts are arranged on the other side of the room. This isn't the auction house—it's a treasure room.

"Oh no," I murmur. "This is...too easy."

"There are the swords." Rhys motions to a stack of them in the corner. "Take a look. I will stand guard."

"Will do." But I can't shake the sinking feeling that things are going too well, and it's just a matter of time before it all comes crashing down. Hopefully not literally. Though I question the structural integrity of the room.

No time to waste on that now.

The swords are in the back corner, so I'm not too concerned about being seen, but there's hardly any light over here. I have to unsheathe every single sword and run my hands over the metal to check for an engraving. None of them have tassels, though I'm not sure if that even matters, since it's something that can be taken off. The engraving, I would assume, is the magical part. But as I check the swords, I have zero luck finding anything resembling the Divinities Sword.

The door opens with a creak just as I put a sword back on the shelf. Rhys barrels over to me and shoves us both into an empty crate nearby, closing the lid just as someone enters the room.

Being in a confined space, our bodies squeezed together, would probably be romantic in any other circumstance. But I'm 80% certain the smooth surface I'm pressed against is a coffin. So are we really "alone" in here?

Bleh. Dealing with zombies on the ship should have

desensitized me, but…come on. A corpse is a corpse, and I don't want any part of it, reanimated or not.

By the sound of the heavy footsteps outside, there are multiple people in the room. Their voices are gruff but crystal clear, as only a piece of wood barricades us from the auctioneers. However, they aren't speaking Elvish. It's another language I'm not familiar with.

My cheek presses against Rhys' chest, and I can hear the loud thump of his heart. I can't move, can't make a sound, as someone stops by the swords right next to us.

I hold my breath, waiting for them to rip open the crate and stab us. But they don't. Instead, they move back toward the doorway with a muttered phrase, slamming the door shut behind them.

Rhys doesn't open the crate until we're certain the auctioneers have left, helping me out first. Taking a step back, I can see I was correct—the crate *does* contain a coffin. Yikes.

"Thanks," I whisper, turning back toward the swords. None of them were the Divinities Sword. My heart deflates immediately; it's a dead end. I *knew* this would be too convenient of a plot point. But I kind of hoped I would find it here anyway.

"You cannot find the sword?" Rhys says in a low voice.

"No. It's not here," I reply, trying not to sound too dejected. "We should go before we get caught."

We walk through the racks of antiquities toward the door, but as we do, I hear a cough from the other side of the room. My head snaps toward the noise, and my body switches to fight or flight mode. Though, let's be honest—it's mostly flight mode.

Did one of the auctioneers stay behind to guard the

room? No. I don't see anyone, at least. Could someone else be trying to rob this room, too?

Rhys steps in front of me cautiously, creeping toward a cloth covering the source of the sound. Peeling back the layer of stained and tattered muslin, an iron cage sits covered in grime. And inside, curled into a ball, a naked child stares back at us.

CHAPTER TWELVE

R hys recoils, turning away from the iron. If the cage elicits that strong of a reaction from him, I'm guessing whoever manages this room isn't a fairy or an elf. Both species are weak to iron, which makes locking a child in this type of cage even crueler. It's torture.

"Stay back," I warn Rhys, my voice coming out more desperate than I intend it to. Images of him in Neil's house flash in my mind like a macabre slideshow, seeing him die next to the ugliest modern art statue I've ever laid eyes on.

No.

I grab a sword from the back, my hands shaking as I shove it through the door handle. That should hold it for now, but I need to work fast. Rummaging through the shelves, I pick up a set of hair pins, using them as makeshift lockpicking tools. Meanwhile, Rhys arms himself, having no qualms about stealing whatever he can use as a weapon. I figured he was the paladin type—a classic hero with steadfast morals. I'm glad he's not; I don't think we'd get along quite so well otherwise.

Then again, this *is* the same guy who suggested we trash someone's bedroom in a petty revenge scheme.

He keeps his distance from the cage, letting me work. Even *he* knows his limits, it seems. After a few minutes, the lock finally clicks open. I steal a sheet covering one of the paintings and wrap the kid inside, holding her small body in my arms. She looks like she's been physically beaten. People who hurt kids are absolute scum. Animal abusers, too.

For the record, I'm not doing this because I'm a hero, or even a good person — I'm doing it because I *have* to. There's not a chance I would be able to think about anything else if I left this kid here and went about my life.

The kid croaks in my arms, lifting her head. She says something in a language I don't understand, her voice a weak whisper.

I shake my head, replying in Elvish, "Sorry, I only speak Elvish."

The kid lifts an arm, trembling as she points toward the shelf behind me.

Rhys follows the kid's shaking finger, taking a book off one of the racks. The kid nods weakly.

"Just take it," I tell him. "Let's get out of here before someone discovers us."

Rhys helps me get the kid through the doorway we came through. We exit back through the shadowy stairwell, pushing the stone wall closed firmly behind us. Making our way quietly up the steps, I hold the child tightly to my chest.

When we finally reach the top of the stairs, I notice the entrance is now guarded. A fairy with bright yellow wings stands outside, his back to us. He's wide and tall, his beige tunic stretched thinly over his muscular arms.

He turns, probably having heard our footsteps. Due to

whatever magic holds the shadows in this stairwell, we couldn't see him until it was too late.

Rhys' reflexes are fast enough to react first, shoving the fae guard to the ground and sprinting ahead. I follow suit, struggling with the kid as I run as fast as my legs can carry us. I can barely see where we're headed, blindly following Rhys down a narrow alley and a maze of buildings. The girl in my arms cries every time my feet beat on the cobblestone. Which, by the way, is *very* uncomfortable to run on. I'm going to file a complaint to the city. Or the shoemaker — these soles are way too thin.

I hate hurting the kid but staying alive tops everything else. I'll apologize later.

The guard is way faster than I thought he'd be, chasing us in circles. Rhys is trying his best to lose him — we wouldn't want to lead the fairy back to the inn — but no chance. Especially not with me slowing us down.

The fairy shouts something unintelligible, pointing to a puddle. The water leaps up, forming an ice wall in front of me. I skid to a stop, trying to avoid crashing. Instead, I topple backward, barely managing to protect the kid in my arms as I fall. My head knocks against the stones, and the kid accidentally kicks me in the stomach when I land. I'm glad I didn't eat beforehand.

The fairy clenches his fists, the ice wall melting into spikes. So this is the magic of a trueblood.

I've *heard* of the type of magic truebloods possess, but aside from Astaroth, I've never seen anything like this first-hand. Shadowborn only have enhanced senses and strength (myself being the exception to that). This is on a whole 'nother level.

I knew that truebloods were supposed to be more

powerful than shadowborn, but compared to the cleaning spells I learned in school, the ability to control the elements is...okay, *fitting*. And not unsurprising. But the power gap between myself and my peers is already very wide, and now, the gap between myself and truebloods is like a gaping chasm. How am I going to defeat Astaroth or Neil with just a damn sword if they can, I don't know, shoot flames from their fingers?

The only power the elves have is detecting lies. The fae can control the elements? How is *that* an equal distribution of power? And how did elves even fight an entire *war* with them?

Rhys, as per usual, seems to be able to read my mind. As if on cue, he picks up a few pebbles from the ground and launches them straight at the fairy. In midair, the tiny rocks no bigger than my thumbnail begin to grow and morph into full-sized stone arrows. The fairy attempts to block them, but he's not fast enough; one of the arrows catches him in the shoulder, eliciting a yowl of pain and a fountain of blood.

Rhys doesn't stop there. He unsheathes the sword at his hip and, without hesitation, runs the fairy through the chest in a single clean blow. The stone arrows on the ground turn back into pebbles as Rhys jerks the sword out of the fairy's body, wiping the blood off on the dead man's shirt and sheathing the sword again.

"I apologize for the gruesome display," he says quietly, taking hold of the child. "That man saw your face."

It was a brutal move, but I can't exactly judge him for it. I stabbed Penny in the neck. If I hadn't, she would have kept coming for me. I don't feel anything in particular for the dead guard, which might be a sign that I'm not a great person—but I think you already know that.

"Come. Let us leave this place before his friends show up," Rhys says.

We return to the inn quietly, entering through the back and going straight to Rhys' bedroom. It's the largest suite in the inn, which is fair since he's a prince and all. He lays the kid down gently on his king-sized bed, mindful of her multitude of injuries.

Now that I'm not running for my life, I can take a good look at her. Her hair is matted with dirt and her bronze skin is marred with bruising, cuts, and boils. She doesn't have elf ears, but she doesn't have fairy wings, either.

"I will call a healer," Rhys says with a grimace. "Are you alright? You took a nasty fall."

"I'm fine." Shockingly. "How bad is the iron poisoning?"

"I am no medic, but this does not look like iron poisoning to me. This child was simply beaten, possibly starved."

"Not iron poisoning?" That's a relief. "Are *you* okay from being around all that iron?"

"Yes. I will be fine." Rhys pulls on a string near the door, which I presume is a call button of sorts. "I apologize. You did not find the sword you were looking for."

"It's fine. It was a long shot, anyway." But now I'm back to searching for it. God knows where else I can look. "I'm sorry I dragged you into this mess for nothing."

What if the Divinities Sword isn't here after all? My time-traveling power is new to me, and this is the first time I've used it without Jenna or Todd's help. This could all just be one massive screw-up.

"I will continue to assist your search. Perhaps there is another information broker we can consult," Rhys suggests kindly.

Theodas finally answers Rhys' summons, knocking on the door before opening it. "Your Highness, you have returned early."

"Theodas, call a healer. Be discreet," he warns, quickly going on to explain what happened. Theodas' expression turns serious as he looks at the child on the bed, checking her ears.

"But this child isn't —"

"Theodas."

"Of course, Your Highness. I will call for a healer at once." Theodas stalks out, closing the door behind him and running downstairs.

Rhys takes a seat at a small table in the corner, removing his face mask. "Are you alright, truly?"

"Do I not look okay?"

"No. You are very calm. More so than me," he admits.

"You just killed somebody."

"I have killed many in battle. It gets easier the more you do it." Rhys grimaces, horrified by his own confession. "My apologies. This is not appropriate conversation."

I sit beside him. "Because you don't like talking about it? Or because you think it makes me uncomfortable?"

"Both."

"It doesn't make me uncomfortable. I understand not wanting to talk about it, though. Sometimes there are things in life which cause such great pain, and no matter how intelligent we are, we can't describe the profoundness of our feelings with words alone. It's like nothing we say can truly capture how we feel, so it's better to say nothing at all than to make our emotions seem shallow."

"Then what is one supposed to do?" Rhys asks. "Keep it all inside?"

"No. Say it anyway. Struggle through the pointless endeavor and hope that there's someone out there who understands your fumbling words."

"Like you?"

"I—"

"My lord." Iacar bursts through the door, followed by a middle-aged elf woman. "I have brought the healer you requested. And, with her, news."

"What is it?" Rhys asks warily.

"We must speak in private." Iacar hoists the child up into his arms, carrying her to another room. The healer follows, her eyes trained on the ground. When Iacar returns, he closes the door. "My lord, men are searching for you and the wench. Someone saw you leave an alleyway where they discovered a corpse."

"So quickly?" Rhys' brow furrows.

"Yes. They will draw a rendering of the wench soon. But I caught word from a servant that men are prowling the streets as we speak. You should go to the safe room."

Rhys shakes his head. "I will have to make preparations. Maria can go into the safe room, and I will join her after."

"Is this really needed?" I ask.

"Yes. Follow Iacar, and bring this with you." He hands me the book he stole from the treasure room. "I must make sure things are taken care of before I go inside. You rest, and I will be there soon."

"Alright." I don't think he would ask me to do this unless absolutely necessary, so I comply.

Iacar pushes the bookcase on the far wall to the side, revealing a hidden passageway behind it. He leads me down, the room below lit up with glowing glass orbs. Unlike the ones throughout the city streets, these provide enough light to see clearly. They're even warm, making the room a comfortable temperature.

The furnishings aren't as lavish as the bedrooms upstairs, but there are two bunk beds. At least Rhys and I won't have to sleep in the same bed. Not that I'm thinking of anything inappropriate. I just think it would be awkward. Because...you know. He's so...

No. Back to the room. There's also a desk and a couch, and a bathroom to the side. It's like a small apartment, minus a kitchenette.

"Don't worry," Iacar says, offering me rare words of assurance. "I'm certain they'll give up soon."

"They had a child in a cage. We stole that child. They'll be looking for us for sure."

"Don't worry," Iacar repeats, clearly as good as I am when it comes to comforting others. Which is to say, terrible. "Rest up. I'll bring ye the Linguist's Orb and some food in a bit."

"Thank you."

After he leaves, I take a seat on the couch and open the stolen book. It's handwritten in Elvish, but the letters are chicken scratch. I can barely make out the words, let alone translate them in my head.

I guess it's not that important. I'm curious about why the kid wanted this book, sure, but it doesn't do much to distract from the fact that I failed tonight. Big time. Not only was I unsuccessful in getting the sword, but now I've dragged Rhys into a manhunt over this kid.

I don't regret bringing her back, but now the auctioneers will be hunting us along with the fae. And I doubt this kid is the only child they've kidnapped. The auctioneers might not have noticed a missing sword, or cared, but the kid is proof of illegal operations.

Which, of course, puts Rhys in a tough spot, too. He just wants to go home, and I'm continually making it harder for him to do that. I *knew* I should have refused his help and gone by myself. Then again, I don't think I'd have been able to escape without him.

The worst part about being useless is, I don't know how to go about fixing it. Training? I've already tried, and my power level is so frighteningly low, I don't stand a chance.

The sword should give me the upper hand against Astaroth once I find it. And figure out how exactly it works. But one step at a time.

CHAPTER THIRTEEN

The hardest part about the nightmares is when I know they aren't real and I still can't stop them. I've heard some people can control the world within their dreams through lucid dreaming, but it's as if my mind doesn't *want* to stop them. Like I'm subconsciously trying to punish myself.

Why not, right? I deserve it.

By the time I wake up, I'm more exhausted than when I fell asleep. Rhys sits in the chair beside me, his eyes closed. God his eyelashes are thick. The kid is tucked into one of the bunk beds, swathed in blankets like a cocoon. At least she's out of the cage for now, but the possibility of other kids being tortured in the same way sends a shiver down my spine.

Rhys slowly opens his eyes, sitting up to look at me.

"Sorry. I didn't mean to wake you," I say.

"I was not sleeping. I was merely resting my eyes."

I don't need to be an elf to tell that's a lie. But, being the kindhearted person I am, I don't call his bluff. "How's the kid?"

"Stable for now," he says mildly. "She needs rest and medical attention. With her condition, she will not be able to travel easily."

The Linguist's Orb must be active, because I can understand every word he's saying without any effort.

"Will there be long-term damage?"

"It's unclear. Her superficial wounds will heal, but it seems she swallowed some sort of substance that makes it difficult for her to speak."

Fuck. "Isn't there a spell for something like this? Any sort of healing potion?"

"For normal wounds, perhaps. But wounds caused by magic like this can take much longer to heal," Rhys says. "We will do our best to help."

"She's just a kid," I mutter.

"It is children who suffer most from the mistakes of adults."

"That's not fair. I know the *world* isn't fair," I add quickly, trying not to sound childish. "But…it's *really* unfair. Kids don't get to choose the circumstances of their birth. They don't choose the color of their skin, how wealthy they are, their assigned gender, or what kind of parents they get. Or don't."

"And yet these things can determine the trajectory of their lives."

"Exactly."

Rhys tosses me a blanket to wrap around my shoulders. "Do you ever wonder how different your life could have been if just one of those things changed, Maria?"

"Yes." More often than I'd like to admit. "My dad…my

biological one… I grew up believing that he was a drug dealer. It turns out he's not. He just came back into my life a few months ago and apparently he's rich. And a total jackass."

"Do you resent him?"

"Yeah. Even though I *know* my life has been better without him. It's not like I wish he never abandoned me. But the fact that he did feels like a personal affront." Being rejected, especially as a child, never feels good. "I hate him. More than I've ever hated anyone."

Even Max—and he taught me just how much animosity I'm capable of having. I never thought anyone else would come close to Max, but Neil surpassed my expectations in the worst possible way. If I haven't even recovered from Max yet, will I ever be able to resolve my issues with Neil? And more importantly, how he makes me feel about myself?

"Even if I hate my biological father, I wonder what kind of life I would have lived with him," I continue, for my own benefit mostly. Rhys probably doesn't want to hear this, but in telling him…I almost feel like he understands better than anyone. "My curiosity feels like a betrayal, not just to myself, but to the family who took me in."

"Because your biological father…hurt your adopted father?" Rhys asks.

I'm shocked he remembers that detail from my truth serum-induced rambling. "Yeah. Before coming here, I told myself that I would do anything to protect them. I failed, though—I wasn't careful enough, and now my dad is dead. That's not something you can undo, no matter how much you want to. As insistent as I've been about needing to find the Divinities Sword, I'm terrified to go back to my family. I know they love me, but how will they feel when they realize that I'm the reason my dad died?"

Great. I'm full-on spiraling now. But this is what happens when I'm Maria. I remember who I really am, how I feel about myself, and just give in to my emotions. Maybe I've been kidding myself with these stupid characters after all. Thinking I can change, thinking I can escape.

And Rhys is here, trapped and forced to be polite while he listens to how crazy I am. How *pathetic* I am. If this doesn't turn him away from me, I don't think anything will. At this point, I'm a walking, talking red flag.

"I'm sorry," I apologize quickly. "I didn't mean to get so heated."

"You have nothing to apologize for," Rhys replies softly.

"No, I'm oversharing. Sorry. It's hard to stop once I've started. I guess seeing kids getting hurt triggers me. It just brings up a lot of stuff. But I'm okay now."

I'm lying, but this time, Rhys doesn't call me out on it. Instead, he asks, "Can I tell you a story?"

"You want to tell me a story?" I repeat. "Is it a happy story?"

"No. But you are fond of telling stories, yes? I thought I might try my hand at it."

I nod. "Okay. I'm listening"

"Once upon a time, there was a boy born in an elf village on the peninsula of Eidera," Rhys begins. "His parents were impoverished healers who believed that elves had an obligation to help any guests who came to their land. A code of honor, so to speak. Eidera was peaceful at the time, and his parents were not very cautious.

"One day, the boy and his mother went to the mountains to collect herbs for her healing potions. On the way back, they happened across a stranger. He was injured, so the mother brought him back and nursed him to health in the village. The mother told her son that it was his *duty* to help others, because there is nothing more precious than a life. Once the man healed, he thanked the villagers for their help and promised to return. But they did not expect him to return so soon, and with reinforcements.

"The injured man revealed himself to be a fairy duke of the Summer Court. He began burning the village to the ground and pillaging the houses. The boy was terrified, and his parents sent him to nearby village on horseback to get help. When the boy arrived, he begged the village head for aid. They had the means; they were warriors, and their numbers were strong. But they refused to help and sent the boy on his way. The boy did not stop. He traveled to three more villages, but no one was willing to lend a hand. When the boy finally returned to his home, all he found was a pile of rotting corpses and half burnt buildings. Not a single elf survived the attack, and the boy was alone.

"Without any means of surviving, the boy became a beggar. He was beaten for eating fallen food scraps and sleeping on the street. When people passed, they looked at him with utter disgust. And he thought to himself that his mother was wrong. Life is not precious—one's *own* life is precious. Everyone else only looked after themselves. They held strict beliefs around morality, but at the end of the day, they were selfish. If nothing was to be gained, they would never lift a finger to help.

"The boy grew up resentful and feral, more animal than elf. It was only by chance that the elf king found the boy, sleeping in a bush and covered in dirt. The king extended his hand and told the boy that his parents once saved him on the battlefield. The king wanted to adopt the boy as his son and make him a prince. The boy was apprehensive at first, but the king brought him back and truly did grant him a royal title. The prince was cleaned and given etiquette classes. Those who scorned him in the past now worshipped at his feet. But more importantly, the prince had a family again—a place where he belonged. Life was good, until the war began. The prince begged the king to let him fight. He promised he would have his vengeance on the fae, and the king easily agreed.

"The night before the prince was set to leave for war, he overheard the king speaking to an advisor. The king told the advisor that he did not bring the prince back because he owed his parents. No, the king had heard rumors of the boy and thought he would make a good sacrifice. Whispers of war had existed for years. The king hoped the prince would die on the battlefield and become a martyr of the people. A symbol to fight for and nothing more. The king told his advisor that he hoped the prince was tortured. He hoped the corpse would be desecrated, so as to arouse more anger in his troops. The prince realized then that he was never truly part of the royal family. He was a joke of a prince, a puppet, just a tool to be used and discarded as the king willed it. If the king wanted him to die, he was supposed to lie down and do it.

"But the prince did not die. He did not want to play into the king's hands. Instead, he defeated his enemies, driven by spite and resentment. By the end of the war, the king and the prince fought together side by side. The king was injured on the battlefield, mortally wounded. There was nothing that could be done. He feebly reached toward the prince and asked for his final rites, but the prince turned away. Angry and bitter all those years later, the prince left the king to die alone."

I wait for Rhys to continue, but when he doesn't speak, doesn't even *look* at me, I ask, "And did the prince regret his choice?"

Rhys hesitates before shaking his head. "No. He has no regrets. Because like the young girl from *your* story, the prince does not know how to pardon such a deep betrayal. It is expected in elven society to forgive others if they apologize, that redemption is always possible for even the worst criminals. But why should it be? If one commits a truly heinous act against another, why should the offender be exonerated and move on if the victim is still living with that trauma? The privileged act in malice and expect kindness in return. I have no qualms about returning evil with evil. Perhaps that makes me a bad person. But I have yet to find a reason to care—because the world is filled with bad people. What difference does one more make?"

"Then we would both be bad people," I say. "But you know what? I'm okay with that, because I'll never be as bad as my biological father. And you'll never be as bad as your adoptive one."

"And how do you know if you are reaching that point? How do you know if you have gone too far?"

"My sister," I answer immediately. Tasha's face surfaces in my head, and I can't help but smile. "I have a sister, Tasha. She's always been with me, even when I didn't deserve her company. She's honest with me and, even though she's been through worse than I have, she's incredibly kind. She's the type of person I respect the most— someone who turns conflict into opportunity and is still able to maintain her morals."

"I have a sister, too," Rhys tells me. "She is strong. I have not seen her in two years, but I look forward to reuniting. She is the reason I wish to return to the palace."

"I'm sorry that I threw a wrench in your plans. I mean, I'm sorry your travel is delayed now." I scratch my head. "You must be eager to see her."

"This is important," Rhys says firmly. "She will understand, I am sure."

"If she's your sister, does that mean she's the king's daughter? A princess?"

"Yes. She helped me grow accustomed to living as a noble," Rhys explains. "It was quite different from living on the streets, as you can imagine."

"Oh, definitely. Whenever I went to a new home, the parents always expected me to be a blank slate. They were disappointed when I had my own habits and opinions. Adapting quickly was the key to gaining any sort of affection."

"It is astounding how little empathy adults can have. Siraye was a child herself, but she was more patient with me than any tutor. Unlike everyone else, she never made me feel less than because of where I came from. She never wanted to erase my past."

Although our experiences are obviously different, they align in all the important places. For the first time, I don't feel bad after talking about such a heavy topic. Actually, I feel *understood*. Understood by an elf prince, who throws me a smile that lights up the entire room.

It's not just that he's handsome. I haven't felt this connected to someone since meeting Tasha. And unlike before, when my attraction to him scared me, I'm oddly calm now. My body feels like it's floating.

"You shouldn't smile at me like that," I warn him. "I told you, when you smile at me, it's too dazzling. Like staring at the sun."

"Is that so?"

"Yes, and there's no need to be so smug about it."

"I am not smug."

"Now *you're* the liar."

His smile widens. Damn it.

"Did you figure out what the book says?" I ask, finally changing the subject. I point to the tome in his lap, which he must have fallen asleep reading. "I couldn't decipher the handwriting."

"I read a few chapters, but it just seems like an ordinary book," Rhys admits, thankfully going along with the shift in conversation. "It tells the story of a magic tree in the heart of the Everwildes, the Wisdom Tree. I heard of the tree as a boy, but only as a legend. It is not *real*. The information contained within these pages would be something one could find at any bookstore."

"What *is* the Wisdom Tree?"

"Legends say that the tree is omniscient. It can answer any question," Rhys explains. "But no one has ever seen it. All who seek the tree never end up finding it."

The kid groans from her bed, opening her eyes weakly. "Map…"

"What?" I kneel beside her, leaning in closer to hear her voice. "What did you say?"

"Tear out the pages…makes a map…"

"I did not see any map." Rhys hands the book back to me, and I flip through the pages. There isn't a map, but each chapter has a weird, abstract illustration. I tear out the beginning of each chapter and lay the pieces on the floor, putting the picture together like a puzzle. When I'm finished, I look down at...

A blob of nothing.

"I didn't just damage some priceless artifact, right?" I mutter.

"No." Rhys switches a few of the pages around. "Now it is finished."

"What am I looking at?" It's still just a massive blob of ink to me.

Rhys hesitates, circling around the pages on the ground before finally answering. "Maria, this is the continent of Eidera."

CHAPTER FOURTEEN

"I'm no cartographer, but those look like mountains."

"You are quite a keen observer."

"Are you being sarcastic?"

"Would I dare, Maria?"

"So that's a yes, then." The Linguist's Orb doesn't do a great job of picking up on that, but I think I know Rhys well enough to tell when he's being sarcastic. Which is insane, since I've known *my* Rhys for much longer than Prince Rhys over here. Then again, after our little heart-to-heart, I *do* feel closer to him.

One of the major differences between Prince Rhys and my Rhys is that the prince smiles a lot more easily, even when I continually warn him not to. It isn't good for my heart.

I try to chalk it up to being confined in a small space with him for the past three days. He should come with a warning: Excess Rhys exposure could cause crush to develop.

Not that I have a *crush* on him. Because kids get

crushes, and I'm not a kid. I'm eighteen. I just...get a heart flutter when he's close. And feel super comfortable sharing my innermost feelings with him. That isn't a crush. Right?

Worse than his smiling is his laughter. There should be some sort of rule to prevent good-looking people from having nice laughs. Especially when they're laughing at my stupid jokes. It's inflating my ego way too much.

Of course, we haven't just been joking around. We've been studying the stolen book, going over every single line written, and reviewing the map.

"Do you think the journey will be too difficult to complete?" Rhys asks me, though I know he's not asking out of genuine curiosity. He's just teasing me, something he's grown far too comfortable doing.

"Of course I think it's too difficult." That doesn't mean I won't do it, but I'm sure as hell going to complain to my heart's content! "I have to trek halfway across the continent, over a bunch of mountains, and cross several rivers all to get to a talking tree and ask it one question?"

"You may ask it *three* questions."

"Not the point. And before I get to enter this super-secret grove the tree grows in, I have to pass three tests."

"Correct. Each test will be more terrible than the last," Rhys says.

"Does it really say that in the book?"

"No, but it is implied. The first gatekeeper will give a test of knowledge. The next, a test of strength. The third, a test of wills."

Wow, that sounds super fun. *Not.*

"It will be difficult to do alone," Rhys continues.

"I know. But I *am* going alone," I insist. "Once I get my

backpack back, that is. Oh, and after those auction house goons stop patrolling the streets for us."

Which, according to our intel (aka Iacar), they have been doing 24/7. But that's beside the point.

When I can finally escape this city, my next move is finding the Wisdom Tree. The first thing Rhys asked when he found out my plan was if he could come along. I shot him down, obviously. I've already delayed him enough, and I don't want to drag him along on some dangerous side quest. It wouldn't be right, and it wouldn't be smart.

But then again, when have I done the *smart* thing here? I've acknowledged what *would* be smart options, and then I do the exact opposite. For example, I told myself that I should be distant and cold to Rhys. Instead, we're growing closer with every passing hour and finding more things we have in common. It's like being with him puts me in a love-struck trance, and pulling away from him is the most unnatural thing in the world.

Like we were *destined* to be together, or some crap like that.

Before, I could have written off his desire to help me as an obligation on his end. But I would be a total idiot to deny that there's something more between us, and it doesn't scare me anymore as much as it should. The ending of our little story has already been spoiled, and despite knowing what's going to happen, I find myself falling…

You know what? It would be in my best interest *not* to finish that sentence.

I don't get it. It's never been particularly difficult for me to be cold to others. But with him, I can't find it in me to be intentionally cruel. Not just because we're trapped together in a room alone for God knows how much longer. I guess the kid is here with us, but she hasn't provided much riveting conversation, on account of her injuries. She sleeps most of the day away, only getting up to eat and go to the bathroom. Which, trust me, has *not* been fun.

The door to the safe room opens, snapping me out of my thoughts. I expect Theodas again, bringing us a warm meal, but it's not. It's Lyari, closely followed by another elf I don't recognize.

The last time we met…not to brag, but I saved Lyari's life. I didn't expect him to throw himself into my arms sobbing or anything, but a word of thanks would have been appreciated. Instead, he looks at me like I'm dirt on the bottom of his shoes.

"Oh, you're still alive," he says.

Yeah, nice to see you, too, little brat.

Lyari shoves my backpack into my arms, unable to meet my eyes. "Here's your stuff."

"Thanks." For the backpack, not for the attitude.

He ignores me and turns his attention to the prince, his demeanor changing completely. "Your Highness, I apologize for arriving so late. Theodas explained everything to us."

The other elf, a balding man with a beer gut and a large medallion hanging around his neck, pats Lyari on the back. "The fae were on our tails, but we managed to lose them for a bit. They were tracking us ferociously. They'll be here within three days."

"Thank you, Kolvar. Has Iacar been informed?" Rhys asks, sounding more serious than he did a few minutes ago when it was just us.

The older elf nods. "He has. We are making preparations to leave now."

"No. The Violet City is in neutral territory, but it is still run by elves. The fae will pillage, regardless of whether or not we are here," Rhys explains, pacing the small room. "We must stay."

"Your Highness, you are a prince. Whether you like it or not, your life is worth more than those in the city," Kolvar says gravely. "You must flee."

It's the wrong argument to make, especially with Rhys. Now that I know what he's been through, I understand that Rhys would never show the same disregard that others have shown *him* in the past.

"You know better than most why I cannot." Rhys' voice comes out harsher than I've ever heard it.

"But staying here would be consigning yourself to death!" Kolvar continues, obviously not getting the message. "My prince, please reconsider. You are not just a foot soldier. You are a symbol, a beacon of hope."

"I will not flee while my people are being slaughtered."

"Uh, excuse me?" I raise my hand like a child in school. "I have an idea."

"And who is this wench?" Kolvar asks.

Lyari replies, "She is Maria. The woman I told you about, Master."

"Ah, yes. I can see your point about her eyes."

Hey. "I have an idea that could help without the use of violence. I would need a few ingredients, and an audience with Lord Selnar, but I think we could pull it off if we work quickly."

"Oh? And what, pray tell, is your idea, wench?"

"I'm not a wench," I correct. "Anyway, in high school, this crazy bitch Maya Peterson was out for blood because she thought I smeared peanut butter on her gym clothes. I didn't, by the way. But she wouldn't listen to reason. She was *pissed* and wanted to get me back. To avoid getting beaten to a pulp, I spread false rumors about myself."

"We are using the Linguist's Orb, and yet I do not follow what you are saying," Kolvar says.

"Sorry. I'll get to the point. I began telling my friends that I was scared of black cats. Word got around to Maya, and she thought the best revenge would be trapping me in a car with ten black cats! I pretended to be scared, but really, I love cats. She thought she traumatized me and she left me alone after that. So why don't we spread a rumor that can satisfy the fae troops and get them to leave quickly?"

Kolvar immediately dismisses this. "That would not work."

"I am afraid I do not understand either, Maria," Rhys says.

"I'm not doing a very good job of communicating, am I?" I cross my arms. "Ask Theodas to get me an audience with Lord Selnar tonight. Trust me, I know what I'm doing. I don't usually have good ideas, but when I do, they *work*."

All three elves in the room give me a dubious look. And in unison they tell me, "You are lying."

GETTING LORD SELNAR TO VISIT ME IS EASY—I SIMPLY lure him with the promise of a good business deal, and a bottle of expensive wine. Well, Theodas technically does that, but he's just delivering *my* message. Dirue and Gaelith are pricier, though to be fair, they work at night. I have to pay for their services, which means *Rhys* has to pay for their services, something he isn't too thrilled about. But he does it, because he trusts me. Or, more likely, he doesn't have many other options.

"Ah, little Maria. I see you've acquired a Linguist's Orb," Lord Selnar greets, being the last to arrive in the dining room. I've saved a seat for him at the head of the table, while Dirue and Gaelith are at the other end. The rest of Rhys' men cram into the small room, standing against the walls. "You are not interested in selling it, are you?"

"I'm afraid not, Lord Selnar," I reply. "I'm here to propose a little business idea. I know you are one of the most successful merchants in the city, and in particular, you own the apothecaries and soap-making businesses. What if I told you I could get every single person in the city to buy your soap?"

"I would be intrigued."

"We've received word that the Summer Court prince, Gwyn, and his men will be tearing through the city within the next few days, looking for a client of mine. Unfortunately they will not care how much damage they cause in their search," I explain, looking at both ends of the table. "All three of you would be in danger—your lives *and* your businesses. Lord Selnar, people cannot buy things if they are dead. Likewise with you two, Dirue and Gaelith, people can't buy your services if they've been mutilated or killed by fae. Financially and morally, it would be bad if Prince Gwyn and his group of lackeys were to destroy the city. I imagine, even if he *did* find my client, Prince Gwyn would still pillage."

Dirue's eyes narrow. "Yes. The fae prince is known for his ruthless, sadistic nature. Your assessment is correct, Lady Maria."

"We can't stop him from coming, and if we fight head-on, there will be casualties. But if we make him so scared that he'll pass through quickly? We can minimize damage and maximize profits." I wish I had glasses right now, just so I could adjust them and look as smart as I feel. Which is to say, *very* smart.

"That would be interesting," Lord Selnar concludes, taking a sip of wine. "I agree with you, Maria. Having the violent Summer Court prince searching my city would be bad for business. I also have a family; my wife is pregnant with our eighth child."

"That makes our plan much more important. I need all of your help to pull this off. Dirue and Gaelith, you're known for spreading news to foreigners and locals alike. I need you to tell people that you've heard a plague is quickly sweeping through the city."

"A plague?" Gaelith repeats.

"Yes. And technically it's not a lie, because you're hearing it from *me*. A plague is sweeping through the city," I say. "This plague spreads through the air. The only way to prevent it is to wash your hands with soap from Lord Selnar. People need to wash their hands every time they use the bathroom. Cough and sneeze into their elbows, like so, and avoid going out for a few days. Keeping people indoors and out of Gwyn's sight would be for the best."

"Interesting. But still, we cannot *lie* about these details," Lord Selnar says. "Your little loophole will surely be discovered if there is no proof."

"Right. I'm going to have elf warriors stationed across the city, dressed as homeless individuals with makeup on. They will be armed and ready to protect the citizens should anything happen," I explain. "Let me demonstrate. Theodas, did you get the ingredients I asked for?"

Theodas steps forward, laying out the various bowls on the table. I tested them once before the meeting, but now that I have an audience, I'm a little bit nervous.

Finding gelatin was surprisingly easy, but since I don't have special effects paint or fake blood, I had to make my own using herbs and cooking ingredients.

It takes just a few minutes to create a fake burn on Theodas' arm. I have him go around the room and show it off, proud of my handiwork given the lack of tools. While I won't be calling Hollywood anytime soon, Gwyn shouldn't be able to realize it's fake. Especially if he's looking down at these "wounds" from his horse.

"He truly looks injured," Lord Selnar marvels.

"How grotesque!" Theodas exclaims giddily. "This is disgusting!"

Thanks, I guess.

"With makeup and costumes, we won't have to go into too much detail. And it won't be a lie if you add 'I heard' to these rumors, or emphasize that they are simply rumors," I explain further. "The proof is right here. The only thing I would ask is for the prices of the soap to be kept reasonable. Other citizens will believe this is real, and they might get scared. To price gouge on top of that would be pretty shitty."

Lord Selnar nods. "Your plan is very unique, shall we say, Maria. It seems we have a lot of preparations. Word of this plague must spread quickly, and people truly have to believe in it. How soon can you have these...*actors* out on the streets?"

"By early tomorrow morning. They'll roam around in shifts," I reply to the room. "They need to be seen, but won't approach anyone. Additionally, spread a rumor that a wealthy aristocrat left the city in the middle of the night."

Rhys speaks up for the first time, looking at me solemnly. "Do you truly think this will work, Maria?"

"All according to plan? Of course not. But we don't have many other non-violent options, do we?" Not that I'm a pacifist or anything. After seeing Gwyn's resources, I don't think we have enough warriors to actually fight and win against him. This is the only solution I can think of, aside from running away with our tails between our legs. And Rhys has already refused that.

All I can do now is hope this plan doesn't fail...and subsequently get us all killed.

CHAPTER FIFTEEN

"This is not as easy as you make it seem," Rhys comments, dotting an elf's face with fake blood. "Is this too much?"

I glance over. The elf soldier looks like he's seen some shit, his face covered in (fake) burns with (fake) pus and (fake) blood oozing from (fake) wounds.

"I think you're doing a good job," I tell him honestly. Sure, this would be comically excessive in a movie, but the more grotesque we make it, the less likely Gwyn will want to examine the wounds closely. I hope. This is all conjecture, and we're pretty fucked if I'm wrong. But I'm really trying not to go down the rabbit hole of self-doubt right now. So false bravado, it is.

We have nearly twenty elves dressed as infected beggars scattered throughout the city. With Lord Selnar and the courtesans helping us spread false rumors, some stores have already begun to close early. Theodas reported seeing fewer and fewer people go outside, and by evening, the shopping district is practically empty.

For dinner, we're planning on sending a rush of infected elves toward any areas that still have people. With all these soldiers needing to be made up, Rhys decided he wanted to help out. He's no artist, but he's improved considerably since first starting to help.

I prefer him here with me, anyway. I'm not saying that I *enjoy* his company. Well, I'm not saying that I *don't* enjoy his company. But he wanted to go out on the streets with his men! He's *way* too recognizable, so I've been doing my utmost to keep him busy. Theodas, Iacar, and Lyari are stuck inside, too.

At least Lyari and Kolvar are keeping an eye on the fae kid, who still isn't well enough to hold a lengthy conversation. Not that it matters at this point. In anticipation of Gwyn's arrival, we've disabled the Linguist's Orb again. I guess I can use the Elvish practice, but it's terribly difficult to tell Theodas stories, much less explain the concept of movies to other elves. I've just been telling them they're like plays but better, and half of them don't believe me.

I will say, though, it's pretty entertaining to hear Theodas explain the plot of *John Wick* in Elvish.

"I would certainly hunt down any criminal who dared steal my hound," one of the elves agrees.

"Of course!" Theodas shouts, pumping his fist in the air. "Justice for our animals!"

"You realize no one actually stole your dogs, right?" I point out. "You're getting riled up over a fictitious scenario."

"Yes. The thought of it has my blood boiling."

"That doesn't seem healthy," I note dryly, turning to Rhys. "And Your Highness, that's enough blood."

Rhys puts the container back on the table and sends the

elf on his way, looking like he just encountered Michael Meyers. "At what point should I have stopped?"

"Blood tears."

"Ah. I will keep that in mind next time."

Well, hopefully there won't be a "next time."

It's been a long few days—a long *week*, really—and after finishing up with all the soldiers, I feel dead on my feet. Excusing myself, I retire to my room upstairs for a long overdue nap.

Sleep doesn't come easily, though. No matter how exhausted I am, I can't help but worry about what happens next. In bed, staring up at the ceiling, my mind begins to replay all my greatest failures like some sort of twisted movie.

Those few days with Rhys in the safe room feel years away now, and I'm back on my bullshit it seems. Finally, after torturing myself for a few hours, someone knocks on the door. I throw the covers off and leap up, eager to escape the mental prison I've trapped myself in.

"Come in!" I call out.

Rhys enters, closing the door carefully behind him. He's changed into a plain white shirt tucked into black pants. What, did he just walk off the cover of a romance novel? This isn't like any outfit I've seen in this time period, and it's criminal how well it suits him. Then again, he could probably wear a plastic garbage bag and still look good.

Wow, what's wrong with me? I need to get my head checked out by a gynecologist.

"I apologize if I interrupted something," he tells me.

"You didn't," I reply quickly. "Sorry, did you need something?"

Rhys holds out a dagger in a worn leather sheath. "In case something happens."

The dagger is heavier than I expect, with a jewel-encrusted handle. "Thank you."

"If the need for escape arises, perhaps you can...use it."

To make a portal. I swallow hard. Even if that were possible, I don't think I could leave Rhys. Especially not in the middle of a battle, knowing he's in danger.

I know I'm going to have to leave eventually, but I still haven't done anything to change the future. Should I tell Rhys what fate awaits him? Warn him, somehow? Would he even believe me? Or would he be angry? I wouldn't blame him.

Archer was angry, too, for the secrets I kept. Rightfully so. As much as I hate self-reflection, as it usually turns into a storm of obsession and self-criticism, Archer had a right to be pissed off. Even if my attraction to him was real, nothing else was. Sure, I couldn't tell him about Neil or my family history, but there were other points I could have opened up to him about. I guess the chemistry just wasn't there. But the absence of it is much greater than I initially realized, because whatever I lacked with Archer exists between Rhys and me.

And damn if that doesn't just figure.

"Thank you," I say. "I'll be fine, though. You have enough to worry about—just focus on your people. At the end of the day, I'm not someone who falls within your circle of protection."

Rhys smiles sardonically. "I do not need magic to detect your obvious lies. What are you so concerned about, Maria?"

I hesitate. "Thank you for the dagger. From this point

on, I just want you to know that I can take care of myself. When you have the opportunity to leave, take it. I'll be fine."

"You are so eager to part?"

"No," I blurt. "It's not that. I can't explain it in a way you would understand."

Or accept.

"I understand more than you believe I do." He pauses, studying my face. My skin prickles beneath his gaze, and suddenly I feel like he can see right inside my head. "We are similar, you and I. You feel it, too, do you not?"

"Yes," I reply truthfully. "We're similar. So I would think you of all people would understand that I cannot bear the thought of another person getting hurt because of me. I don't want anyone to be put at risk, more so than they already are, to protect me."

His eyes soften. "And I cannot ignore someone in need."

"I'm not even an elf. You shouldn't feel any obligation toward me."

"It is not *obligation* I feel."

My throat tightens. "I guess that makes us quite a mismatched pair."

"Indeed."

There's nothing left to say, staring at each other wordlessly. Our bodies stiffen, as if we're both standing on an icy lake. If there's any sudden movement, any heat between us at all, the floor beneath us will shatter and we'll drown. Metaphorically, of course.

Rhys doesn't know the future like I do. He doesn't understand just how big of a mistake it would be to…have feelings for me. If he even does in the first place. It would be cruel to let whatever it is between us play out. It would be *selfish* of me. So even though it goes against everything I feel in my heart, I move toward the door. It's as if I'm going in slow motion, reaching for the knob and twisting it open.

"We should go back downstairs," I say quietly, unable to look at him. "Dinner will be ready soon."

"If that is what you wish, Maria." Rhys leaves first, and as hypocritical as it sounds, I hate how easily he walks away from me. But all I can do is watch him go.

GAELITH LOOKS ALL TOO COMFORTABLE IN MY BEDROOM, lounging in the wooden chair beside my bed with a cup of tea in his hand. He wears civilian clothes today—slacks and a tunic, nothing like the sheer garb he wore the night we met. I prefer it this way, when he's not "on the clock," so to speak.

"The Summer Prince has arrived," Gaelith says after a long sip of tea. His dark eyes sweep over me, curving when he smiles. "It seems your plan is working, Maria."

"Have the brothels closed?" I ask. He came without notice, though admittedly it isn't easy to send notice when there are no phones in this time period. He showed up, walked in through the back door, and helped himself into my room. I'm not even sure how he found it, but when I came back from the bath, he was just sitting here like he owns the place.

"Yes." He takes another long sip of tea, and I get the feeling he enjoys making me wait. It builds up the anticipation. "Are you well?"

How do I say, "I'm a nervous trainwreck" in Elvish?

"No," I say honestly, not bothering to lie. "Are you?"

"No," he says with a wry smile. "Your plan is risky and

frankly, I cannot believe it has fooled the fae prince for even a second. But he is not causing nearly as much damage as I initially anticipated, so I suppose I shall commend you on that. However, that is not the reason I have come to pay you a visit. You are looking for a specific sword, correct?"

I nod. "You know where it is?"

"Unfortunately I haven't been able to locate it. But I heard an interesting story from a client that I wished to share," he explains, leaning close to whisper in my ear. We're the only two people in the room, so I'm not sure why he's doing this. "A witch stole a sword from a portal she stumbled across in the middle of the forest. While she could not wield it, she claimed the sword had great power and sold it off to a traveling merchant. It was as you described, with strange spells inscribed on the blade and a red-knotted tassel hanging from the hilt. Due to the strangeness of its construction, it was purchased and passed around. No one kept it for long, though."

That's not exactly a location, or helpful information, but I appreciate Gaelith telling me nonetheless. Maybe I can track down who it was sold to?

"During the war against fae, many goods were seized and returned. Treasures usually end up in the Elven palace and are later distributed to their rightful owners. It is quite possible the sword you seek could be in the palace," he continues.

In the palace. Which would require me to continue traveling with Rhys.

"You are less excited than I thought you would be." Gaelith studies my face, leaning in close. "In fact, you seem troubled."

"It's complicated."

"Matters of the heart tend to be." He smiles like he knows everything, and maybe he does. "I can be of assistance. I'm quite well versed in these things, you know."

"Why help me?" I ask bluntly.

"It pleases me to do so," he answers without hesitation. "You interest me greatly. Is that so difficult for you to believe?"

"Not romantically." I can tell *that* much, at least.

But Gaelith reaches toward me, brushing his fingers across my cheek. "Do you not find me attractive?"

"You're teasing me now." Or fishing for compliments. One or the other. "You're very handsome, and you have a nice voice. I don't doubt that you are the most popular courtesan in the city."

He laughs, twirling a strand of my hair around his finger. I don't mind the contact, in part because I know it doesn't mean anything. And despite his proximity, he's not making my heart race. Not like certain *other* people.

"You flatter me. But I am very serious about you, Maria. I see why the prince is so enchanted by you. Oh, you do not need to act so alarmed. While you did not reveal him, Prince Vesryn is quite recognizable. Do not worry—I won't say a word."

"He isn't *enchanted* with me." I don't know *what* he is.

"In my line of work, Maria, I can tell when one is besotted with another. You seem to be able to as well; you are simply lying to yourself," Gaelith chides.

"Let me get this straight: you're being nice to me because *you think* the prince has feelings for me?"

"It would not be so bad to gain his favor. Though, if that is not the case, I would not mind gaining solely *your* favor."

"I—" I begin, only to be cut off by the innkeeper bursting into the room, bowing frantically.

"My lady, the Summer Prince is on his way here. Please get to the safe room," he says.

Well, that was faster than I expected. Gaelith and I rush down the hall and into the safe room downstairs, locking the door behind us. The lights have been put out, leaving the room in total darkness.

Huddling in a corner, all we can do now is pray the Summer Prince doesn't find us and wait until a servant comes to tell us the coast is clear.

While I can't see him, I know Rhys is beside me. I hear his steady breath, feel his presence like his soul is connected to my own. And in the darkness, his hand finds mine.

Whatever exists between us, this *thing* neither of us is brave enough to name, comes to life instantly. I know that nothing can ever happen between us, but right now, that doesn't matter. Because this room is dark and cold, and even though we aren't alone, no one can see us holding hands. We can't even see each other. All we can do is feel each other's warmth.

CHAPTER SIXTEEN

Gwyn must be an idiot. That's the only reason I can think of as to how my plan actually works. Did he destroy a few shops? Yes. But no one got physically injured, he didn't find Rhys, and Lord Selnar vowed to help any business owners with the money he earned from the soap sales. Not to mention, news of the plague sent the auction house goons into hiding for the time being, so we're now safe to leave the Violet City. All in all, this was a major win for me.

But I'm trying not to let it go to my head as we prepare to depart. *Together*, I may add. With Gaelith's hint about the elven treasury, I'm now on my way to the palace with Rhys and his men.

What I don't understand is why Gaelith and Dirue have insisted on seeing me off. We're not friends, and my plan might have done more harm than good to their brothel. Still, Gaelith smiles at me.

"Your clothing is quite interesting," he comments casually, still dressed in civilian clothes. Dirue stands at his side in a matching tunic and trouser set, her hair pulled back into a braid.

"Do come back soon, Maria," she tells me. "Perhaps you can start a shop with your…interesting fashion sense."

"This is common clothing in my hometown," I reply, zipping up my hoodie. Now that I'm leaving, I don't see a reason to fit in with the others and wear a dress anymore. If I have to travel, I'm going to do so in a hoodie and leggings.

"Come along, wench," Iacar says, opening the carriage door for me. Thankfully, that's what we'll be riding in for the rest of the journey to the palace.

"We will meet again, Maria. I believe fate will allow our paths to cross once more." Gaelith kisses my hand with a smile, his lips lingering on my skin until Rhys exits the inn. As soon as Gaelith sees him, he takes a big step back from me.

"Maria." Rhys holds out his hand to me, but then thinks better of it and withdraws, letting it fall to his side. "Are you prepared to depart?"

I nod. Iacar offers his hand, but I manage to get into the carriage on my own. Lyari and the child sit inside, both fast asleep. I'm grateful for it; I don't imagine either would make lively conversation, no offense to them. Lyari still doesn't like me, and the child can't speak Elvish, though I have a feeling she understands more than she lets on.

She's still healing, with bandages covering her body, but she's taken a bath and received a fresh set of clothes. And she can walk on her own, a major improvement. At breakfast this morning, she tore into her bread roll with abandon. That's something, right?

To be completely honest, I'm relieved she's doing better. I think it's another one of my psychological hang-ups, something I definitely would have talked to Tasha about if she were here. And I *do* wish she were here, in the past. Part of me does, anyway. Though her presence would mean she could share in my misery, her safety would be a constant concern, she wouldn't have the luxuries of modern times, and she would struggle with Elvish. But at least we'd be together.

Growing up, Tash wasn't always in the same house as me. She wasn't always in the same *school* as me, either. But we tended to find our way back to each other. The group home was only bearable because of her—we both suffered for it, but at least we understood each other.

We're not exactly cut from the same cloth, her and I, but we were sewn into the same dress. The only difference is, Tasha turned out radiant. Not without snags, but everyone has those. Even though things were hard at times, especially for Tasha, she became better in spite of that. More resilient, intelligent, and empathetic. Not me, though.

I guess that's another thing I've always hated about myself as Maria. When I'm myself, I can't deny the fact that I've had an easier life than my other friends in the foster care system. But I'm the one who's *this* fucked up inside. Because there's something wrong with me.

I shut my eyes as the carriage begins to move, hoping sleep will sweep me away before I get too caught up in my own head. But once my mind catches on the topic, I can't stop thinking about it. Reliving everything, turning over the memories in my mind like a child flipping over rocks in a garden and watching the bugs scuttle out from underneath.

It's not that I don't have *good* memories. But the bad ones have a deeper hold on me, turning me into a pathetic mess. The worst part is, I don't even remember the pain clearly. I *know* that when my ribs broke it hurt every time I breathed, but I don't remember it exactly. What hurts more now, looking back, is how it made me feel. I remember very specifically every tangle of emotions brought on by all the key events in my life, like they're fresh wounds. It makes me nauseous, which is worsened by the rocking of the carriage. It takes several days to reach the palace, and the first thing I do upon our arrival is puke beside a tree. Very classy.

Once I get back inside the carriage, I barely register my surroundings. My head is pounding, and no matter how much water I drink, my mouth feels dry.

"We are almost there," Lyari tells me, eyes half lidded. He slept for the entire journey, and yet he's still exhausted. I guess he *is* a kid.

I push back the curtain and look out the small window, but night has already fallen, so I can barely make out my surroundings. The moon hides behind the clouds, and the only lights are from torches in the distance. The grounds must be huge, which I'd expect from a palace for royalty, because it takes another fifteen minutes from the gate to the walkway.

Theodas opens the door to the carriage for me, and I don't mind when he takes my hand to help me step out. Mostly because my legs feel like jelly, and I'd be majorly embarrassed if I were to trip and fall flat on my face.

"His Highness has requested I coordinate a guest room to be prepared for you," Theodas says, taking my arm. The exhaustion is clear in his voice, which is fair since he's been on horseback the entire day and slept little the night before.

Rhys is nowhere to be seen, though I imagine he immediately went to meet with his sister. The other soldiers scatter around the grounds, some going around the back of the castle.

Theodas brings me through the grand entrance and up a set of stone stairs. When he leads me to a guest room, I wash my face and change into a T-shirt with the help of a small elf woman. As soon as my head hits my pillow, I fall into a deep sleep. And for once, I don't dream.

IT'S NOT THE FIRST TIME I'VE WOKEN UP TO A GIRL straddling me. It's not even the second or third time. But it *is* the first time a girl has straddled me in my sleep without a can of shaving cream, a tube of wasabi, or a black permanent marker in hand. That's a good sign, right?

"She is awake," the redhead says to no one in particular, staring at me with large gray eyes. She pokes my cheek with her pinky, proceeding to knead and squeeze it. "You have soft skin."

"Thank you?"

"You are welcome." She speaks English, so I assume the Linguist's Orb is activated again. "My brother told me about your travels, Maria. I am Siraye, Crown Princess of Asari."

Asari? Ah. Eidera is the continent name, but the elven nation must be Asari. Which makes this girl Rhys' sister.

"Is it common for elves to greet their guests like this?" I ask.

"I am not *common*. I am a princess. Soon to be a queen," she adds, not moving from her position on top of me. "Oh, rest assured, I am not interested in courtship with you, Maria. But Theodas has spoken about you at length. He says you tell the most marvelous stories. And Lyari says that you are my older brother's intended. So of course, I had to meet you."

Wow, that's a lot to unpack. "How long have I been asleep?"

"It is midday. Luncheon has already passed, I am afraid, but the cook can prepare anything you would like," the princess says. "My handmaidens will assist you with your clothes. There are a few gowns I have that may fit you. My brother tells me you prefer your own clothes, but Theodas and Lyari assure me you have no court-appropriate wear. It is odd for them to agree on anything, you know."

I guess sweats aren't "court appropriate."

"Thank you for your hospitality," I tell her earnestly.

"Of course. When you are ready, the maids will bring you to the sitting room in the west wing observatory." She nods, as if she's agreeing with herself. "Yes, that will be rather lovely. We will have tea and biscuits, and soup and rolls. And cake."

She continues listing foods as she pops off the bed and walks out of the room. As she leaves, three elf women rush in and draw open the heavy curtains.

The room is quickly filled with light, revealing extravagant tapestries covering the walls and lush velvet-cushioned furniture. To the side of the room is a fireplace with a massive mirror above it, and in the corner, a painted partition makes for a decent changing area.

The maids do everything from washing me to dressing me. One even tries to brush my teeth for me, but I decline and do it myself with the toiletries in my backpack. They manage to wrangle me into a dress—another velvet number in a deep garnet red. As for shoes, I wear sneakers. The maids nearly have a fit, but since the dress is long, my shoes won't show anyway.

The west wing is a ten-minute walk inside the palace, which is just as lavish as my bedroom. Various paintings hang on the walls, to the point where it looks more over-crowded than stylish. But the entire place is buzzing with elves dressed in all different types of clothing, from tunics to armor to gowns. The servants wear tunics and either a skirt or leggings underneath, all in a royal purple shade to differ-entiate themselves from others in the palace.

The observatory is detached from the main palace, a glass greenhouse filled with plants growing wild. In the center is a gazebo of white metal, providing shade and seating.

The princess lounges at a small table flooded with sweets, helping herself to cookies. The crumbs stick to her small lips and settle in her lap, though she doesn't seem to mind as she sweeps them off her skirt with a hand.

Rhys sits on the sofa beside her, wearing a loose white shirt tucked into brown trousers. He stands when he sees me, though I can't tell what he's feeling by that blank expression. "Maria. Have you slept well?"

"Very," I reply curtly. "It was a long journey."

The princess looks between us. "Come, sit beside me, Maria. I sent Theodas to fetch us fresh rolls."

"Thanks." I take the chair beside hers, mindful of my posture. Rhys might be a prince, but I am hyperaware that the girl sitting next to me is a *princess*. You can see it in every graceful flick of her wrist—a regal aura, so to speak, that instinctively makes me throw up my defenses.

"Rhys tells me you seek a sword," the princess says casually.

"Your Highness," Iacar admonishes, appearing from behind me. He and Theodas bring a basket of rolls and set them on the table, though one is suspiciously missing. And there are crumbs in Iacar's beard. Hmmm.

"We are among friends, are we not?" Princess Siraye retorts. "Besides, my brother prefers that name. I do not understand why Father, bless his soul, insisted on changing it to Vesryn. It is an old family name—my grandfather's generation, Maria. Does it not sound odd to you?"

"Calling His Highness by that name is too intimate in front of current company," Iacar continues to argue. "The wench—I mean, Maria—must show some decorum before royalty."

Princess Siraye sniffs, crossing her arms. "She is practically family, Iacar. Is my brother not courting her?"

Rhys' eyes widen. "I am unsure of what you have heard, Your Highness, but that is not the nature of our relationship."

"Maria is a guest in our lands," Iacar agrees, nodding his head at me. "Besides, she is…well, look at her."

Hey.

"She is turning red. Is that not a sign of affection?" Princess Siraye leans in close, studying my face. "In all the romance novels I've read, particularly the erotic ones, the heroines blush when they are near their lovers."

Jeez. Having her point out that I'm blushing makes my face heat up even more, if that's possible. I'm in danger of catching fire at this point.

"Romance novels are hardly accurate," Iacar rebuffs. "She is just easily embarrassed."

Theodas gives me a sheepish grin. "Now, now. Maria did

not come here to discuss that. She wishes to see the treasury and find the sword she seeks."

"Of course. But today should be about relaxation and recovery," the princess instructs, staring pointedly at her brother. "It has not been easy in the palace without you."

A pained expression flickers over Rhys' face, but it leaves as quickly as it appeared. "Your Highness —"

"Please. Enough of that, Rhys. Just call me by my name. You, too, Maria. At least in private, we should address ourselves less formally." She grins, and when she does, she looks childish. She can't be much older than me, if at all. Or maybe elves just age *really* well. "Maria, do tell me about your homeland. I am very interested in all kinds of countries. I haven't been able to travel much, outside of the books I read."

"There isn't much to tell," I reply, taking a bread roll. "I'm afraid I'm incredibly boring."

"That cannot be true."

"This bread is delicious." It's both sweet and salty, and with the orange marmalade on the table...I'm in citrus heaven. "We don't have royalty where I'm from. This is all very extravagant."

"Then, who rules your nation?" Princess Siraye asks, tilting her head to the side.

"We elect candidates and vote on them." Though maybe I'm not the best person to ask about politics, given how little I know on the matter. I go for another roll instead, all too aware of the princess' eyes trained on me.

But my attention is drawn to something crawling across my skirt, and when I look down, I wish I hadn't.

I scream, jumping up and dropping my roll to the ground. "What *is* that!"

"What?" Iacar picks up the squirming insect with a laugh, holding it in front of my face. I back up, skirting around the table. You would, too, if you could see it. It looks like a fly, a white spider, and a centipede had a baby. So many legs. And worse, it has wings. It's about the size of a sparrow, too, so I can see all the grisly details and hairs. Ick.

"That is just a bug," the princess assures me. "It will not hurt you."

"It's hurting my peace of mind," I mutter.

"They are rather cute, and helpful to the environment," Theodas comments. Iacar lets the insect go, and it flies right toward me.

I'm not embarrassed to say I scream again, dropping to the ground with my hands covering my head. It's not even that I don't like bugs (I don't), but when they're that big... no. No way.

Rhys, at least, gets a good chuckle out of it. He extends a hand to me, smiling at me for the first time in days. "It is gone now, Maria."

Absentmindedly, I take his hand and allow him to pull me to my feet. "I wish I could un-see that."

"You don't like looking at them, but you don't mind eating them?" Iacar asks with a hearty laugh.

"Do not tease her, Iacar," Rhys admonishes, noting my pale complexion. "Maria, we do not eat them, rest assured."

"I'm not assured, actually. I'm the opposite of that. I'm *unsure*." I eye the treats on the table warily. "And now, I am full."

Chapter Seventeen

As a debutante, I had to wear the ugliest hand-me-down wedding dress to my cotillion. The puffy sleeves and high-neck lace collar were reminiscent of Princess Diana's, except of course that I'm *not* Princess Diana, so I didn't pull off the style well at all. I still have the photos back home.

I didn't think I could look any worse than I did in that dress. Today, I'm proven wrong. The dress the maids choose for me makes me look like a fancy blueberry. It puffs and cinches in all the wrong places, and there are so many ruffles it's a wonder I haven't drowned in them yet.

"Are you certain this is…in style?" I ask cautiously, spinning around in the mirror slowly. The skirts are so thick they could stop a bullet, and will certainly prevent me from running away should the need arise.

"Of course," the head maid replies smoothly, pushing one of my many hairpins into place. "The prince's homecoming banquet is a very important matter, Lady Maria.

Many nobles will be coming from across the region to attend. Her Highness has given us strict instructions to ensure you assimilate well."

I'm not going to blend in. I don't have elf ears, my Elvish is barely passable, and this makeup gunked on my face makes me look like the fifth member of KISS. Black lipstick just doesn't suit me.

My face is plain without makeup, but I decide to wipe it all off anyway. A bare face is better than whatever it is the maids have done. I know, I know. "When in Rome" and all that. But I'm already on edge because of everything happening with Rhys. I don't need another reason to be more self-conscious.

With the face paint cleaned off, I head downstairs. The halls are more crowded than a seedy underground rave, except instead of dancing, the elves are conversing in rapid Elvish. I weave through the crowd, no easy feat in this princess skirt, in a feeble attempt to find Siraye. Instead, Theodas spots me first and waves frantically at me.

"We match," he says delightedly, dragging an older woman by the arm. It's true—we're all wearing the same shade of blue, and with our warmer complexions, it's not very flattering. But I *do* notice the woman at Theodas' side isn't wearing any heavy makeup. In fact, none of the party guests are. Were the maids just screwing with me earlier?

"Hello, Theodas," I say.

Theodas grins, patting the woman's hand. "Mother, this is the girl I was telling you about. Maria. Maria, this is my mother, Duchess Tinesi Aeynore."

The older woman bows her head and drops into a low curtsy. She doesn't resemble Theodas at all, with her blonde hair and sharper facial features. "How do you do?"

I mimic her, trying to be polite, but Theodas bursts into laughter.

"Mother, I'll part with you now. I am going to escort Maria."

"Very well, dear." The duchess curtsies again before departing, exchanging her empty glass of wine for a full one from the waitstaff stationed around the hall.

"Have they given you the grand tour yet?" Theodas takes my arm, guiding me to the next room with relative ease. Unlike a few minutes ago, when I was fumbling through the crowd, the elves move away when they see Theodas coming. Not because they're trying to avoid him — it looks more to me like they're trying to show respect.

The room we enter is a gallery of paintings, with chairs and sofas pushed against each wall. Only the older elves sit down, surrounded by younger aristocrats and servants.

"I didn't expect to see so many people," I begin. "I'm not sure what to do with myself."

"His Highness thought as much. He requested I accompany you tonight," Theodas replies. "I can hardly refuse the prince."

"The prince did?"

I thought, given his long-awaited return, Rhys might have forgotten all about me. Understandably so — I'm sure he wants to spend time catching up with his sister and any friends he left behind in the palace.

Theodas nods vigorously and mimics Rhys' deep baritone. "'Theodas, see to it that Maria is entertained this evening, and no one pesters her.' How was my impression?"

"Spot on."

"I've been at Rhys' side since he came to the palace. My father and his forced our companionship, though it never felt that way," Theodas explains. "My father is a duke, but I am untitled. My sister will inherit eventually, thank the gods. Heirs have so little freedom, and I've not done my share of traveling yet."

"Is that your plan? To travel?"

"It has always been my life's plan. Travel, make friends along the way, see all the great things this world has to offer." He gestures to one of the paintings hanging on the wall, depicting an elf holding a bowl of fruit. "Surely there must be more than this. Do you ever wonder, Maria, what else is out there?"

Not really, but I can't say it aloud. It seems pathetic. To be honest, I've always been so focused on myself that I never really cared much about exploring new paths. Any curiosity I had was satisfied with a simple Google search. With the internet, I can access a ton of different artwork, movies, books, and what have you, all on my phone.

"Have you always wanted to explore the world?" I ask.

"Yes, ever since I was a boy. But when the war efforts were desperate, my father enlisted me. He wanted me to fight alongside the prince," Theodas says casually. "It is an honor to die with royalty, according to the nobles."

"And you agree?"

"No, but I had little choice in the matter. Oh, do not mistake me — I do not regret leaving," Theodas adds hastily. "But now that matters are relatively calm, I plan on enjoying my newfound free time by exploring my areas of interest and passion. Unlike Iacar, I do not find any beauty in battle."

"So you're going to return home?"

"Yes, tonight. The trek up north will be another few

days, but I will use the time to speak with my sisters. I haven't seen them since the war began. Unlike Her Highness, my sisters stayed home for the entire war. They did not venture onto the battlefield."

"I will miss you, Theodas," I admit. We take a turn around the room, and he slows his pace so I can keep up. Not easy, with this skirt. We spend the rest of the night walking around the palace critiquing the paintings. I don't see anyone else I recognize, not even in the banquet hall for dinner. Rhys and Siraye are nowhere to be found, but I imagine they are busy greeting all their guests. I don't spot them at the table when we're ready to eat.

The distraction with Theodas was nice and all, but the small talk served as a reminder that I'm straying too far from my original purpose: grab the sword and book it back to the future. Not that there's anyone waiting for me at home. Neil doesn't count, obviously—he isn't waiting for *me*.

Meanwhile, I feel more kinship toward people I've met in the last couple of weeks here than anyone at Southeastern.

Eventually, Theodas is pulled into conversation with another set of nobles, and I take the chance to slip away. I should be good at goodbyes, but I'm not. It's important to admit your faults, isn't it? Even if you're just admitting them to yourself. Since I'm no good at goodbyes, I leave Theodas without one and head upstairs to my room. I'll go to sleep early, get some rest, and check for the sword in the morning. If it's not in the treasury, I'll leave. Maybe I'll go back to the Violet City and search for more clues.

When it comes to Rhys' fate, I'm not sure how to stop

the future from happening—is it even possible to change an isolated event so far in the future without screwing *everything* up? And even if that's the case, Todd Glass told me that I can't go back and prevent someone from dying. Otherwise, Luke...

Shit.

"Maria." Rhys calls me from the bottom of the staircase. He makes his way up slowly, cautiously, as if I'm a deer in the headlights about to bolt. "I have been searching for you."

"You have?" I ask, not hiding my shock.

He nods, stopping when he reaches two steps below me. He's dressed more like a prince now, complete with a silver crown atop his head. It matches the embroidery lining his jacket, the pale colors making his eyes look more purple than blue.

"You sound surprised," he notes.

"I am. I was just with Theodas earlier, and he was being dragged into conversation left and right," I say. "This entire party is for you. Everyone downstairs is here to talk to *you.*"

"Hardly. They are surprised I survived. I am merely...a spectacle. My parentage is no secret, especially amongst the nobles," he explains. A group of maids pass by, arms filled with towels, and Rhys shifts to the side. "Perhaps we may speak in private."

That's not a good idea. But I nod along anyway.

Rhys doesn't touch me as he leads me down the hall and through a set of French doors, outside to a balcony filled with flowers. And, most likely, giant bugs.

"The larger insects will not fly this high. Not when the garden is directly below us," Rhys assures me, reading my mind. He leans with his back against the railing, eyes fixed on me. "I have been thinking a lot."

"That's a good thing."

"You seem troubled lately. More so than before. I thought, given your victory over the fae prince, you would be in high spirits."

"It's not exactly a victory. I still haven't found the Divinities Sword. And even if I do, I'm not physically strong enough, or powerful enough, or even intelligent enough to defeat Astaroth on my own."

"Having never met this villain Astaroth, I must disagree that you are not *enough*. But there is no shame in asking for help."

"Haven't I told you?" I laugh sardonically. "Back home I have no allies, and I've driven everyone who would have potentially assisted me away. Which is just as well—nothing is free and no one will help without a good reason."

"And me?" He looks at me so earnestly, for some reason I feel like I could burst into tears. "Why will you not ask me for help? Am I not reliable?"

"I've relied on you more than I should have. Anyway, you just returned home," I say. "We've both known from the start that this…is temporary."

"Yes. Even if it is evident to me that you do not want it to be."

I draw closer to him in spite of myself, walking toward the edge of the balcony until we're only standing an arm's length away. "What I want has hardly ever mattered. There was a time when I was selfish, more so than I am now. I thought focusing on myself would make me happy. Instead, I hurt those around me."

"You fear you will hurt me?"

"I know I will." And that knowledge, those memories, plague me.

He inches closer, and my heart beats rapidly at his proximity. It makes me want to give into him, to ignore all the warnings in my head and just exist in this moment, in our own little bubble where nothing and no one else matters.

How does he manage to do these things to me? To make my body and mind react in such a way that my desire overrides my sensibilities?

Rhys pauses for a long moment, his voice trembling as he asks, "Do you care for me?"

The question freezes me in place. I want to answer—the immediate response that comes to mind is "Aren't we beyond questions like that?" But what's the point of denying it or being vague? Maybe I'm just tired or going crazy from all this planning and constantly worrying about what's going to happen next, because my brain completely blanks. Everything else seems so much less important, and all I can think about is myself and Rhys.

"Yes," I say plainly. "It's a bad idea. I think we both know that. And given the short amount of time we've known each other, it doesn't make sense to me. But I can't pretend that nothing is going on between us. Even if it scares the living hell out of me."

"Am I so frightening?" he jokes. But I can't even bring myself to smile.

"No. I'm scared of myself. After pretending to be someone I'm not over the last few years, wearing masks and desperately trying to forget, it's been a long time since I felt something this intense. I don't know what to do. Logically, I know what's right. Morally, too, if you can believe that. But, true to form, my base instincts are much more powerful."

"You are making the situation more complicated than it needs to be," Rhys decides.

"Probably."

"I wish I could put your mind at ease."

"You can." I close the short distance between us, pressing myself to his chest and wrapping my arms around his neck. It's stupid. Idiotic, really. Is being an idiot worse than being stupid? Whichever one is worse, that's me. After all that hemming and hawing about protecting him and pushing him away, here I am, doing the opposite. This might be the biggest mistake I've made here, but it doesn't feel like one. It feels *right*, like we should have been doing this all along.

Rhys pulls me against him, his arms winding around my waist as if it's the most natural thing in the world. The kiss is soft, almost tentative at first, as his lips brush mine. Everything else seems so much less important now, and I lean into him, tilting my head. My heart races as my lips slowly part.

His touch lights a flame inside me, burning through my body like wildfire. He tastes so sweet, kissing me deeper as our tongues meet. I can barely breathe, and yet I can't get enough. It's as if everything I've felt for Rhys since the moment I met him has been slowly building in my mind, whether I was aware of it or not, and now the floodgates have swung wide open. I don't want to stop, even if it's the smart thing to do.

Rhys pulls away first, both of us flushed and breathless. It takes a moment for us to come back to reality, and when I do, I'm horrified. Whatever invisible line I've worked hard(ish) to maintain has been crossed, and there's no turning back. To make matters worse, the kiss was much better than I imagined. Not that I thought it was going to be bad. And not that I've been spending my time imagining how kissing Rhys would feel. Maybe my feelings for him are more severe than I'd imagined.

And if that's the case, then I have to leave as soon as possible. I'm just not sure how.

CHAPTER EIGHTEEN

You should all be proud of me. I didn't run away this time. Was my walk back to the guest room brisk? Yes, but technically it wasn't *running*. And I said good night. My voice was squeaky as hell, and my palms were sweating, but I said the words. I think that counts for something.

I *know* you didn't expect some grand declaration of love, right? Because I'm not even sure if I'm in love with him. I don't think I'm *not* in love with him. Like, I'm not *disgusted* by him. Obviously. And that kiss was certainly...pleasant. More than pleasant, if I'm being totally honest. Maybe I'm not in love with him now, but it's moving in that direction, which is dangerous in and of itself.

I don't have a right to be in love with him. Not just because he's going to die for me. But part of the reason why I find myself so attracted to him is because of the experiences we shared in my timeline, in the future. Is it really fair to fall in love with someone based on events that haven't happened to them yet? And what if they end up *never* happening because of my meddling? And if everything *does* go according to how I remember, then why did my Rhys pretend not to know me? Does something bad happen with us between now and then? Then and now?

Ugh, it's clear I'm not going to get any answers — or sleep — tonight.

The worst part about this whole situation is, despite everything, I don't regret kissing him.

I sit up in bed, throwing the covers off. I need to get up and take a walk. The guests should be gone by now, and the palace is filled with guards, so I'm not very concerned about my own safety for the time being. Shrugging on a sweatshirt and shoes, I trudge downstairs. I'm not sure what my plan is — not for tonight, and not for the future. I wander like a ghost between the rooms of the castle, which have already been cleaned up by the staff. The guards standing at the front entrance nod in acknowledgment as I pass.

The lights in the halls are dim, but I manage to navigate through without tripping over the carpets. By "navigate" I mean, of course, get lost and go in circles, but pretend that it's all intentional. By the fourth time I circle the front entrance, the guards no longer acknowledge me.

"Maria?"

I spin around. Princess Siraye stands at the end of the corridor, wrapped in a thick knit shawl. "Your Highness."

She smiles. She looks younger without makeup on, standing there in her nightgown with her hair loose around her shoulders. "You cannot sleep?"

"I'm a bit restless," I say. No thanks to your brother, I think.

"Ah, so we are both wanderers of the night. Come, let us walk." Princess Siraye motions for me to join her, and I see no reason to refuse. We're both awake.

She knows the grounds like the back of her hand, unsurprising given she probably grew up here. The night chill doesn't bother us for long, as we walk out the back door and directly into another building. Unlike the stone castle, this structure is painted white. A circle of marble columns surrounds it, and when we venture inside, I realize it must be some sort of house of worship. The large room is circular with rows of white pews centered around a white marble statue in the center, right under a dome of glass.

"That is our goddess," Princess Siraye tells me. "One of them, at least. Vessa, the Hooded Mother. She is both the goddess of fertility and the goddess of the underworld."

White lilies bloom from the statue's head, somehow growing out of the marble. White vines wrap around her curvy figure, forming a tight dress. In one hand, she holds a wooden scepter topped with a fist-sized diamond. In the other hand, a skull sits perched on her palm.

"Was this made by hand?" I ask.

Princess Siraye shakes her head. "The artisan used magic for certain parts. The flowers, for example, are artificial—but they look real, do they not? That is a simple trick, a spell used by the sculptor."

"Do you come here when you can't sleep?"

Princess Siraye sets her candle down on the table and sits in the front pew, motioning for me to join her. "My mother was a devout believer in the gods. She was to be a holy maiden before my father ruined her. He built this chapel for her as a wedding gift, but it did little to ease her anguish. She died shortly after my birth."

"So did my mom. According to my father," I clarify. "I don't know if I can trust half the things that come out of his mouth."

Not that I particularly care. One biological father is bad enough — I don't need more complications.

Princess Siraye smiles sadly. "My father was a bad man. It is said that we should never speak ill of the dead, but if they are truly bad people, I do not see why I should lie about it. The way he treated my brother and me was abhorrent. But I know you understand this well, Maria."

"Did the prince tell you about me?"

"My brother is very tight-lipped when it comes to matters regarding you. He would not tell me, or anyone else, such private matters," she explains quickly. "I can just *tell*. I am a bit intuitive. That is the kinder word for it, anyway. Forgive me if I have insulted you."

"No, you're right. My biological dad is an asshole. Worse than that — but I don't have a word strong enough for how much I hate him."

"Those who love us can often inflict the worst damage. But I have always found solace in prayer. Do you pray, Maria?" she asks.

I shake my head. I've never prayed much. When I have, it was never for anything good — and my prayers were hardly ever answered. If they had been, that stupid bitch Alison Dolittle would have turned into a blueberry, like the girl from *Willy Wonka*.

"Not many people do, nowadays," Princess Siraye says. "But I do. Not because I am devout, or I believe in the goddess. It makes me feel closer to my mother, though. And sometimes, just for a fleeting moment, I feel something beyond myself. Whether that is truly a divine being or an act of nature, it calms me."

"That's a...nice way to look at it," I say, struggling with my words. "You aren't afraid?"

"Afraid? Of what?"

"Of putting your wishes out into the universe. Not everything you wish for can come true, but what if the exact opposite of what you wish for happens? What if it's a sign that there *is* some divine power, and it just hates you?"

"I do not think often of those scenarios. It is quite a conundrum you've concocted."

Translation: you're being weird as shit right now.

"Sorry. Forget I said anything," I say shyly.

Princess Siraye merely laughs. "I will have to think about it and return to you with an answer. But for now, Maria, I choose to believe that any higher power which exists is not malevolent, or even good, but neutral. I believe the same with people—generally, they are neutral. Some twist and harden over time, and some are born that way due to factors unknown by my people. My brother is not of a similar mindset. Rhys believes that people are, by nature, cruel. Do you believe the same?"

"Most people," I clarify. "Not all."

"Do you include yourself in that?"

"Yes." I'm not the *worst* offender, but I'm no saint. "If I were a better person, I would have never accepted His Highness' help."

"You needed his help."

"Yes, I did." I wouldn't have gotten this far without it. Actually, I'd probably be dead two times over. "Tomorrow, I need to see the treasury. If I can't find the sword, I have to leave. It's for the better."

"You are welcome to visit the treasury. But I recommend speaking with Rhys before gallivanting off on your own. If you leave without word, he will surely follow," Princess

Siraye says. "I have a feeling you have something you need to tell each other."

"Is that your power of intuition?"

"No. Observation," she replies casually. "During the party, I went outside for fresh air and caught you two necking. It was quite the spectacle."

Oh. Oh no.

Oh, fuck no.

"D-Did anyone else...?"

"See?" Princess Siraye finishes. "I imagine two dukes and one very scandalized young lady saw. Myself not included, of course. I am now twenty, and cannot consider myself a young lady, nor am I scandalized by your heated embrace."

Heated embrace? Hey, if there's actually a goddess in this chapel, can you just strike me down right now? I'd rather die by a lightning bolt than by this slow, simmering embarrassment!

"Not to worry, Maria," Princess Siraye says, patting my back. "You may have stolen my brother's lips for the first time, but I do not disagree with this love match. Should you both find harmony, I will gladly welcome you into the family as my sister-in-law."

AFTER LAST NIGHT'S "FUN" REVELATION, THE FIRST THING I do after breakfast is try to find Rhys. It shouldn't be too difficult—one would think, anyway. I toured the castle grounds twice and went around the main building lord knows how many times last night. But I still manage to get lost for an hour today, trapped in a guest room, and finally, back to the dining room.

"My lady, His Highness is training outside," a guard finally tells me, taking pity on my poor, directionally-challenged soul. "If you walk straight out that door and turn left at the stables, you will find him."

"Thank you." I try to follow his directions, but no path leads me directly to the stables in the first place. If they weren't painted red, I would have gotten lost again.

I just need to talk to Rhys. I don't know what I'm going to say, which is impressive considering I spent the rest of last night thinking about it.

I pause at the stable doors, trying to gather my thoughts, when a sudden onslaught of rain pours down from overhead, drenching me. Cursing, I fling the doors open and take shelter with the horses. Unfortunately, one of the doors doesn't shut all the way, and instead the wind rips it straight off its hinges. It doesn't instill much faith in me about the structural integrity of this building.

I shiver, backing away from the doorway. The rain is so heavy I can't see outside, and I know I won't be able to make it back on my own. I'll have to wait until it lets up a little, though I have no idea how long that will take.

At least I'm alone with my thoughts again, not that it's ever been very helpful. Princess Siraye was right last night —I have to tell Rhys *something*. Something to keep him here, safe. Relatively. I've learned that the Veil is hardly safe, but at least it's his *home*. He belongs in this realm, and I belong...

Well, as a shadowborn, I'm not sure where I belong. Not in the Veil. And certainly not in the past. But in the present, I never really belonged either—in either realm. Even without all this magic and shadowborn nonsense, have I ever really fit in with other people?

I sit on the dirt floor, hugging my knees to my chest. It's hard to pinpoint exactly where I fucked up, because there's not a single instance where I haven't made awful decisions. And even beyond the whole Rhys situation—let's say I find the Divinities Sword and go back to my own time period. What then? Isabelle, Tash, and David are still hostages. Neil has every power over me, and now that my secret is out and Faith is dead, I have no allies. Allegra probably hates me, rightfully so. No one at Southeastern will be willing to help me because I have nothing to offer. I'm just a bastard. Provost Mathers got hurt when *he* tried to help me. And Jenna and Todd have helped, but they don't answer to me. They answer to a higher power, one that wants me alive for some reason.

"Maria!" I look up toward the open doorway. Rhys stands in the rain, searching the room until his eyes land on me.

"Holy shit! Get in here!" I jump to my feet and drag him inside, away from the storm. "What the hell?"

"I have been searching for you," he says. Rain soaks his clothes like it does mine, his white shirt nearly transparent. Water drips down his face from his hair, and all I want to do is brush my fingers across his wet skin. I need mental help.

"Why?" I ask dumbly.

"Gowin told me you went outside."

"I was looking for you, but I got caught in the rain," I explain, searching the stable for a clean towel to help dry him off. We'll catch our deaths at this rate. "I was going to come back inside once the storm calmed down."

Lightning streaks across the sky in response, followed

by a bellow of thunder. So maybe the rain won't let up anytime soon. And now that Rhys is here, we're trapped together. *Great.*

Rhys finds a set of blankets on the workbench further inside, and while they smell like horse, they're better than nothing. He drapes one over my shoulders gingerly. "When it comes to you, I do not think rationally."

"That much is clear." And dangerous. "We need to talk, anyway. About last night."

"I agree. After what happened, we did not get a chance to properly speak. I feared I had upset you."

"It didn't have anything to do with you," I say quickly. "I mean, I'm the one with problems. Not you."

"I disagree. Were you bothered I did not properly court you first?"

"Not at all. I'm the one who started it, which was a mistake on my part."

"You disliked it."

"No, no that is not it. I'm really screwing this up, aren't I?" I take a deep breath. "It's not a question of enjoying it or not. Just so there's no misunderstanding, I *did* enjoy it. More than I should have."

The rain pounds harder on the roof. Rhys takes a moment to think before speaking, something I should probably try out more often. When he does finally talk, his voice comes out low, so quiet it's nearly drowned out by the storm. "You say that, and yet you look morose. As if being here with me is the last place you would like to be."

"That isn't true. It's just…the circumstances," I say lamely. "What I want doesn't matter, in this case."

"And what do you want?"

I answer without hesitation. "I want to kiss you. But—"

He cuts me off, sealing my lips with his own. The cold from the rain disappears immediately, his touch scorching as he cups my face in his hands. It isn't long before my entire body flushes with heat, and instinctively I sink into him.

Words aren't enough anymore. Instead of speaking endlessly about how he feels, Rhys is showing me, engraving his passion into my soul with this single, hungry kiss. It's clear, painfully so, that my feelings are reciprocated in this regard.

I can't allow myself to get carried away again, no matter how much I want to. I put a hand on his chest and push him back.

"I need to tell you something." The words tumble from my mouth before I can stop them. "I'm not who you think I am."

"Maria…"

"I'm not just from a foreign land. I'm a time traveler from the future," I blurt. "I know, it sounds insane, but listen to me. You can tell if I'm lying, can't you? I'm not. In the future, we meet somehow. I still haven't worked that part out yet. We meet, and things don't end up well for you. I'm the reason you die."

"Maria, I know."

"No, you don't understand," I insist, shaking my head.

"I do," he says. "Listen to me. The night we first met, I confiscated your satchel and searched it for weapons. I did not find any, but there was…a letter."

"A letter?" I repeat. "What kind of letter?"

"A letter from my future self."

Chapter Nineteen

"What did the letter say?" I ask, my voice hollow.

Rhys grimaces. "It requested that I protect you and help you in whatever way I could, because I am destined to fall in love with you."

Well, it's worse than I ever could have imagined.

"I admit, I was drawn to you from the moment we met, but I had my doubts about the letter," he continues. "Now, I have come to realize that it is true."

What's true? The fact that he loves me? Or that he's falling in love with me? Does that mean that the Rhys I met in the future...that *my* Rhys...loved me all along? That he somehow traveled to the future in the hope that we could be together, only to die before I even realized the truth?

"Take it back," I demand.

"Maria—"

"*Take it back.* You don't love me. You never did, and you never will. *Please* take it back. Because if you don't, if you truly feel that way about me...it will ruin you," I say. "We don't end up together in the future. Because I'm an idiot and a bitch, and the last thing I did before you died was yell at you and accuse you of something you didn't do! You saved my life for what—nothing! I'm not *worth* it, I promise you."

Pain spreads from my chest to my entire body, and I want to scream in a feeble attempt to let it all out. But there's no possible punishment I could inflict on myself to make up for my ignorance. I just want to wash it all away. The emotion bubbles from inside me, boiling over until I can't do anything but run outside. At least here, in the storm, my tears mix with the rain.

"Maria, wait! You will fall ill if you stand out here for too long," Rhys says worriedly, following me.

"I'm sorry!" I shout, turning away from him. I could spend my entire life apologizing, and it wouldn't be enough.

I close my eyes, wishing I were back home. Not back at Neil's house—*my* home, with my family. With Luke *alive* and ready to give me advice on what to do.

Rhys' arms wrap around me from behind, his voice right in my ear. "Maria, I did not regret it. I *will* not regret it, any of it. And I am not afraid."

"Then I'm afraid enough for the both of us! I'm angry, and scared, and angry again because this *shouldn't have happened*. It wasn't supposed to be like this!" I sob. "It isn't fair to you!"

"Maria, please do not cry."

"I'm *not*," I lie.

"I want to be with you," Rhys says earnestly. "Even if it means the future you know will come to pass. But I promise I will do everything in my power to prevent that, so we may be together if you wish it."

I hate the way he's reassuring me now, because I want so badly to believe him. I actually *do* believe that he'll do whatever it takes for us to be together, but I don't know if he'll succeed. And knowing my track record, he won't. Because even if he avoids death by Faith, he'll still be in danger because of me. Neil would kill him or use him as a pawn against me, and I can't guarantee his safety. I can't even keep my own family safe, let alone Rhys.

But even if I push him away, if I act cruel toward him now, will that really solve anything? I don't think I can bring myself to hurt him, even if it means saving his life.

"I'm sorry," I choke out, because after everything, that's all I can really say. "I'm so, so sorry."

It's a wonder my eyes aren't swollen shut.

I try not to cry because of this very reason. It's hard to stop once I've started. Before I know it, four days have passed. Luckily, the princess doesn't comment on my condition when she invites me to the treasury.

Iacar, however, is not as sensitive. "What happened to you, wench? Allergies?"

"No," I mutter.

"Iacar, you must learn to be more delicate at times like these," the princess chides, waving her hands at the guards stationed by the door. "Here we are, Maria."

The treasury is in the west wing of the palace, in a separate building that looks like a warehouse from the outside. Metal shelves go up three full stories, but that doesn't seem to be a problem. Elves working in the warehouse float on marble slabs powered by magic. There are at least fifty workers there, cataloging and moving items from a giant pile off to the side to their proper shelves.

As soon as the princess introduces me, one of the managers makes quick work of bringing me up to the swords. Several of the workers help me unsheathe them, but after going through what must be 500 different blades, none of them are the Divinities Sword.

Damn it!

If I don't find the sword, how am I going to return to Neil? How can I defeat Astaroth?

"I am sorry, Maria," Siraye says when I come back to the ground. "I know you need that sword. I will liaise with several historians and scholars and see what we can do. But it will take a few days."

"Perhaps you should rest, wench," Iacar says gently. Gently for *him*, anyway. "The maids tell me you've been screaming up a storm at night. You look exhausted."

Nightmares. Worse than I've had them in years.

"I'll be fine," I lie. I don't know why I bother—maybe because I want so badly for it to be true. But I don't know what "fine" really is. I've pretended to be fine, though that pretense has shattered along with my characters. "I suppose I expected this outcome. Thank you, Your Highness. I'll pack my things and leave quickly so as not to inconvenience you."

"You are a *guest* here," Siraye says, bewildered. "You do not have to go. In fact, I wish you would stay. At least until my brother feels better. He will want to bid you a proper goodbye."

"The prince isn't feeling well?" I ask in alarm.

"It is nothing serious," she says quickly.

All the more reason for me to go. *Of course* he's sick—I made him stand outside in the rain. Oh God. Do people die from a cold in this era?

I caused this—Rhys got hurt because of my selfishness and indecision. Would it be better if I left tonight, didn't tell him where I was going, and just...disappeared from his life? Or would he look for me and put himself in further danger?

Goddamn it.

"Don't be impulsive, wench," Iacar says. "Make a plan first before you go off running into danger. Finding the sword will be difficult to do if you're dead."

Tell me something I don't know.

RHYS DOESN'T TELL ANYONE HOW HE GOT SICK. I IMAGINE if he had, I would be barred from visiting him. He asks for me and I feel guilty thinking of refusing. But Guilt and I have become close friends in recent days. We're now in a throuple with Shame.

The guards escort me to the prince's chambers, but I enter the room alone. Surprisingly, it's not much bigger than my guest room. The shades are open, but it's been storming for days on end, so hardly any light enters the room.

"How are you feeling?" I ask, approaching the bed. I shove my hands in the pockets of my sweatshirt to hide the fact that I've been biting my nails, a nervous habit I thought I'd kicked in grade school.

Rhys lies in bed, pale as his sheets. He still has a high fever, but the royal physician said he'd make a full recovery soon. I thought truebloods wouldn't get sick so easily, but here we are.

"I have seen better days," he acknowledges, sitting up. "I was afraid that you would take my illness as an opportunity to leave."

"I considered it," I confess, "but I didn't want to hurt you. More than I already have."

"You have not," he assures me, but I can't tell if he's lying. "This was simply bad luck on my part."

"No, it's definitely because I'm an idiot and made you chase me into the rain. But I appreciate your kindness." I manage a crooked smile. "I've been thinking a lot about what happened over the last few days. What you told me and stuff."

"And?"

"You know, when I first came here, I was going to push you away. I didn't want to get close to you, knowing your fate. I hoped that, by being cold, I could prevent your death somehow. If you didn't care about me, I figured you wouldn't step in to help," I explain. "I also considered lying to you."

"You have not been forthright," he agrees. "But that is understandable, given your circumstances. I also hid the letter from you. I was concerned about how you would react."

"On a scale of one to ten, how bad was my reaction?"

"A hundred."

"That's a fair assessment," I say. "Look. I don't know what's going to happen, or how you get to the future. I don't know if I can change your death or not, and there's no possible way to figure it out until I return. But as I tortured myself over all the possible outcomes, I realized something: I'm dumb as shit. Like, *really* not smart. And that's not even factoring in my wild emotions and my poor decision-making when I panic. So I was left with two options: One, deny everything and try to solve this issue on my own. Or two, be honest with you and try to work together to save you."

"And? What have you decided?"

"I remembered that one of my least favorite romance tropes is when the love interest tries to push their partner away to protect them," I babble. "It always struck a chord with me because being in a relationship means partnering with someone on equal footing. And you can't be equal if one person is making decisions unilaterally."

"You have a good point." Rhys' lips twist into a smile. "What do you propose we do, then?"

"I was hoping we could figure it out together. You know —teamwork makes the dream work. Did that translate well?" I ask.

"No, not at all. But I completely agree with your assessment of our situation," he says. "Does this mean you will allow me to court you?"

"Oh, definitely not," I reply without hesitation. "Technically, *I'm* courting *you*. Prepare to be…courted. Whatever that involves."

"The one who confesses their intentions first is typically the one who courts."

"Yeah. I confessed first. You asked me if I cared for you, and I said yes. Plus all the romantic crap I just spewed a moment ago. Was that for nothing?"

"That hardly counts."

"Um, it *totally* counts," I argue.

Rhys scoffs. "I told you I *love* you just three days ago."

"This fever scrambled your brain, because it was *four* days ago, and you said that you read in *the letter* that you were falling in love with me. You didn't outright say 'I love you.' There's a major difference."

"I did. The Linguist's Orb is simply not doing its job translating nuance in language."

"Oh, you're going to blame the orb?" I laugh for the first time in days. "Alright, fine. Let's compromise: we're mutually courting each other. We can switch off courting duties. After you explain to me what courting is."

"You do not practice this where you are from?"

"We have courting rituals. They're just not as fancy schmancy as yours."

"You do not even know Elven courting rituals. How do you know if they are fancy or not?" Rhys challenges, some color returning to his face.

"It's *fancy schmancy*, and that's an assumption based on your position and this time period. Though I'm not quite sure what year it is, translated to *my* time. I think we use different calendar systems," I say. "What's courting like for you?"

"If we were to follow proper social etiquette, an older male family member would introduce us. Due to my status, I have the right to refuse an introduction. Though if I agree, we would converse at a social gathering. We would take walks, chaperoned, and meet at parties until a betrothal is extended. From that point on, we would be able to make house calls—chaperoned."

"Oh wow. That sounds fun."

"You are being sarcastic, I take it."

"Bingo."

Rhys chuckles. "What does courtship in your era look like?"

"We don't have to be properly introduced. And we don't need chaperones. If I meet someone and I like them after talking with them for a little, we can—" I stop abruptly. "Actually, my idea of courtship might be a little skewed. I've never been in a *real* relationship before."

Sadly, my little thing with Archer Kinsey was the closest I've come to a normal relationship. Oh my God.

"But you *have* been in a relationship that is not 'real,' I take it?" Rhys presses.

"To be perfectly up front with you, yes. In my time period, it's normal to have casual physical relationships with other people. Which I have done. Does that, uh, bother you?" I ask nervously. I had been so focused on the whole "I'm the reason he's going to die" thing that I forgot about all the other obstacles in our path. Culturally, we're probably so different. And Rhys is a trueblood elf—I'm a demon shadowborn. If I remember correctly, there's bad blood between the different shadowborn species.

But Rhys sets my worries aside immediately. "Not at all. You and I have not followed proper courting protocols so far. Perhaps we should forgo some of the more archaic rules and do what we are both comfortable with."

"What do you have in mind?"

"When I am back on my feet, perhaps I could teach you how to make the bread you enjoy so much," he suggests. "Do you enjoy baking?"

"Yes. I didn't know *you* did." Then again, Rhys used to make breakfast for me. He was a great cook. "Okay. It's a date, then."

Rhys smiles softly at me. "I look forward to it."

CHAPTER TWENTY

R iding a horse is *not* like riding a bicycle. Not that I know how to do either.

I cling to the horse's neck for dear life, trying to come up with a good reason as to why I agreed to a lesson in the first place. Independence? Girl power? Or because Rhys asked if I wanted to learn, and I was too distracted to refuse? Oh yeah—it's that one.

But it's easy to get distracted where Rhys is concerned. Now that he's my…boyfriend? Courting partner? Whatever. We haven't figured out the labels yet, and I'm not in a rush to define anything. I'm having *way* too much fun just being together. It's like a weight has been lifted off my shoulders. This is how, in my dazed bliss, I found myself agreeing to a horseback riding lesson from hell.

"This horse hates me," I tell Rhys, who seems all too amused by my failure.

"The horse does not hate you," he reassures me. "Horses do not hate people."

"Is one of your powers horse mind-reading?"

"No."

"Then you don't know for sure if this horse hates me, do you?"

At least the storm has finally cleared up. There's not even a cloud in the sky, almost like it never rained in the first place. And Rhys is feeling better, otherwise he wouldn't be out here teaching me a supposed "life skill." When he asked if I wanted to have fun today, I thought he wanted to make out or something. It looks like we'll have to revisit his definition of "fun."

Then again, maybe this *is* fun. For him. It's not fun for me, or the horse, I imagine.

"Maria, you must sit up."

"I'm going to fall."

"You are not. If you do, I will catch you."

"I doubt it! I'd crush your arms!" I exclaim. "All I've been eating lately is bread and cheese, and I haven't exercised since coming here. My heart, maybe, but not my body."

"Should I be flattered?" Rhys teases.

I shake my head vehemently. "I was talking about all the dangerous situations we've found ourselves in as of late, but go ahead and flatter yourself if you'd like. One of us should feel good about something this morning."

"You are doing much better than you think."

"I'm ready to come down now," I tell him, reaching out. He takes my arm and manages to help me off the saddle, but I can barely feel my legs. Sitting in the grass, I shield my eyes from the sun with my hand and squint up at him. "That was…interesting, to say the least. But I think I'll keep riding with you, if that's okay."

"And if I am not available to help you?"

"Then I'm screwed. Not in a fun way," I add. "Did that translate well?"

"Not particularly, but I understand the gist." He sits beside me, but since we're "unchaperoned" he keeps an arm's length of distance between us. Like we haven't kissed twice already. Even before that, we've been alone a bunch of times. I tried to tell him that it doesn't matter—what the hell do I care if my reputation is ruined in this era? I'm not going to be staying anyway. But Rhys insists, because according to him, he's a gentleman. Yeah, I can't tell if that translated incorrectly, or if he's full of shit. Either way, he's been pretty chaste with me.

Not that I'm a raging horndog or anything, but now that I read that back, it sure sounds like it. Damn, where's the delete button on this thing?

Anyway, I'm fine with taking things slow. I've never been in a real relationship before—that time with Derick Lowry doesn't count, because he was just playing a prank on me at the request of that stupid bitch Alison Dolittle—so I'm not sure what a healthy romantic relationship is even supposed to look like. Obviously I've seen *movies*, but those are hardly shining examples, right?

How do you tell if a guy likes you other than when you have sex with them?

I don't even have Wi-Fi to ask Reddit this very important question. How did people survive before the internet?

I know what it looks like when a guy *doesn't* like you during sex. Going on their phones, calling some other girl's name, shoving you out the window right after because his girlfriend knocks on the bedroom door... All *very* clear indicators that he's not "the one." Frankly, I have a hard time believing Rhys would do any of the above. But what if there are other, more period-appropriate methods to show disinterest?

Am I just overthinking this? Is this what it's like to be in a relationship? Good lord.

"Where's Her Highness?" I ask, trying to change the subject. "I didn't see her at breakfast this morning."

"My sister is attending to matters of state. With the treaty's signing, there is still much work to do," Rhys explains. "And you can call her by her given name when we are alone. She prefers it, especially since you are not her subject. I feel the same. I call you your name often, but you never say mine."

"You just like to see my reaction when you say my name," I accuse.

"That is true."

"Besides, what would you prefer I call you? You have a plethora of titles." Yeah, yeah, I get the irony here. "What's appropriate to call you?"

"What did you call me in the future?" he asks.

"Everyone called you Rhys," I begin. "But you never introduced yourself to me formally. Does only the princess call you that?"

He gives a slow nod. "Siraye calls me my given name because she knows I prefer it. The late king renamed me Vesryn—he said 'Rhys' was a commoner's name. Perhaps it is. He wished for me to forget my lowborn roots."

"No matter what you call yourself, at your core, you can't forget who you really are." I should know that by now, right? "Well, Rhys it is. That's what I call you in my head, anyway."

"Do you spend a lot of time calling my name in your head?"

"An appropriate amount of time, I'd say."

Rhys rises to his feet, dusting himself off. He extends a hand toward me, which makes me scoff.

"Is this amount of contact acceptable, or will we be caught by the hanky-panky patrol?" I tease, lacing my fingers through his as I stand.

"I am helping you, as is appropriate," he says evenly. Is it just me, or is he blushing? The sunlight makes it hard to tell.

"Should I help myself?" I don't let go of his hand, and to my relief, he doesn't pull away either. "How about now? Is it still okay?"

"You are too close, according to the rules of courtship," he says quietly, standing stock still.

"Oh? And what happens if we break the rules?" I grin.

"I do not see anyone here to tell on us," Rhys replies, lowering his head.

"I am here, and I will *definitely* tell on you," Princess Siraye calls, standing just a few feet away. "Iacar is here, too."

Rhys and I leap apart, startled by the sudden intrusion. What the heck? Someone should put bells on that princess.

"Sorry to interrupt your ruination, wench," Iacar says, shoving a biscuit into his mouth.

Technically I'm already ruined in their eyes, an archaic concept if I've ever heard one. But I have a feeling Iacar is just joking.

"I thought since the treasury did not contain the sword you seek, we could hold a strategy meeting," Princess Siraye suggests, looking between us as if to measure the distance from our shoulders. "If you are finished touching my brother, that is."

"I'm not *finished*. Just putting it on hold for now," I whisper to Rhys.

"Is that a promise?" he asks.

"Definitely."

"I heard that," Princess Siraye says. "Come—there will be plenty of time for flirtation later, when you have a proper chaperone. Let us adjourn to the East Gardens for tea. I have been pondering your issue, Maria, and I believe I have come up with a solution."

Which issue? Because I have a bucketload. "You have?"

She guides us all down a stone walkway, through walls of tall hedges. The East Gardens are near the greenhouse, but there's an outdoor gazebo with a table already prepared for us.

"Your troubles with the sword," Princess Siraye clarifies, sitting down. She waves a servant over to pour us all a cup of tea, and proceeds to dunk a cookie in hers. "Why not journey to the Wisdom Tree and ask for the sword's location? You have the map, do you not?"

"It is a dangerous journey," Rhys responds immediately, sitting beside me. "Even if Maria manages to find the tree, who's to say that the tree won't ask for something in return? Magic is never free, and the Everwildes are filled with deadly creatures."

"That is true. It will not be an easy journey," Princess Siraye concedes, staring at me. "But she has more questions, Rhys. Things that she must know in order to attain her goals. She can ask the tree for guidance."

Well, she has a point. If this tree really *can* answer any question, I could see the value in speaking with it. But it also doesn't slip my mind that a well-connected elf princess is suggesting this. I've tried searching for the sword and haven't come up with any good answers, so maybe this is the only way.

Plus, I can ask the tree how to save Rhys. Despite wanting to talk about the future with him, I'm having a hard time broaching the subject in further detail. How do you go about telling someone they're going to be murdered? Moreover, I'm actually enjoying the short time we've spent together so far. "Courting." I don't want it to end. And at the same time, I'm eager to go home and get everything over with—killing Astaroth and Neil, and getting back to my family so I can tell them what I did to Luke.

"Is this something you want to do?" Rhys asks me, searching my eyes.

I nod. "I think it could be enlightening. It's worth a try, right?"

"Then I will join you," he says firmly.

I glance toward Princess Siraye awkwardly. "What about your family? You just returned."

"Oh, do not mind me." Princess Siraye smiles. "I just *know* I will see you both again."

"Is that intuition or hope?"

"Both," she says decisively. "You shouldn't leave right away, though. Stay a few more days here and prepare for your journey. We can find some soldiers to accompany you, as well. I am sure there will be a trustworthy group willing to attend to you, for the chance of asking the Wisdom Tree a question."

"Is that...a good idea?"

"I will vet them to ensure they are trustworthy. Do not fret, dear Maria."

Now that it's settled we're going to the tree, I spend the rest of the day thinking about what questions I'll ask it. What if it's like a genie, and you have to get the phrasing precise in order to attain the proper answer? This is…stressful to say the least.

I sit alone in my room well into the evening, thinking, but the paper at my desk remains blank. Suddenly, there is a knock at the door. I rush to answer, finding Rhys standing in the doorway.

I can't help but grin when I see him. "Isn't this against the rules of courtship?"

"When have you shown much care toward rules?" he replies, leaning against the door. "I thought you might be awake, torturing yourself over the Wisdom Tree. Or other matters."

"Good guess. Would you like to come in?"

"I would, but to trespass into your bedroom might be *too* risqué, even for me. Would you care to take a stroll around the pond with me?"

"Unchaperoned? How scandalous!" I pause. "There won't be any bugs, will there?"

"I will keep them away." Rhys takes my hand and leads me downstairs, out the back door. We walk past the gardens, coming across a small pond. The surface glitters in the moonlight, making the water look magical.

"Is this what constitutes a date in this era? Strolls outside?" I ask.

"And mingling at gatherings. Must not forget about public social events," he says.

"With all these rules around courtship, and you having left for war at such a young age, am I the first you've courted?"

Rhys hesitates before replying. "I did not have any dalliances during the war. You are not just the first woman I have courted, but the first in every regard."

Wait. So when he kissed me, that was his first time *ever*? Did I steal his first kiss?

What if he only likes me because I'm his first experience? He doesn't know what's out there.

"You are thinking something irrational. I can tell," he says. "Does this bother you?"

"It doesn't bother me, but you're not the first guy *I've*, er, courted," I blurt. "Does that bother you?"

His brows rise. "Are other men courting you right now, Maria?"

"Well, no."

"Then it does not bother me."

"It's different with you." For some stupid reason, I need him to understand that. "In a good way, obviously."

"Different how?" he probes.

"Well, with my last boyfriend... He wasn't really even my boyfriend. We just kissed a few times," I explain, babbling now. "I lied to him a lot. He wasn't who I thought he was. Everything kind of fell apart."

"Did I know this...boyfriend? In the future?" Rhys hesitates. "I apologize. Perhaps you should not answer that."

"No. I can tell you about it." Even if it's super awkward, he should know what he's in for. "I don't want to spring all this future information at you, but if you ask, I'm not going to lie. Anyway, the short answer is yes, you did know Archer. You didn't like him very much, though."

"I would imagine not."

"He dated my half sister before me," I continue. "I guess we should talk about that whole situation, since that's partly what puts you in danger."

"I agree, but perhaps another time," he suggests lightly. "Right now, I just wish to enjoy this moment with you."

CHAPTER TWENTY-ONE

As it turns out, we're not going to be the type of couple who bakes together. Rhys' future cooking skills apparently don't translate into baking skills, and my lackadaisical attitude toward measurements has left the palace kitchen…let's just say worse for wear.

Pots, pans, and trays clutter the countertops. The wooden cutting boards are caked with flour and other ingredients, much like my apron, and empty bags and boxes are piled in a corner on the ground. More concerningly, a basket of burnt baked goods steams by the open window. Not even the animals outside dare touch it. I doubt they recognize it as food.

"Perhaps we missed a step," Rhys suggests, poking the latest burnt loaf of bread with the handle of a wooden spoon. The *last* clean utensil in this entire palace.

"That's an understatement," I reply, wrinkling my nose. "Is that thing growing out of the side *cheese*, or sausage?"

"Cheese." But he doesn't sound so sure of himself. "Why is it green?"

"I added some herbs. For flavor."

"What kind of herbs?"

"No idea." It looked like cilantro, but now I'm not so sure. Is cilantro supposed to smell sweet when you bake it? "This is your fault, you know."

"*My* fault?" he says incredulously, pointing to himself. I'm glad the servants and chefs let us use the kitchen by ourselves, so at least Rhys can preserve his dignity as a prince. He's a mess of flour and dough, though to be fair I'm pretty sure my face is just as smeared with ingredients. "You were quite distracting when I attempted to knead."

"Hey, I resent that accusation. You started it! You were *laughing*," I sputter. "Your laughter is too melodious!"

"If I recall correctly, *you* were the one who told the joke in the first place."

"Yes, and it wasn't very funny. I doubt the orb translated it well enough to produce even a *pity* giggle from you."

"It was not," he concedes, "but the way you told the joke, that motion you did with your hands, looked ridiculous."

"So you were laughing *at* me, not with me?"

He nods, completely unapologetic. But at least he feels comfortable enough to speak with me so openly. Over the past week, between teatime with Princess Siraye and preparing for our trip to the Wisdom Tree, we've spent practically every waking hour attached at the hip. You'd think we'd be bored of each other by now, but with Rhys, there's always something new to learn about him. For example, he can't bake for shit. He also can't tell the difference between a Southern accent and a general American accent.

This honeymoon period has to come to an end one of these days, though, and I have a feeling that point will be reached when I broach the topic of his death in the future. So far I've avoided it like the plague, trying to pretend like it's not always at the back of my mind. But there's no avoiding it forever. When Rhys asks me what I'm thinking about, I tell him.

"You and me," I say. "Our future. Uh, not in a weird way."

"Oh? The future, as in my death?" He says it casually, like we're going to talk about the weather or something. "To be quite honest with you, I have not thought about it much."

I'm glad if that's truly the case. I don't want him worrying—I'm doing enough of that for the both of us.

"I can't *not* think about it. I mean, it was pretty terrible. And I don't want to kill the mood, but if something were to happen… Look, something could happen at any time," I babble. "I've been so enjoying being with you, and I don't want to ruin that. But I guess we need to have this conversation in case something unexpected happens. I just don't even know where to begin."

"Begin where you feel it necessary, and we will fill in the gaps along the way," he encourages gently, taking a seat at the counter.

"Okay, then." Time to rip off the Band-Aid, I guess. I launch into a recap of my life since stepping foot on the SS *Athena*. I even tell him about Archer, though I leave out the unnecessary details. So much has happened, it takes a whole hour of lecturing to cover everything. Even then, I'm sure I'm missing a few details. Rhys, to his credit, listens without interruption. "In the end, Faith stabs you with an iron knife and you die."

Rhys needs a moment to digest everything I've thrown

at him. Finally, he says, "There are several things that do not make sense to me, Maria."

"Sorry, I don't think I'm the best explainer."

"No. It is not your explanation that is faulty. Rather, the events you describe. I cannot figure out why Faith attacked you at the house in the first place. The previous methods she used were attempts to sully your name."

True. "But she tried to shoot me in the cafeteria that one time."

"Yes, but she ended up stabbing another student and attempting, poorly I may add, to frame you. Her methods were never as direct as your final confrontation. It makes me wonder what changed." He pauses. "If Neil is as strong as you say, and as powerful, then how did Faith manage to pull off these attempts without his knowledge? Was no one investigating these incidents?"

"Faith said that Neil tampered with the evidence. But in that case, I have a feeling he *did* know about her involvement and just…didn't do anything about it."

"You also mentioned that Faith was stronger than she should have been. Along with that, your half sister has an unusual condition that requires her abilities to be sealed. Perhaps Neil had a hand in both of those rare cases."

"Are you suggesting Neil *did* something to them?" I wouldn't put it past him. "Shit."

"He is a dangerous character," Rhys says darkly. "I do not look forward to working with him."

"Then *don't*. Avoid him, and —"

"If I do that, what will happen to you?"

"I'll figure something out. Todd and Jenna need me alive, for now."

"*For now*," he emphasizes. "That is yet another thing I do

not understand. You say Neil is a demon, and your mother is human. If that is the case, where do your time travel abilities come from?"

"No idea. The only people who seem to know anything about my powers are Todd, Jenna, and Neil. After you were injured, Neil and I argued. He threatened to kill my family again unless I came up with a reason why he shouldn't. I told him I'd go back in time and find the Divinities Sword."

"And how did he react?"

"He was happy. Not surprised, though. He might have known beforehand that I'd be capable of it."

"There are many questions left unanswered. But there is one thing I am confident about," Rhys says. "Avoiding my own demise."

"Really?" I ask, trying not to sound too hopeful. "You think you can avoid it? How?"

"Iron poisoning can be treated through other means," he explains. "Not by magic, but with time and care, it isn't as immediately fatal as you describe. You do not need to worry or feel guilty about this any longer."

I give him a wry smile. "I'll stop worrying once I see you alive and well in the future."

"Fair enough. But on another subject, the child from the Violet City has been asking for you. She is well enough for a visit; perhaps you would like to see her?"

As much as I want to press him on his so-called plan for avoiding Faith's knife, there's nothing he could say at this point to reassure me when there's no guarantee anything we do will work. So I let the topic go for the time being.

"I haven't even thought about the kid since we got here," I confess, feeling a little bit guilty for being so caught up in myself. "Your sister is letting her stay?"

"Until she makes a full recovery. For political reasons, we might at some point have to send her back to her own home," Rhys says, wiping his hands with a towel. "Would you like to speak with her?"

"Sure, why not?" I would like to learn why the kid was in that treasure room in the first place. But before we can go see her, Rhys and I try to clean up the mess we left in the kitchen. The explosion of ingredients, pots, and pans cluttering the countertops would give the palace staff a heart attack, especially since when we first started this morning, the kitchen was pristine.

Rhys and I make quick work of washing up. Once the kitchen is clean and we're both changed into a fresh set of clothes, we head upstairs to one of the guest rooms.

It's not as large as the one I'm in, but it still has a queen-sized bed, a full wardrobe, and a private bathroom. It's bigger than my room back home in Georgia, at least. And it's nicer than my basement dorm room at Southeastern. Not looking forward to going back *there* after this is all over.

The child sits by the window, a book propped in her lap. Behind her, Lyari braids her garnet-red hair into a tight plait.

"Your Highness, I did not expect you," Lyari says, getting up quickly.

"I did. One of these days," the child says. Dark scars mark her warm, olive-toned skin. She looks older than I initially thought, now that she's cleaned and dressed. And, you know, not unconscious. She could be around Lyari's age, and they're around the same height. "I am Chaela. You are...not as big as I thought."

Pot, meet kettle.

"I'm Mar. Short for Maria."

"What an odd name. But I suppose it's fitting."

Is she looking to pick a fight?

"I thought you would have come to visit me sooner." Her dark eyes slide to Lyari, a hint of a smile on her lips. "I had to make do with Lyari as my companion."

"*Make do?*" Lyari squawks. "I've been reading you every book you've wanted to hear for the past few weeks! I've been your *errand* boy, dressing your injuries and feeding you soup! Your Highness, Lady Chaela has been the most *annoying* patient I've ever had the displeasure of caring for!"

His harsh words don't ruffle Chaela in the slightest. Instead, she focuses all her attention on me, studying me. "My mother wrote the book you stole—the one with the map to the Wisdom Tree. But when news of her research got out, a man cloaked in black killed my family, took the book, and imprisoned me as collateral. They tortured me because they wanted to find the map."

"Do you know who did it?" I ask.

Chaela shakes her head. "I did not see the man's face, but I know he is only using the auction house as a front. He was never originally part of it; he was just a traveler in the Violet City. He wanted the book more than anything. Even at the cost of my family's lives."

"I'm sorry." The words don't seem like enough, but they're all I can muster.

"I have long since accepted my fate, Maria. I knew it would come to pass because my mother and I visited the Wisdom Tree before. It told us many things," Chaela says. "It instructed my mother to write the book and allowed us safe passage to the Violet City. The tree is waiting for someone, you see. The Timekeeper's daughter."

229

Timekeeper? The phrase sounds familiar. I know Jenna and Todd are Time Agents. Could it be related to that?

"You did what the Wisdom Tree said, even though you knew it would cause the death of your family?"

"My family's death was fate's design," Chaela replies sadly. "But the Wisdom Tree told me it needed you. It said that I needed to give you the book no matter what, and if I fulfill my role in the grand design, I will be happy. It also told me that you would make a face and think to yourself, 'Why is it that everyone I meet has to be so cryptic? Can't they just tell me information clearly and concisely?'"

"Good guess. Did the tree have an answer?"

"No. It said you have to visit yourself." Chaela yawns. "You'll have to tell me all about it when we meet again. Now, I want to rest."

With that, the girl dismisses me, leaving me once again with more questions than answers.

I can't help but think about what she said, even as I lie in bed later that night. The Wisdom Tree is real, and it's waiting for the Timekeeper's daughter. I'm going to go out on a limb and say that I'm either the Timekeeper's daughter, or I'm somehow connected to her. But assuming it's the former option, then what does that make Neil? The Timekeeper?

If Neil is the Timekeeper, then I guess he's who I inherit my powers from. But if he has the same powers, why would he even *need* me in the first place? I'm more of a liability than anything else. And he has no qualms about killing.

My biological *mother* could be the Timekeeper. No one said it had to be a man. In this scenario, Neil would need my powers because my mother is dead. Or so Neil claims. She's either dead, or she escaped his grasp and left me to rot with him. Neither scenario is particularly good.

But it all comes back to what Neil's true goal is. After I kill Astaroth, what's going to happen? Neil won't possibly let me go. When we had that first conversation in his car, he told me that he was keeping tabs on me to ensure that my powers didn't develop. But he detected something several months before I went on the cruise ship. I assumed that implied he orchestrated my acceptance into the South-eastern summer program and that he wanted me to be on the ship to keep a close eye on me.

What if he knew about the cult of Astaroth being on the ship? And he purposely set it up so I would get involved with them? He wouldn't have me free Astaroth just as a *test*, right?

If that's true, which I sincerely hope it's not, then I'm even *more* confused about his true goal. And what that means for me and the people I care about. Not just my family, but Rhys...

Sitting up in bed, I can't shake the thought of him from my head. Even though it's not "appropriate" courting behavior, I'm on my feet and heading toward his room before my head can catch up to my heart.

But as soon as I knock on his door, I feel absolutely idiotic. I'm in a T-shirt and shorts in the middle of the night, looking to talk to him about my constant concerns. What if he gets sick of me worrying so much?

Rhys answers, still dressed in his clothes from earlier. It's the middle of the night—why is he up so late?

"Hi," I say lamely. What the hell? Did I think I was just going to throw myself into his arms or something? *Get a grip, Mar!* "I, um, hope I'm not disturbing you."

"No. I could not sleep, so I was reading," he admits. "Is there something wrong?"

"I wanted to see you. I've been thinking more about the future, and our situation with Neil."

"Let us speak in private."

I thought he was going to invite me inside, but instead, he closes the door behind him and leads me to the balcony where we first kissed. The moon hangs bright and full in the sky, illuminating the gardens below us.

Rhys takes my hand, sitting us both down on a bench by the railing. "What troubles you?"

"I was thinking about how Neil is holding my family hostage. And if he knew about us, he would do the same to you—hold your wellbeing over my head. Or vice versa," I say. "In the future, you absolutely cannot let anyone know what our relationship is."

Not that *I* even know, at this point. We're courting, but that doesn't make him my boyfriend, right? I don't think they even *have* boyfriends and girlfriends in this era.

"What if you misunderstand?" he asks.

"I won't. Probably," I add. "I just want to make sure you do what you need to, to survive. Long term, you know? Be cold to me. Don't smile, don't show compassion toward me. Nic Woolridge will report everything he sees to Neil, and Allegra might accidentally say something to her father again. I don't want to put you in danger."

All assuming he survives Faith's attack, of course.

"This whole situation is complicated," I continue. "I know that I'm asking a lot from you. If you had fallen for a girl *here*, like Lensa or someone, it would be so much easier. Maybe you'd be happier, too. Putting in all this effort for me just feels silly, now that I think about it. I wouldn't blame you if you walked away right now. Seriously."

"I will not leave, even when things get difficult," Rhys says.

"I'm going to get beat up," I warn him. "Like, a lot. You can't do anything about it. You're just going to have to watch. Don't react—don't give anyone a reason to even *suspect* you."

He brushes a strand of hair out of my face, the calloused pads of his fingertips caressing my skin. "I will try."

"Being with me isn't easy." Not romantically *or* platonically. I have a string of failed foster homes, failed friendships, and failed *relationships* in general, as proof of that. When the going gets hard, most people leave. I can't even blame them. I don't really bring anything of value to the table.

Oh God. Did that just *reek* of abandonment issues?

"Being with you *is* easy. It is the most natural thing in the world. Being apart from you, having to watch as others wrong you without being able to do anything about it, will be hard," Rhys admits. "But when I think about the future with you, all the struggles we will face do not even cross my mind. Whatever fate has in store for us, I am prepared. Because for me, there is no one else but you."

CHAPTER TWENTY-TWO

The trip should take us two weeks on horseback, but I think at the rate we're going, it'll be longer. Now, I'm not blaming the horse, but I swear to God it loves Rhys and *hates* me. Don't ask me how I know that—it's, like, animal instinct or something. A human being is a type of animal, right?

Anyway, I can look into its eyes and just *know* it hates me. Rhys thinks I'm being ridiculous, but he doesn't see the glare the horse gives me sometimes. I thought things would get better after a few days of traveling, but no such luck. And we're still quite far from the Wisdom Tree, according to the map.

There's only so much we can do with just the two of us. I can't ride on my own, and the horse is also carrying our supplies, so the weight of everything is slowing us down. Not that I can complain—I'm the one who insisted on this trip being a two-person mission. I'm just shocked Rhys agreed.

Before you say anything, I doubt his reasoning was

romantic. To be perfectly honest with you, I thought it was at first—but he hasn't made a single move on me. And, because I'm a feminist and all, you can trust that I've made moves on *him*. But he'll usually bring up the rules of propriety, courtship, yada yada, and doesn't reciprocate my advances. I've concluded that he only wanted to travel as a pair because he felt bad asking a guard to attend to us.

By nightfall on the third day of our journey, we make camp under the stars. It would be a lot more romantic if I *liked* camping. If I've learned anything about myself on this trip, it's this: I was *not* built for the outdoors. I am a girl made for Wi-Fi, sweet tea, and A/C. In that order.

God, I miss sweet tea. I never thought I'd say that, but then again, I never thought I'd be leaving Georgia for this long. I don't think *anyone* did, actually.

In school at the end of the year, we always had yearbook superlatives. We also had unofficial superlatives published online, and sometimes printed and pasted on the girls' room stalls in the second-floor science wing. I've won Most Likely to be a Crack Whore twice, Most Likely to be Found Dead in a Ditch all four years, and Most Likely Never to Leave Douglas County. People in my town, and I guess in the county, either make it big and move to Atlanta or never leave and start families early. I guess this is one area where I subverted others' expectations. Even my own.

As strange and horrible as this whole "finding out I'm the daughter of a demon" thing has been, I can also feel myself changing more than I ever did in Georgia. Whether that's because of the challenges I've faced—and I use "faced" pretty loosely since I've done a ton of running away —or the people I've met, I'm uncertain. I don't even know if I'm changing *for the better*.

Rhys makes me want to be better, as cheesy as that sounds. I'd never tell him, because if I did, I'd have to get into the whole issue of worrying that I'm not good enough for him.

If he's having second thoughts about being together, I'd never know from how he acts. Which means I'm making a huge deal of nothing in my head. Or he's so blinded by emotion that he can't think rationally, or I'm his first crush and he doesn't understand his own feelings, or he's really good at hiding regret... The possibilities are endless and, frankly, negative.

"What are you thinking about, Maria?" Rhys asks, rousing me from my self-deprecating thoughts. "You are making a face."

I pick up another arm-length stick from the ground, part of what is quickly becoming our nightly routine. I could lie to him, but he would be able to tell. I could also dance around the issue. Instead, I blurt, "I'm thinking about how I have no helpful skills, and you've pretty much been doing everything since we left."

"But you are gathering materials. That is very helpful."

"I'm picking up sticks. It's not anything complicated. Is this enough?"

He nods, taking the bundle from me. Finding a flat surface, he sets down the bundle and picks out a single, skinny branch from the ones I've gathered. Holding it in front of him, the wood flattens and grows into a solid plank. Setting it on the ground, Rhys continues to pump his magic into it, making one wall of a small shelter for us to sleep. Each stick I picked turns into a wall, and the last one functions as a roof. It's no architectural achievement—it's a

SAM GAO

wooden box—but it will protect us from the elements, at least.

"See? Your powers are so convenient," I say, bringing our bedrolls inside. He insisted on packing two, so we'd each have our own separate one. I wouldn't have minded sharing, but Rhys barely likes the idea of staying in the same *room* as me. He only does it for safety reasons, apparently. "On top of this, you've been hunting and cooking for us."

"I am used to it. You are clearly not," Rhys replies casually. He lies near the door, allowing me to rest further inside. If I reached out, I'd be able to brush his back with my fingers. "Maria, do not worry about this."

"This is just a small issue," I relent, "but it speaks to a bigger one. I know we have no clue what's going to happen, but chances are, you're going to be taken into the future against your will. You're going to be forced to leave your home, work for Neil, lose your status as a prince, lose your *family*...all for what? Me? And now that I say it aloud, I realize how insecure and pathetic I sound."

"We do not know what is going to happen in the future," Rhys says firmly. I can't see his face well in the dark, but his voice doesn't tremble. Not like mine. "There is no use concerning yourself with these things. My royal status is not precious to me, nor has it ever been central to my identity. Likewise, I lost my home long ago. The palace is where I reside, but I have no attachment to it. And my family and friends will still be alive in your era. We elves are long-lived. We value time differently."

"That's another thing! I'm just shadowborn, Rhys. Half human. You know that I'm not going to live as long as you, right?"

"I did not." He goes quiet for a moment. Of course he

238

doesn't. He doesn't even know what a *human* is, and I haven't brought up my lifespan before. "How long do your kind live?"

"I don't know the average. Eighty years, maybe?" I mutter. "It's not nearly as long as you. And I'm going to get old faster, I imagine. You're going to uproot your entire life, and I don't even have anything to give you in return."

"You are not lying, but that does not mean your words are true. In an ideal world, we would have met in the same time period, in the same realm. But the world is hardly ideal, and because of that, we share similar experiences which bind us," Rhys says. "I have not met another who…understands as deeply as you do how painful it can be to grow up in an indifferent world."

"I'm not sure what to do."

"Give me your hand."

We reach for each other, our hands bumping together. If I stretch out my arm fully, I can barely reach him. When he meets me halfway, our fingers lock together.

"We will make the best of whatever situation is thrown at us. Do not get discouraged, Maria. Let us enjoy what time we have together."

"Alright," I relent, because I have to. Because he sounds like he really believes in us.

It's not that I don't. God, that's not it at all. I just don't have much faith in myself. And I can't shake my fear that Rhys will wake up and realize what I already know: I'm not good enough for him.

A few days later, we stop for lunch. "We *have* to be halfway there by now," I say, holding up the map. We're still in the middle of the Everwildes and fresh out of jerky, so we've rerouted near a creek to fish. Rhys taught me how to scale and debone a fish, which is easier and somehow less disgusting to me than preparing rabbits and birds.

"That is upside down," Rhys comments, twisting the map in my hands. "We are here. The Wisdom Tree is here."

"So we're…a third of the way?"

"About. But this area of the Everwildes is particularly dangerous. We will have to take care," he warns, folding the map back up. He places it in the horse's saddle bag. "There are more beastbloods. Most will leave us be, so long as we do not disturb them."

"I don't know much about beastbloods." Just the basics. They're like truebloods—magical creatures originating in the Veil—except they aren't humanoid. They're more like animals. "What species are local to this area?"

"Chimera. Talking animals with elemental abilities. Snakes and insects." It's the wrong thing to say, and as soon as the words leave Rhys' mouth, he follows up with, "I will, of course, protect you from any insects, Maria. They will not bother us."

"Insects? With stingers?" I ask nervously. "Oh jeez. It's going to be like a Stephen King novel, minus the mist."

"I am still surprised you are so afraid," Rhys muses. "From what you describe, smaller creatures seem far more menacing and difficult to destroy. And the spray you use to kill them can be toxic to other living beings. It is nonsensical. At least you can slay a larger insect."

"*You* can." And he has, with his little turning-rocks-into-arrows magic trick. He tried to show me how to do it, but of course, as a shadowborn I couldn't. "All I've got is a dagger. And daggers are used in close-range combat."

"When we return, we will continue swordsmanship lessons," he promises, a smile tugging at his lips.

Continuing on our way, we finish our fish sticks—that is, fish on a *literal* stick—and continue riding. By sunset, we make camp in a large clearing, with Rhys putting extra effort into our shelter for the night. This time, he creates a cabin large enough to fit his horse inside.

"When did you learn how to use magic?" I ask.

Rhys unfolds a blanket to lay over his horse, who shoots me a glare. Of course, Rhys doesn't notice this. "When I went to war. I knew how to do simple things—making plants grow faster, for instance—but the conditions on the battlefield taught me very quickly how to use magic in more useful ways. Fae have powerful magic, but it is derived from glamour. They can create powerful illusions and potions, but they aren't real. Elves can manipulate nature itself."

"So if a fairy had created this shelter, it would just be an illusion?"

"Correct. It would not actually protect them at all. The difference in our abilities is yet another point of contention."

"Isn't that usually the case?" I muse, rolling out our bedrolls. Despite the extra space in the room, I put them right next to each other. For warmth. "In the future, when you tutor me, you never mention much about elves and fae. Otherwise, I would be able to tell you how political relations are in my time period."

"It is better this way. I would prefer not to know just yet." Thankfully, Rhys doesn't say anything about the bedrolls and lies down beside me. "Tell me more about *us* in the future."

"There isn't much to tell. You're cold as ice, but in a sexy way."

"You have said that before, but I am still unsure what you mean."

"You never smile at me. Maybe if you had, I would have fallen for you," I tease, curling into his side. He puts an arm around me, drawing me closer until my head rests against his chest. I can hear the steadiness of his heartbeat, which calms me. "Allegra probably has."

"Your half sister? Am I not her servant?"

"Pretty much. You take care of her and, from what I can tell, you're her only companion. But all of us are around the same age, and you took care of her for years. It makes sense she'd have feelings for you." I remember talking to Allegra about those dating rumors, but what happened a few months back feels like a lifetime ago. "When I asked if you were dating, though, you were pretty quick to deny it."

"I should hope so. Regardless of what our relationship is, or is not, I would not pursue another."

"No, I don't think you would either. You're too honorable to do that. And besides, you're mine," I declare.

"Yours?" he murmurs.

My cheeks heat up at my own words, which sound super cheesy now that I think about it. "Yeah. That's how you signed your letters to me. 'Yours, Rhys.' And despite my mounting insecurities, I think of you as...mine? I'm not sure how else to put it. I know that people don't 'own' each other or anything, but..."

"Perhaps it is just the limit of your language. In Elvish, what you have said does not necessarily imply ownership, but belonging," he explains. "Two people who fit together in a way that is beyond comprehension."

"Exactly. Like soulmates. Not that I ever really believed in that, or anything," I add quickly. "It's just...I don't know how else to describe the connection I feel toward you. It's taken years for me to feel this way *platonically* for other people, and even then, it's never been so fierce."

God, normally I would *never* talk about stuff like this. Not even with Tasha. Telling someone how much you care for them is terrifying; it's like daring the universe to take them away from you. And I guess the universe *will* be taking Rhys away from me, sooner or later. But I didn't tell Luke how much I loved him, and then... Well, now I'll never have the chance to.

I won't be making the same mistake. Rhys needs to know because no matter what happens in the future, there's no guarantee of anything. All I can give him is now.

Rhys, however, has an entirely different opinion on the matter. His hold on me tightens, and he says, "I look forward to our future, Maria."

"Really? But what if...something bad happens?"

"I cannot stop the bad things from happening. That is inevitable," he relents. "But I promise you that I will fill our lives with so much joy, the good will outweigh the bad, and that will be more than enough."

CHAPTER TWENTY-THREE

I'm right about the journey to the Wisdom Tree taking longer than it should. I just got my period again, which seems to be the only semi-reliable way to track how much time has passed. Thank God for menstrual cups.

Rhys and I slow our pace considerably the deeper into the Everwildes we get, and for good reason. The insects *are* huge nightmare fuel, and so are the beastbloods. We don't have to fight any, thankfully, but avoiding herds makes it much more difficult to cover a lot of ground quickly. Especially on horseback, when the forest becomes impossibly thick.

When we reach the first grove, I'm not even certain we're in the right place. *This* is supposed to be the first trial of the Wisdom Tree? It looks like any old meadow. Not that I was expecting a gilded fountain or dancing unicorns or anything of the sort.

Okay, maybe I was. But can you blame me for wanting to see some beauty? My eyes were defiled by a cross between a wasp, a praying mantis, and a monkey the size of a bear cub. I don't have my cell phone, so I can't bleach my eyes in the form of cute puppy videos.

"What's the first test, again?" I ask Rhys, looking around at the thicket of trees.

"A test of wills," he replies, just as confused as I am about the emptiness around us. He gets off the horse first before helping me down. "I am certain this is the correct place."

"Hello?" I call out. "Is anyone here?"

No one responds. In fact, it's eerily quiet. Shouldn't there be animals moving around and wind blowing, or some other nature sounds? Instead, there's total silence. Just like a horror movie right before a jump scare.

"Should we come back?" I walk around the edge of the meadow, searching the trees. The problem is, there's no way to move forward. The trees create a wall surrounding us, growing so close together that I know it can't be natural. "Can you use your magic to make them move?"

Rhys shakes his head. "There is already some sort of magic spell cast over this place. I cannot use my own."

"Oh, even better," I mutter. At least we can still use the Linguist's Orb.

Finally, I hear something behind us. Turning around as the footsteps draw closer, my hand flies to my dagger.

The newcomer is a tiger. Except this is the Veil, so it can't just be a normal tiger—it's six feet tall on all fours. Its fur is a particularly neon shade of orange, unlike the tigers I'm used to. Which is to say, the ones I see on the Nature Channel on TV.

The tiger walks past us, its eyes skimming over our shocked faces before it makes its way to the center of the meadow and lies down in the grass.

"You must be here for the Wisdom Tree," the tiger says finally.

"Uh, yeah. Are you the guardian of this grove?" I ask.

"Guardian?" The tiger snorts, rolling its amber eyes. Its mannerisms are entirely human. "That's a nice way to put it. Yes, I'm the *guardian* here. The tester of wills."

"Great. I'd like to see the talking tree. Go ahead. Test my will."

"Your will?" The tiger considers this. "Oh, who the hell cares?"

"What?"

"My girlfriend dumped me again," the tiger continues. "She said she couldn't see herself getting serious with a workaholic. It's not like I *want* to be soul-bound here for the rest of time. I'm supposed to be giving anyone who comes to my grove a test of wills, but this job is testing *my* will to live! Life sucks. People suck. It's not like I have anything to do all day. Whenever we don't have visitors, the guardians get together, but lately I feel like Owl and Savel are avoiding me. And now you two come in during my lunch break, no less, and I can just *tell* you're a couple. Well, screw off. We're closed for the day."

Good God, that's a lot to unpack.

"I don't think so," I say with a derisive laugh. "We came all the way here to see the tree, so we're seeing the tree. We won't leave until we do."

"You're not getting past me."

"Good. Then this really *is* a test of wills."

"Maria, perhaps we *should* come back," Rhys says.

"Oh, Rhys. Sweet, patient Rhys. Don't worry about a thing. You've been working hard this whole time," I say.

"Now, it's my time to shine. Trust me, we're going to get through."

Rhys gives me a dubious look, but this is one area I have full confidence in.

"So," I say, whirling around to the tiger beastblood. "You're a talking tiger. Was your girlfriend also a talking tiger?"

"Enough. I don't want to talk about it," the tiger replies glumly. "Just leave me alone."

"I can't do that. So you might as well tell me about your life. Unless you want me to talk about myself? Let's see. Well, my name is Mar. It's short for Maria. Maria Rochester, like the book *Jane Eyre*. Maria can mean 'bitter' or 'beloved,' but I think 'bitter' suits me better, because I'm a pretty bitter person. Oh, that sounded kind of like a tongue twister! Anyway, we did this project in fourth grade where we had to explore our family origins and make a poster about it. And, true to form, Raina Cochrin started making fun of me for my name with some pretty racist stuff she probably learned from her parents. Anyway, I ended up shoving a bottle of glue right up that crazy bitch's nostril and—"

"My gods, shut up!" the tiger snaps. "You cannot expect to pass by simply *annoying* me into submission."

My jaw drops. "Excuse me? Annoying you? Are you saying that my talking about myself is annoying to you? Jeez, no wonder your girlfriend broke up with you! Are you this rude to everyone you meet for the first time?"

"Excuse me?"

"I was trying to be *nice* and I asked you about yourself, but since you wouldn't answer I thought I would tell you about myself. As a means to *relate* to you in some way. But

I'm glad to know you find me annoying!" I say sarcastically. "And to embarrass me in front of Rhys like this...you're just *mean*. The whole 'nice guys finish last' is a total myth. Women actually enjoy partners who care about them, listen to them, and are kind and considerate. It's clear that you're none of those things!"

"You—"

"No, you!" I point at the tiger. "If you want to win your girlfriend back, try being nicer to others! You say you lost her because you're a workaholic, but then you don't even want to do your job? You're spending all this time soul-bound here, and for what? To mope?"

"N-not just to mope," the tiger says in a small voice. "I crochet as a hobby."

"Well, I think you should reevaluate how you treat others and better yourself before trying to get back together with your girlfriend. I also think you should just let us through. But if you won't, I understand, I guess. We can just sit here and talk about all the ways you can improve yourself. Or all the ways you've caused me emotional distress by calling me *annoying*."

The tiger looks at me, and I think he's trying to discern whether or not I'm bluffing.

Spoiler alert: I'm not.

"You won't find what you seek inside," the tiger warns.

"I'll worry about that later."

The tiger sighs, waving its paw. The trees behind it begin to move, the ground below us rumbling as a path forms in the forest.

"Thank you!" I chirp, grabbing Rhys' arm. "Onto the next trial!"

"What just happened?" Rhys asks, dazed. "Should we be

leaving the horse there?"

"Yes, he'll be fine. I passed the test of wills!" I beam. "That was *so* easy."

"Not for the guardian," Rhys says under his breath. "Alright, the next trial is a test of intelligence."

"I'll let you handle this one." It's best to know one's strengths and weaknesses, right?

"Let's be careful. There could be some trickery involved. I do not think it will be as easy as the first trial."

No, neither do I. The tiger was probably a fluke, but I'm confident that between the two of us, we'll be able to pass through to the Wisdom Tree. We don't have much choice in the matter. If we fail now, we'll have wasted time, energy, and supplies, and I won't be any closer to figuring out where the sword is.

We move to the next grove, which is quite different from the first. There's a log cabin off to the side with a pond right next to it. An owl sits perched next to the pond, watching the water's surface despite no fish swimming below. He doesn't look up. He doesn't even acknowledge us until we're standing directly in front of him. I have to crane my neck to look into his eyes, because like the tiger, this owl is abnormally large. I wouldn't expect anything less from the guardian of a talking tree.

"It appears you have passed the test of wills. I wonder how many years it's been since anyone's passed," the owl says. "Here is your riddle: what has one voice but goes on four legs in the morning, two in the afternoon, and three in the evening?"

"Uh, a human?" I guess, remembering the riddle from high school.

"Congratulations." The owl sighs, bored. "You may

pass."

"Really?" I can't believe that worked! I thought I was gonna have to write an essay or something.

"Yes, yes. See you again in five years." The owl waves its wing, parting the trees ahead to form yet another path.

Rhys looks as shocked as I do. He squeezes my hand, a slow grin spreading on his face. "Impressive, Maria."

"For me, that was nothing short of a miracle," I reply.

We walk along the next path into a third grove, where a brown bear waits for us. But to our surprise, there is a path beyond the bear already open.

"Greetings," the bear says, more enthusiastic than his other two coworkers. He's the same size as a regular bear in the mortal world, making him slightly less intimidating than the previous guardians. Don't get me wrong, I don't want to wrestle a bear whether it's "normal-sized" or not—but this is a test of strength. I think I'll leave this to Rhys.

"Hi," I answer politely. "Um, I'm Mar. This is Rhys."

"You're new. You've never been here before." The bear tilts its head to the side. "I would have remembered a funny-looking thing like you."

"Thanks, I guess."

"Maria does not look *funny*," Rhys interjects coldly. "She is beautiful."

"I appreciate the gesture, but this is a pick-your-battles situation." I nod pointedly toward the bear. "That's a bear."

"My name is Savel," the bear supplies.

"Savel," I correct. "So, you're the one who's going to administer the test of strength?"

"Oh, we *did* have a test of strength at one time. But then I threw my back out, and it was a whole thing. There are no doctors here, so I was just on the ground for a week until I healed. It was awful," Savel says. "Visitors came by and beat me while I was on the ground already. No one offered to help. It made me feel horrible about myself."

"Uh, I'm sure it did."

"People are *monsters*."

"Tell me about it."

"Anyway, I don't want any trouble. Go ahead, I guess," Savel tells us. "I'm sure we'll meet again."

"Why does everyone keep saying that?" I ask.

"Because everyone comes here again." Savel shrugs his furry brown shoulders. "Once you exit the Wisdom Tree's grove, you forget everything from the first grove on. That is the cost of infinite information."

"Wait, *what*?" You don't remember anything once you leave the Wisdom Tree? Then how the hell am I going to use the information the tree tells me? What's the goddamn point? "Wait, I've *met* someone who remembers speaking with the Wisdom Tree."

"There are a few exceptions," Savel relents. "You don't look that exceptional to *me*. No offense."

"Full offense taken, actually."

"There isn't much I can do about that."

"Come, Maria. Let us see what the tree says," Rhys urges gently, tugging my hand. "I am sure there is a solution."

"Yeah, yeah. Alright," I grumble.

I guess the trials could have been way worse. I should be grateful I can even speak to the tree at all. But does it really matter if I'm going to end up forgetting everything I'm told? How the hell am I going to find the Divinities Sword this way?

And more importantly, how am I going to save Rhys?

Chapter Twenty-Four

The Wisdom Tree reminds me of the talking tree in Pocahontas, which is to say, it's nothing short of downright terrifying. Its facial features are etched in the grooves of the bark, but it barely resembles anything human. Its eyes are glossy black beads, and its mouth is stretched wide in a way that can only be described as grotesque.

The weeping willow's trunk is so large, Rhys and I could both wrap our arms around it and our fingers still wouldn't touch. It sits in the center of the grove, its roots spread and its branches budding with glowing blue flowers.

"Welcome," the tree rasps, spreading its branches like arms. "I have been waiting for you, Maria Alison Rochester. Mary Alice. Mar. Marilyn. Mari. You have many names, it seems. But *I* know the titles you have not yet heard, the ones whispered behind your back: the Timekeeper's daughter. The girl who should not exist. The Serpent Queen."

After all those titles, all I can muster is a lame, "Hi."

"And I see you have met your mate, your fated pairing. The prince in name only, Vesryn. Or shall I say Rhys?"

Okay, is it just me, or was Rhys' introduction worse than mine?

"Uh, yeah. I'm Mar. That's Rhys." I don't let go of Rhys' hand as we approach the tree, needing his warmth now more than ever. "If you're omniscient, then you already know why we've come here, right?"

"Of course, Maria Rochester. I know even more than the fates. I can see their blind spot. I know the reason you have come is not the reason I have summoned you. The Timekeepers don't want you to know the truth, and yet they needed you to visit me so I could tell you where the Divinities Sword is. Beware of those who would keep knowledge from you; they do it to take your choices and seal the fate that is rightfully yours to write."

I have a lot of questions, but the most important one right now: "Where *is* the Divinities Sword?"

"It is in the lake you landed in. You will find it by unlocking your full abilities, but in doing that, you will open a door that cannot be closed. Not by you."

I exchange a glance with Rhys, relieved when he looks as clueless as I feel. "How do I unlock my abilities?"

"How did you unlock them the first time?"

The first time? "I used my blood to open the rift. Do I need to bleed into the lake and open a gateway there somehow?"

The tree's branches rustle with the wind. "Maria Rochester, the sword is not the right key to your lock."

"If you're omniscient, then you must know how to speak normally." Stop with the cryptic crap, please!

"The sword cannot be used by someone like you, no matter how special you may be."

"Someone like me? Shadowborn?" I guess. "Does it have to be used by a trueblood or something?"

"A sword crafted by a mortal monster can only be used by one. But the Timekeepers do not like that. They fear the White Swan, the Butcher, a creature whose destiny rivals yours in its dreadfulness. The blind spot."

"Again, I don't know what *any* of that means." I didn't even know I had a destiny to begin with! "Rhys, why don't *you* try asking it your questions?"

Rhys hesitates. "You say Maria and I are mates. What do you mean?"

"Maria Rochester is the Timekeeper's daughter. She is the girl who should not exist. She was never part of the grand design the fates originally laid out," the tree explains. "Because of that, the grand design needed to be altered. Many died because of it, and many were born when they were not supposed to be. Her existence changed everything. And you, Rhys Torren, are Maria's goodwill gift, a prize the Timekeepers will hold over her head until her mission is complete. They chose you out of every single creature in the Veil born throughout time, because you are her perfect match. And she is yours. Thus, I can think of no other way to describe you but as soulmates."

"*What?*" I sputter, dropping Rhys' hand like a hot potato.

First of all—oh my God. What? I wasn't supposed to exist? What does that *mean*? According to a talking tree, if I'm understanding correctly, fate is real. Like God's plan, in Christianity. Except, it's not Christian God's plan, because we're in the Veil. So for some reason, a greater power decided I should be born one day. And then because of that, the timeline after my birth changed, causing a ripple effect in everyone else's fate.

Rhys' fate was also changed because I was born. Was he supposed to be with someone else? Did all that bad stuff happen to him because of me? Because he needed to be my "perfect match"? Let's be real for a second here—Rhys is a good match for me because, in a way, we have similar cynical viewpoints on life. I don't think he's as insecure as I am, but there's something morose about him that draws me in. Was his life ruined just so he could be my match?

"Maria Rochester, Rhys Torren's life was fated to end early. Because of you, it has been extended. The Timekeepers' wish is to keep you happy and compliant, and they will use him, along with the rest of your family, as a means of doing so."

Rhys recoils, taken aback by the revelation. "I—"

"He has no choice is what you're saying?" My voice grows shrill. "He *has* to be with me because *fate* decided it?"

"Your romantic troubles are secondary to the true horrors you will face, Maria Rochester."

Well, if the *talking tree* is telling me that I should focus, then I guess I should focus, right?

Wrong!

"You look ill," Rhys comments worriedly.

"I'm just trying to process all this. How are you okay?" I search his face, but he looks completely fine, except for his concern about *me*. Because I'm freaking the fuck out. "A sentient tree just told you that you were forced to fall in love with me by some unseen power beyond your control."

"I believe it said that you and I are perfect for each other, and that 'some unseen power' merely allowed us to meet."

"That's hyper-optimistic, especially coming from you."

"What can I say? You bring out the positive side of me."

"Yeah, *positively* stupid!"

Rhys chuckles, which pisses me off even more. Why is he making light of this situation? How can he laugh when his choices aren't even his own? Not to mention, if I don't follow my fate, what's going to happen to him? Will these Timekeepers hold Rhys hostage, just as Neil is holding my family hostage? Is *Neil* the Timekeeper, or is it my biological mother? Or are the Timekeepers related to me more in a symbolic way, because they arranged for me to be born despite going against the original "grand design"? What even *was* the grand design, and what is it now? Why was I born?

"What 'true horrors' will Maria face?" Rhys asks, turning his attention to the Wisdom Tree.

"She will destroy the world."

What's that, now?

So, to summarize, I:

1. Wasn't supposed to be born, so my birth caused a bunch of people to die who weren't supposed to

2. Changed Rhys' fate and he's now practically forced to be with me

3. Am going to destroy the world at some point

Great. As if I didn't already have enough to look forward to.

The tree goes on. "Maria Rochester's fate should be sealed, but there is a wild card. The Timekeepers have blind spots. The sword is one of them, and the Butcher is another. When you are in fate's blind spot, the rules do not apply to you, and destiny is yours to write. You are both fated to destroy the world, but together, you can save it."

"Alright," I say, "I've heard enough. Where's the thing you do to make me forget all this crap?"

"Maria Rochester—"

"Seriously, I'm waiting." I point to my head. "Are you going to give me a good old bonk on the skull?" I haven't had *that* happen yet in this book. I've been waiting for it. By now, head injuries are my trademark.

"No, Maria Rochester. You will not forget. You will open a rift here and leave with Rhys Torren, your memories intact."

But I *want* to forget, desperately. I won't even be mad if the tree takes my memories of Max away or the very specific image in my head of Luke's death. Maybe then I'd stop seeing them every night.

As much as I don't want this knowledge, I know deep down that I need it. I'm not sure what I'm going to *do* about any of it yet, but I'll fumble through it, I guess. With or without Rhys.

"Fine," I say, my voice clipped. I pull the dagger out from my waistband and cut my palm, welcoming the sting of pain it brings. It's better than how I feel inside.

Rhys lets out a surprised yelp, grabbing my wrist. "What are you doing?"

"I need to use my blood to make the rift." I shake off his hand, trying to ignore the hurt expression flickering over his face as I slash through the empty air.

Marilyn could pretend this never happened. Any of my characters could. If I could change into them and shove all these worries into the back of my mind, I would be able to move on and make better decisions. But my long-term thinking skills have completely fizzled out, replaced by panic and fear so familiar you'd think I would know how to deal with it by now.

But no one taught me how. Not that it's any excuse.

Actually, I *was* taught, indirectly, how to deal with problems: blame others, manipulate the situation, and lie until you reach a suitable outcome. All the toxic things people have done to me have stuck with me, clearly. And despite how happy I've been as of late, reality has a way of crashing down so hard it'll make your head spin.

Even as Maria, for a few precious moments I forgot how awful I really am. Rhys made me feel better about myself, just like how my family makes me feel. But I know that without their support, I devolve into this negative, insecure, whiny bitch. It's the core of who I am, and no matter how hard I've tried, I can't change.

Maybe I'm not supposed to.

My very existence was a *mistake*, and it's caused strangers to suffer. All for what? A girl who's going to destroy the world?

I tear open the rift, my eyes stinging as I attempt to maintain my composure. And fail.

"Maria—"

"Don't." I can't deal with Rhys' gentle words, or his feelings. Because no matter what he says, I know that I don't really deserve his love, and he's *blinded* by it.

If we're not together, then what? Is he going to die if he rejects me? He's my "prize," right?

The sad thing is, I still care for him. I want him to choose me regardless of this fucked-up situation. But I will *never* know if he's choosing me because he wants me, or because he has no other choice. I know what it's like to be forced onto someone. As a kid, some of my parents didn't even want me, despite volunteering to take me in. And that's what it all boils down to, right? That's what my therapists always asked—how was my childhood?

Not worse than any other kid in the foster care system. But I made the worst out of the situation instead of the best, and now I'm a dysfunctional young adult. And Rhys is the sorry soul cursed with me.

The gaping rift ripples before me, and I take Rhys' wrist mostly out of necessity. I've never traveled with another person before, so I'm really hoping this works. The tree wouldn't suggest it otherwise, right?

"We will meet again, Maria Rochester," the Wisdom Tree says, branches waving as Rhys and I pass through the portal.

I don't have it in me to say goodbye.

When we get to the other side of the rift, we're not back in the Everwildes. We're not by the lake, either. We're in the Infinity Hallway. The white halls haven't become any less uncomfortable to look at, each end of the hallway going on seemingly forever.

Now, suddenly, everything is clicking into place. How Rhys gets to the future...

"Ah, Mar. I was wondering when you were coming by," Jenna Cooper greets. She's in her late twenties now, her long brown hair braided over her shoulder. She's not wearing a business suit like last time, but her dress and heels are still quite professional. The bag of pretzels in her hand, however, is not. "Rhys Torren. Is this the first time we've met? I'm Jenna."

"I'm Todd." Todd Glass, the skinny human boy from the ship, introduces himself. He's young now, compared to other times I've seen him, with the same dark hair and spray of freckles across his face. He wears a polo and khaki shorts. "Mar, are you alright? You look pale."

With a trembling hand, I take out the Linguist's Orb and hand it to Rhys. He just stares at it in his palm, like he doesn't know what he's looking at. I think we're both in a state of shock.

"I was wondering when you two would pop up," I say with a shaking voice. "I didn't think you would even make an appearance at this point. But I guess here we are, with your timing just as convenient as ever."

"Wow, you're in a pissy mood. Total 360 from what we just saw."

"Jenna, it's a 180, not a 360."

"Details." She shrugs. "What did they say about the sword? Where is it?"

"The lake I landed in when I first got here," I answer absentmindedly. "It doesn't matter."

"It does, actually." Jenna looks between Rhys and me. "Oh. I guess you figured out where this is heading, huh, Mar?"

"Yeah, well. It's not hard to put two and two together. I guess I'm growing," I say. Not in a good way. "Rhys, this is the part where Jenna and Todd take you to the future. The part where you endure years of servitude and suffering, only to die at the hands of some crazed bitch."

Rhys shakes his head. "We should discuss what the Wisdom Tree said. I do not believe you are thinking about this rationally."

"Probably not," I agree. "I feel *sick* over this, Rhys. I can't believe that this is what fate has in store for you. You deserve *so* much better. And I want to give it to you, but I can't. All I can ask is that you refuse, right here, right now.

Don't go to the future. I promise I will find a way to let you live a happy, healthy, full life no matter what—so choose yourself, Rhys. If you pick me, you will be miserable."

"As touching as this moment is, Mar, we don't have time for it," Jenna interjects, opening a door in front of me. "Let's go."

"Wait—"

But Jenna pulls me forward, and the last thing I see is Rhys reaching toward me.

CHAPTER TWENTY-FIVE

"What the fuck, you bitch!" I scream. "I was just talking to Rhys. Did you have to cut me off like that?"

"Wow. You were *way* nicer when you were Mary Alice," Jenna says with a snort. She holds the bag of pretzels out to me. "Pretzel?"

I smack them to the ground and stomp on them.

"Hey!"

"Go back," I demand. "Go back right now and tell Todd not to screw with Rhys. He should be allowed to make his own decisions. I don't care what anyone else says—not the tree, not the Timekeepers, and certainly not you and Todd."

"Haven't you ever heard the saying, 'Free will is the greatest illusion'?" Jenna leaps back as I take a swing at her. "Wow, I never knew you had such a violent temper!"

"Fuck off."

"*Language.*"

"Kindly fuck off."

She's brought me to the lake, where this whole adventure began. Surrounded by the Everwildes, the lake is peaceful like I remember, and the sky is cloudless and blue. A brighter blue than in the mortal realm, I note. Far brighter than what I've seen of the modern-day Veil. But the cheery atmosphere doesn't match my mood at all. I just want to throttle her for cutting me off, especially since that might be the last interaction I have with Rhys.

Beyond Jenna is the door to the Infinity Hallway, standing freely on the shore. It's open just a crack, but before I can sprint toward it, she steps in front of me and glares.

"You know what you have to do, Mar." Jenna picks up the crushed bag of pretzels off the ground.

I do—but that doesn't make me any less angry. Not just because of her—I'm also angry at myself. Notice a pattern?

I'm a *time traveler.* I should have plenty of time, and yet I am constantly running out of it.

"You want to go home, right?" Jenna goads.

"Southeastern isn't my home," I spit. I don't know if I'll ever get to go back *home* again. Not after what the Wisdom Tree told me.

But without Rhys here, there's nothing left for me but the sword. I should be grateful I don't have to wrestle a beastblood for it—all I need to do is bleed. And I'm already doing that.

I walk to the water's edge, hold my bloody palm out, and let a drop fall. Just a single drop doesn't work, though, so I have to cut open my other palm. My hand stings as I squeeze my eyes shut, envisioning the Divinities Sword rising from the water.

The ground beneath me begins to shake. My eyes fly open and I fling my arms and legs out, trying to steady myself as the water in the lake begins to go down like a sink drain.

"I didn't just irreparably damage the ecosystem, right?" I call Jenna, turning around. "Jenna?"

What the hell? That bitch is gone! She just disappeared! The doorway to the Infinity Hallway is gone, too.

"Jenna!" I screech again, but she doesn't come back.

In front of me, the lake is nearly drained. I begin walking, crossing the sand until I reach the center. There's not a single dead fish or animal at the bottom, and thankfully no dead truebloods, either. Instead, there's a gaping rift.

Um, didn't I just envision the sword coming out of the water? Isn't that how spells are supposed to work — I use my blood, think hard about what I want, and then it happens?

There's no way I'm going into that rift, right?

I search the lake for the sword, hoping desperately I'll find it trapped somewhere in the sand, but there's nothing. All that's left is the rift.

The surface is reflective, like a mirror, and I can't see through to the other side. I stick a long branch in, just to make sure I won't be jumping into a pool of acid, but it comes out clean and dry. That's as much reassurance as I'll get.

I now have two options:

1. Go into the rift and hope the sword is there

2. Leave without the sword and face the consequences with Neil

Damn it. I can't go back empty-handed. The Wisdom Tree told me that I'm not meant to use the sword, but the Time Agents seem to want me to. Well, even if I can't use the sword, I might be able to find someone who can. And it will buy me time with Neil.

Ripping off the metaphorical Band-Aid, I jump into the rift. No time like the present.

Wind pushes back my hair as I pass through, landing on my feet. The air is crisp and cold, a thick fog settling over what appears to be a forest. I can barely make out the trees around me.

A light shines up ahead, and I follow it to a house. The walls look like white stucco with dark wooden beams and a curved roof. A lantern hangs by the wooden door, the source of the light. Not hearing anyone, I open the door quietly and creep inside.

The furniture is all hardwood, as are the floors. There aren't many decorations and no photos, but I'm guessing I'm not in modern times yet. Against the far wall, next to the bookshelf and a painted wardrobe, is a table filled with decorations. Mounted on a wooden stand in the middle of it all is a sword.

I know it's the Divinities Sword from the moment I lay eyes on it, though it's different from the replica I saw in the Veil. A red tassel hangs off the hilt, vibrant vermillion, with a jade bead and a silver bell attached. The blade has an engraving on it, but unlike the depictions of the Divinities Sword, the "spell" carved in the blade isn't a simple squiggly line. It's some sort of East Asian script. Considering the fact that I'm culturally ignorant, I'm not going to just *guess* where it's from. But it's definitely not a squiggle.

The other things laid out on the table with the sword make me pause. A battle rattle. A doll. A jade bracelet. A small dress. A tiny pair of embroidered shoes. These are baby gifts. The sword is probably meant for a child when she grows up.

But I need the sword *now*. For saving the world (probably).

Reaching for it, I grab the hilt and try to take it off the stand, but it's impossibly heavy. It's not any larger than a regular sword, but try as I might, I can't lift it. I end up knocking the gifts to the ground as I struggle, breaking the rattle in half and cracking the bracelet. I nearly drop the blade on my foot, but I manage to bring it to the ground and slide the sheath on. To make matters worse, I'm bleeding everywhere due to the cuts on my hands.

I have to drag the sword across the floor, struggling the entire time to get it out the door and back to the rift. Sweat drips down my back by the time I manage to return to the lake, though the sword doesn't get any easier to carry in the Veil.

Am I just weak? Or is the sword spelled? How am I going to kill Astaroth with this when I can't even lift it?

"You found it!" Jenna squeals, the traitorous bitch having returned. This time, she has an ice cream cone. Despite being exhausted from bringing the sword back, I still have enough energy to knock the cone out of her hand. "Hey!"

"Why did you *leave* me?" I snarl. "I could've used your help!"

"I thought something was going to jump out and attack you," Jenna says bluntly. "I'm not supposed to fight your battles for you, so I left to watch from a safe distance. And you owe me an ice cream cone *and* a new bag of pretzels."

"You'll be waiting forever."

"At least get me some hardcore yaoi manga."

"I don't know what that is, and I don't want to," I say dryly.

"Is that it?" Jenna asks, pointing to the sword on the ground. She doesn't wait for me to reply before picking it up, or trying to. It's a bit gratifying to see her struggle with it, too. "Oh wow. That is *really* heavy."

"No kidding."

"Well, buck up. You're almost finished. I'll bring you back to your correct time. I think you'd pass out from blood loss if you tried to open another portal."

"Thanks." My hands are already a mess, and now that I've been struggling with the sword, they're throbbing.

Jenna opens the door to the Infinity Hallway, helping me drag and kick the sword with us. I know it's kind of disrespectful to treat the sword this way, but it's just not easy to carry.

Back inside, Todd greets us. My heart deflates a little when I see that he's alone.

"Where did Rhys go, Todd?" I ask him. I try to prop the sword against the wall, but it falls to the ground with a heavy thud. "You didn't force him into the future, did you?"

"We can't *force* him, Mar." Todd shakes his head. "You'll figure that out sooner or later."

"You still have your mission," Jenna adds. "Go back, find Astaroth, and kill him. Now that you have the sword, things should go a lot more smoothly."

I point to it on the ground. "*You* can't even lift that, Jenna. How am I going to kill Astaroth with a sword I can't carry?"

"You'll figure it out...somehow." Jenna shakes her head. "Unfortunately, that's one thing we're not privy to, so you don't have to look so pissed off. We're not being mysterious on purpose."

I beg to differ.

But the Wisdom Tree said the sword is a blind spot; I guess this is what it meant. Not only did Jenna and Todd not know where it was, but they also can't see how I'm going to use it. *If* I even can.

"I'll figure it out? That's the best advice you can give me?" I ask, letting the frustration fully seep into my voice. I know it's not Jenna and Todd's fault—they're just following orders. But I need to lash out at someone, and they're easy targets right now. "I don't know *anything*. No one will give me straight answers. The Wisdom Tree told me things I can't comprehend, and I still haven't gotten answers from *you* about what happened on the ship."

"What happened on the ship?"

"Are you playing dumb right now, Jenna? You tried to *kill* me. You're a *necromancer*, you made a zombie who looks like Provost Mathers, you attacked and drugged me, and now you're here trying to help me. I don't understand."

"Didn't you hear enough from the talking tree?" Jenna mocks, her frustration matching my own. She puts her hands on her hips, brow creasing. "You're *special*, Mar. I told you before. When the Timekeepers created the world and everyone in it, they wrote out every single event that would happen like a novel. They had lists of everyone who would ever be born, how their lives would play out, and all the nitty gritty details. But something changed, and they began making edits to the manuscript. They wrote *you* into existence. You're the reason this hallway exists. You're the reason Todd's fate was rewritten, ending in an early grave.

You're the reason *I* was born in the first place. Without you, the world is going to end."

That's the opposite of what the Wisdom Tree told me.

"I've known about my fate since I was a kid, Mar," Jenna says gravely. "You want to know why I joined the cult of Astaroth? Because I *founded* the cult. I used the hallway and blood magic to gain powers and organize a rebellion of Time Agents against the Timekeepers. Against *you*. I wanted to kill you before you fulfilled your destiny."

"Jenna," Todd warns, "you need to calm down."

Jenna isn't listening. "I'm sorry. Is that what you want to hear? It wasn't *personal*. Despite what you might believe, I have a certain fondness for you, Mar. But I knew what I was in store for, and I hated it. I thought I could change things if you died because you're the reason everything is happening right now. You were *chosen*."

"I didn't ask to be chosen. Not by fate, anyway. I just want to go home."

"I know. I'm sorry." This time when she says it, I truly think she means it. "But if someone asked *you* to go back in time and save Neil's life, would you? Would you help him knowing that he kills Luke in the future?"

"Neil?" My heart lurches in my chest. "I might be a horrible person, but he has crossed a line that I would never touch."

"I know you wouldn't do something like that on purpose. But that doesn't change anything," Jenna says sadly. "I tried to scare you off the ship. I tried to hurt you, and then, yes, I tried to kill you. But now I see that nothing I've done has made a difference. I played right into the Timekeeper's hands. It took me years, but I finally accept my fate. You have nothing to fear from me anymore."

Not because she doesn't *want* to kill me still, I note. Clearly, if she could do something about my fate, Jenna would. She sounds more dejected than anything else.

"Jenna, what am I supposed to do to you? What is written in my fate that you're so scared of?"

She smiles, opening another door in the hall. "You're going to go back to the future. You're going to take that sword, and you're going to kill my dad. And I get to watch, knowing I did whatever I could to help you do it."

CHAPTER TWENTY-SIX

The doorway brings me through the front door of the Foley-Hill Plantation. A baby statue is the first thing to greet me, its white plastic face contorted in a painful screech. The head is attached to a metal spider's body, hanging from the ceiling in place of a chandelier. I have to walk under it to leave, dragging the Divinities Sword along with me across the marble floor.

I follow the classical music to the dining room. The curtains are drawn back, revealing a bright and sunny day in Georgia. Neil sits at the head of the table, basking in the sunlight with a newspaper. A breakfast spread sits untouched, clearly too much for one person to eat.

I take a seat beside Neil, flipping over a glass and pouring myself ice water from an ornate pitcher. One of the household staff members eyes me curiously, but due to Neil's complete lack of a reaction, the man doesn't say anything.

"Can I have a glass of sweet tea, please?" I ask him, my stomach grumbling.

The older man looks to Neil for guidance. My biological father lowers his paper, glances at me, and then says, "Go ahead. Bring a washcloth for her hands, too."

The man nods and heads to the kitchen. A moment later, a young woman brings me a warm, damp towel in a bowl.

"Thanks." I take the towel from her and pat my hands, which are caked in dry blood. Wincing, I wipe my hands and face clean.

"I take it the trip went well?" Neil asks casually. He wears a navy suit, his blonde hair slicked back and his tie securely fastened. Does he have somewhere to be? Because he certainly isn't acting like it. Maybe he dresses like this all the time.

"I didn't get eaten," I offer, spooning eggs onto my plate. They're still warm, thankfully. There's nothing worse than cold eggs. "I got the sword."

"Hmm. Did you see anything interesting?"

"Not really."

"Where was the sword?"

"Under a lake."

"How long were you in the past?"

"I don't know. I didn't have a phone." I shrug, buttering a piece of toast. The male staff member brings me my sweet tea and I down the whole glass before continuing to speak. "I got my period a few times, but my schedule has been completely messed up by time travel."

Neil is completely unruffled. "I imagine that was unpleasant."

"It was," I agree. "I need a bath. How long have I been gone?"

"Oh, just a little bit over a year," Neil replies.

"A *year*?" My eyes widen. I didn't think that much time would have passed.

What about David? He was ten when I left him. He's probably grown so much now, and I missed it. And Tasha is already in her second year of college.

I'm technically still in my *first* year. And I missed my nineteenth birthday. I'm going to be *twenty* this spring.

"Not much has changed," Neil continues. "Except, perhaps, that you missed the first death anniversary of Luke Porter. What a shame. They're still looking for his killer, you know."

My entire body freezes. He's just trying to get a rise out of me—and it's working. How *dare* he bring up Luke? I didn't think Neil cared enough to taunt me, especially not like this. But now he's watching me, amused, waiting to see what I'll do. He *wants* me to explode in anger, and I wouldn't want to disappoint him.

I throw the plate of eggs at the window, shattering both the plate and the glass. The pancakes are next, followed by the fruit bowl. I don't care if it's hurting my hands or if none of this makes a difference. He's rich and he can get anything I break fixed as if nothing happened—I'm well aware. But I can't attack him; I don't have a death wish *just* yet. All I can do is play into his hands by throwing a massive tantrum.

To my surprise, Neil begins laughing. He takes the water pitcher and smashes it against an ugly painting on the wall. This only serves to piss me off further, because whatever pain he causes me is just a game to him.

It feels good to see his things break, to destroy them with my own bloody hands. Literally bloody—the wounds have reopened yet again. After I'm finished, there's nothing left on the table. Food covers every surface of the dining room, the tablecloth has been ripped off, the windows are smashed, and the staff members have fled. All Neil can do is smile in the middle of the room, satisfied by the carnage we've caused.

"As much as I've enjoyed this father-daughter time with you, unfortunately there are other matters I must attend to," Neil tells me calmly. "Clean yourself up and take a rest upstairs. I've had a proper room prepared for you. Now that you are my daughter, to keep up appearances, I'll be forced to treat you better. Consider it a reward for bringing back the sword."

"What happens next?" I ask dully.

"I'll need a few days to prepare the paperwork, but you will be re-enrolling in Southeastern University with your older sister. The semester starts at the end of the month, but due to certain circumstances, Nic and Allegra have been taking a winter hunting course for extra credits and are already at school. You, my dear, will be able to move in close to the beginning of the semester. Use the time to prepare for your upcoming courses. You'll be taken out of remedial classes and placed with the general population. And despite being my daughter, you are still a bastard. Trust me when I tell you that no one will welcome you back with open arms but me."

How could I expect anything different?

MY NEW BEDROOM HAS A PRIVATE BATHROOM, WITH heated floor tiles and a soaking tub with jets. Now that I'm officially recognized as Neil's daughter, the staff have gone above and beyond, bending over backward for me. They even prepared my bath while I was in the shower, filling it with fresh flower petals and salts. By the time I get out and dry off, I smell like I've just blossomed.

After getting dressed in a clean set of clothes and having my hands bandaged, one of the female staff members comes in to take away my dirty laundry. Unfortunately, I left most of my supplies with Rhys' horse, which is still in the Everwildes.

"Miss Maria, there were boxes of your things collected from the guest house and dormitory last year," the middle-aged woman says nervously. "We were ordered not to touch anything. They're still stored away. Would you like to go through them?"

"Sure. Thank you," I say politely.

"Mr. Abbott also informed us that he is issuing you a black card. His secretary should be getting that for you soon, but until then, he said that I should accompany you to the mall tomorrow and purchase a new cell phone and laptop for you for school."

Seriously? I know he's rich, but he was pretty tight-fisted about money before. He didn't give me anything. It's suspicious that he would want to provide for me now.

"You represent the Abbott family now," the woman explains, noting my confused expression. "He cannot be looked down upon, even if you are illegitimate. Pardon the language, miss. I am to take you to several beauty and spa appointments as well, in preparation for school."

"Thanks for the heads up. Can my boxes be brought to my room? I'd like to go through them in private." Not that I have anything private in there.

The woman nods. "Of course. Let me arrange that for you immediately."

And by "immediately," she really *means* "immediately." Within minutes, cardboard boxes are hauled into my new bedroom and set down by the desk while I sit on the bed watching television. Once everything is inside, the staff members give me privacy and close the door.

I turn on a sitcom for background noise and walk over to one of the boxes. None of them are labeled, but there are only about ten of them. I open the first box and find that it's clothing from my dorm. I throw half of the clothes in the laundry bin and the other half away—some of them are cut up, presumably by my oh-so-kind roommates. The dress Archer gave me for the Halloween dance is in another box, but it didn't even fit right. I'll have it washed and donated.

I'm not looking forward to seeing him again. Or anyone at Southeastern, really. I'm relieved that Allegra and Nic aren't here. Despite Neil's presence, at least he's leaving me alone.

While I go through my things, I make a list of supplies I'll need for school. I'm worried that Neil is going to make me pay him back somehow if I spend any of his money, but I don't have any of my own, and I don't have a job. The last time I tried to get one, I was shot at by Faith. So I've decided that I'm only going to buy things I absolutely need.

Going through the final box, underneath another pile of cut-up clothes is a wooden box I don't recognize. A tree is carved into the top, with five rubies embedded in it. I set it down carefully on my desk and open it. Inside, there must be hundreds of envelopes, all addressed to me. Maria is written in big, loopy cursive.

I cautiously pick one up, dated back to three years ago. Opening it, I read the contents carefully. It's in Elvish, so I have to go slowly.

Tears prick my eyes, but I take a deep breath and put the letter back in the envelope and begin reading another. And another, and another. Like a woman possessed, I read every letter in that box. By dawn, I've finished, and I've added one more thing to my list of supplies: a set of stationery.

THE NEXT FEW WEEKS ARE A WHIRLWIND. NEIL WANTS ME to look better, so he makes appointments for me to go to the hairdresser, nail salon, dermatologist, dentist—everything you can think of. He even hired a personal trainer to come in and help me lose my cheese weight.

You'd think doing all this would garner some goodwill between Neil and me, but instead, I'm just resentful of the wealthy. Because I've never looked better in my life.

What the hell? So all I needed was *money* to be pretty? I'm not even wearing a lot of makeup. I don't need to, thanks to the fancy (and painful) skincare treatments, eyelash extensions, and microblading. And my hair? Totally shiny. It's still shoulder-length and dyed dark, but I have no split ends and it actually feels *soft*. I don't have any product in it, but after a keratin treatment, my hair is frizz-less even in the Georgia humidity.

I'm a brand-new girl when I get off the ferry on Kingsmarch Island. And at the same time, I'm still just Maria. Hopefully that will be enough for what I have to do this semester.

Dragging my luggage behind me, I follow the map on my phone to my new dorm house. It's a white Victorian with a rose bush outside, the flowers in full bloom. Just like me.

My heart pounds as I walk up the sidewalk, my heels clicking on the ground. The necklace Rhys gave me feels warm against the hollow of my throat, my very own protection amulet. I'm not sure if it actually has powers, but it gives me the courage I need to continue.

Last semester, I was thrown into a world I knew very little about. Now, armed with more knowledge and a very powerful sword, I'm ready for a new chapter.

I raise my hand to the door and knock.

Maria,

I am unsure whether or not you will receive these letters. My hope is that you will, one day, and we can read them together. After you recover from your anger, of course.

As you might have guessed, I have chosen to follow you into the future. Siraye and the others will still be alive and well, but I cannot wait centuries to meet you again. I have been given three years until you turn eighteen and board the SS Athena. Three years to become fluent in English and find employment with Neil.

I impatiently wait until I can see you once more. You will not remember me, but I will do my utmost to keep you safe and ensure the timeline remains unchanged. This means I cannot be too familiar with you. Forgive me if I am cordial. Understand that behaving in such a way is all I can do to put distance between us, though my heart desires the opposite.

Not because a sentient tree said so, or because the fates willed it. No matter what the circumstances will be, I am yours eternally.

Rhys

EPILOGUE

A llegra Abbott knew from a very early age that she was fated to die young. Everybody told her so, and perhaps that was why she felt "special." Unlike everyone else, she knew her time was limited and did her utmost to live life to the fullest.

That was easy to do, considering the Abbott family's wealth. She wore the nicest clothes — as long as they covered her scars and wounds — and was doted upon by her parents. She had a goal as well: become her father's heir before she died. A noble, if not lofty, endeavor. Everyone had to have something to work toward, or so she thought.

That was not to say Allegra had a carefree life. Her illness took its toll on her body, along with the secrets surrounding it. The shame of being born invalid. She smothered it as best she could, but ableism was ripe in the shadowborn community.

Still, Allegra was more often content than not, despite her own frustrations with the body she was cursed with.

Weak, vulnerable, and defenseless. At least, she reasoned, she had people around her who loved her.

And then Mary Alice Rochester—or *Maria*—showed up and ruined everything. Allegra lost her mother. She lost Rhys. She would not lose her father, too.

She stormed up the stairs of the Foley-Hill Plantation, past the very spot her mother died, and swept into her father's study without knocking.

Neil looked up from his desk, surprised. "Allegra? Where on earth are your manners?"

"Father, it's about Maria," she began. "I know you told me not to, but I—"

"A sentence should *end* with that, Allegra. Not begin with it," Neil chided, leaning back in his chair. "I told you not to do something, so you are not to do it. I believe the rules of this household have been made clear to you."

"This is important," Allegra stressed, on the verge of tears. Ever since her mother died, at the hands of her father no less, their relationship had been strained. Rightfully so, though Allegra thought *she* should have been the one upset about it. Instead, her father seemed to lose patience rapidly with her.

She didn't understand why. Maria was gone. And if Allegra was being completely honest with herself, her father was the one who killed her mother. Not Maria. But Allegra needed to place blame on someone, and at the time, Maria was an easy target. An outsider.

"What is it, then?" Neil asked, exasperated. He raked a hand through his blonde hair, staring at his daughter coldly. "Speak your piece."

She didn't need to speak. She threw a manila folder on his desk, just as dramatically as she'd pictured doing before coming in. She went over the scenario countless times in her head, but never thought…

Neil raised his brows and opened the folder, glancing at the single-page letter typed inside. Then, as if nothing were wrong, he dropped the letter directly into his shredder.

"Hey—" Allegra began, but Neil's glare silenced her.

"This changes nothing," Neil snarled. "If it does, then you won't like the outcome, I assure you. Have you told anyone?"

"No, but aren't you going to explain that to me?"

"Do I owe you an explanation?" He laughed. "My darling *daughter*, I owe you nothing. Things will continue to progress, and when Maria returns, you will keep an eye on her as promised. Or do you want to end up like your mother?"

Allegra recoiled. Her father had never spoken to her like that before. Tears stung the back of her eyes, and pathetically, she fled the study. Running to her room, she shut the door behind her and flung herself onto her bed.

In the corner of the room, something moved. A chair scraped the floor. Allegra lifted her head, startled. And then, she smiled.

"What? Come here to gloat?" she asked, the bitterness seeping into her voice. It was yet another thing she hated Maria for. Before *she* came along, Allegra was always able to hide her emotions. Now, they overwhelmed her with their intensity.

Nic Woolridge stepped out from the shadows, wearing the same insincere smile he usually did. "I didn't come to gloat. I just came to confirm something."

"Well, you were right." Her father didn't even deny what was in the envelope. Instead, he threatened her, which made

Allegra even more convinced that the letter was true. That Nic was actually correct, that it was all some twisted conspiracy by Neil Abbott.

That Allegra was just...

"Of course I was right," Nic concluded, crossing his arms. "The question is, what are you going to do about it?"

Allegra hesitated. "When do you think Maria is coming back?"

"I don't know. She left months ago. Maybe she's already dead."

"No. She isn't." Allegra didn't know for sure, but she had a *feeling* her so-called sister was still alive and kicking. "We need to move before Maria returns. I'll do whatever you say — I just want my body fixed."

"Even if it means defying fate itself?"

Allegra nodded slowly. "Fuck fate. I'm doing things my way."

Nic's grin widened. "Good girl. We'll begin tonight."

Dear Ms. Abbott,

The Northeastern College, Elisa Goldberg College of Genetic Sciences, has processed your request. Based on the DNA analysis of the provided specimen, there is no evidence that the Alleged Sister [Allegra Abbott] is the biological sister of Maria Rochester.

Details are attached.

Sincerely,
Sabine Everleigh, Ph.D.
Professor and Research Lead
Elisa Goldberg College of Genetic Sciences
Northeastern College of Magic

Special Content: Rhys
Just in Time, Chapter 18

Nothing quite prepared him for seeing her again. Rhys Torren spent three years thinking about it, with both longing and dread. Longing, because for gods' sake it was *Maria*. And dread, because now, he would have to pretend like they were strangers.

But when he caught sight of her boarding the ship, his heart felt like it was finally beating again. He could feel it in his chest, pounding so hard it might burst.

She was the most beautiful woman he had ever laid eyes on. It was silly to even *think*, much less admit aloud, but it was true. He hadn't seen her in years, but now that she was in front of him, not just a memory, he was struck dumb by her appearance.

Her hair was longer, darker, and her eyes were a rich shade of brown. She glanced around the lobby, lost for a moment, before she noticed the elevators to the side. Rhys' eyes followed her retreating form as she made her way toward the elevators.

They encountered each other several times after that,

though just in passing, and always from a distance. The closest they came to seeing each other was in the infirmary, when Maria was looking for the restroom. Separated by just a thin curtain, Rhys wanted to introduce himself. But he didn't know what would happen if he acted according to his desires.

Maria had explicitly told him that he was to be cold to her. He didn't smile at her, nor did he laugh or behave in an overly familiar way. This was probably for the best, but Rhys still didn't like it. Especially not with that awful Archer Kinsey sleazing about, *exposing* himself like a pervert to *his* Maria. The thought of it made Rhys insatiably angry, but he couldn't very well beat the boy senseless. Even if he desperately wanted to.

Nic Woolridge was another fly buzzing around Maria, his own *cousin*. Sort of. Rhys loathed Nic more than any man before, even perhaps Prince Gwyn.

Rhys waited as Maria had bid him to, however. And then the Fourth of July came, and Rhys wound up alone with her in the sickbay. *Handcuffed to a bed*, prone and unconscious.

It was not *his* idea to handcuff her. That idiot Kinsey suggested it, and everyone else agreed. Yet another reason Rhys wanted to punch Archer straight in the face. But he was too preoccupied with Maria at the moment.

She woke with a groan, the handcuffs shaking as she moved.

"Fuck," she muttered under her breath. It was a slip of the tongue, a breach in character that made Rhys smile.

Sitting up, she looked herself over, turning her arms and twisting her legs to see how badly she was injured.

Rhys held up a book to his face in a weak attempt to

shield himself from her. He couldn't control his expression and was concerned she would find the look of utter relief on his face odd. They weren't supposed to know each other.

He thought he would be able to hide his emotions from her upon their reunion, but he wasn't as disciplined as he originally thought. Not around *her*.

"Stop moving around," he commanded, his heart leaping to his throat. This was the first time he was speaking to her in her mother tongue, without the Linguist's Orb. "I can hear the handcuffs rattle. It is rather annoying."

Maria immediately replied, "Not a problem. Just uncuff me and I'll be on my merry way."

The sound of her voice sent a chill down his spine, and he wondered how she managed to have such an effect on him. He tried to ignore her, turning a page in the book he was clearly not reading.

Maria huffed and stood on shaking legs, steadying herself with the bed rail. She moved across the room, rummaging through the drawers in search of something.

"What are you doing?" Rhys asked, trying to keep his voice level.

"Trying to get these handcuffs off," she replied, as if the answer was obvious.

"You will not be able to. Just wait here patiently. This is the safest place to be, for now." Rhys would make sure of it.

Maria had told him a lot about the future, but she was sparse with details when it came to her time on the ship. Rhys wasn't sure how he was "supposed" to behave, so he merely followed her general guidelines: be cold (in a sexy way) and don't smile. He had to convince Maria that he was indifferent to her, when in fact the opposite was true.

He remembered their last few interactions, the look of

concern etched deeply into her face as she admitted her anxieties to him. Now, in the future, he wanted to reassure her that his feelings hadn't changed—that he didn't regret a single thing. But the current Maria before him had no memory of him, and no love for him, either.

"No," Maria said. She fumbled around the room for the light switch, unsuccessfully flicking it on and off.

"The power is out," Rhys said. "That is another reason why I suggested you remain here."

"Handcuffed."

"Yes."

"And if someone comes in and attacks me?" Maria challenged. This version of her was more guarded than the one he first met, as if there was a wall of ice between them.

"I will shield you." It wasn't even a question.

"Why?" she asked, curiosity lighting up her voice. "Who *are* you? How do I know you're not my enemy?"

Because he could *never* be her enemy. Rhys wanted to tell her that. Instead, he said coldly, "I may not be your friend, but you can trust that I am not your enemy."

"Prove it. Uncuff me."

"You are persistent." He liked that about her. "I have been instructed not to."

"Do you always do what you're told?" she teased.

A smile tugged at the corners of his lips. "Sixty percent of the time. The provost has instructed me to keep an eye on you, despite my protests. Everyone else is busy, it seems, rounding up the cultists who attacked the ship."

"And have they been successful?"

No. The ship was currently in total chaos. No one was prepared for the attack, which made Rhys' head spin. He knew this was a pilot program, but the shadowborn were incredibly arrogant when dealing with humans. Most thought of them as "lesser beings," even though shadowborn weren't particularly powerful. Humans had guns, which leveled the playing field considerably.

But Rhys didn't particularly care about any of the shadowborn on the ship. Allegra, perhaps. He had grown fond of the girl, in a platonic way. She was sweet but too naïve. She lacked knowledge of the world in a way that was almost proactively oblivious, and despite her intelligence, she was culturally ignorant. Neil's fault, mostly. Rhys worked to get Allegra off the ship as quickly as possible so he could focus his attention on Maria.

This version of Maria was special. She knew nothing of magic or the shadowborn—she thought herself to be human. Her desperation to escape the ship, and her desire to return home, made his heart ache for her.

"I have not received word from anyone since arriving here with you," Rhys answered finally.

Just as he said that, the door to the infirmary opened. A cultist in black robes paused in the doorway before lunging toward Maria. Rhys grabbed ahold of her, reaching her first with his inhuman speed. He covered her eyes, pulling her toward his chest and grasping the chain of her handcuffs.

The handcuffs melted off her thin wrist and turned into a sword, just in time to deflect the cultist's blow. Rhys spun Maria behind him, shoving the cultist against the door. Maria, her vision impaired, ran over with a fire extinguisher and knocked the cultist in the head.

Rhys quickly turned the sword back into the set of handcuffs and let them drop to the ground.

"Do you have a flashlight?" she asked casually, as if she hadn't just hit a man over the head hard enough to kill him.

Well, his Maria was always braver than she gave herself credit for.

Rhys fought a smile, turning around so she wouldn't see. "No."

Maria dragged the body toward the window to get a better look at his face. When she didn't recognize him, she began to pat him down for weapons, finding a knife in his pocket. Of course, she took it for herself. His Maria was always so resourceful.

"We should go," she said. He loved how she used *we*. For a long time, he wondered if they would ever be "we" again. "Before anyone else comes."

"Where, exactly, do you plan on going?" Rhys asked.

Her silence said all he needed to know: Maria had no idea what she was doing.

"I'm not going to be a sitting duck," Maria argued. "You can send the provost my apologies."

"How? I will be coming with you," Rhys replied.

"I didn't invite you," Maria pointed out, though her words weren't barbed. They were more...teasing.

Rhys resisted the urge to laugh. "I'm well aware."

"I don't trust you."

"You would be a fool if you did," said Rhys. "I imagine you do not know who I am."

"Should I?" she asked.

"Not now, no." Someday, though. Soon. And until that day, Rhys would be at her side as much as he could, preparing her for what was to come.

"Why are you facing the window?" Maria asked, not beating around the bush.

He adored her honesty, even though she thought of them as strangers. But he wasn't prepared for the question, and fumbled out a reply. "I do not want you to see my face. I'm…ugly."

"That's the stupidest lie I've ever heard."

"It might be a lie, but I have my reasons. None of which I can disclose to you at this time."

"So, let me get this straight: you can't show me your face because of secret reasons you can't tell me now, but plan to in the future?"

"I do not *plan* to tell you. You'll figure it out on your own. Now, must we waste more time on this meaningless bickering?"

"Bickering? Can't you tell that I'm flirting with you?" Maria asked.

His heart stuttered. He knew she only said it as a joke, but still…

"If we're going to go together, give me a reason to trust you," she continued.

"The provost tasked me with keeping you safe," Rhys lied, knowing just what to say to get her to believe him. "If I fail, I will be punished. There is no reason I could give you to trust me, a stranger, but trust that I will protect my own self-interest."

Maria considered this an acceptable answer. "You're going to lead me off the ship, then. You take point."

Rhys was careful when walking around her, not wanting to show his face. Maria followed close behind; he could feel her presence at his back.

"What should I call you?" she asked.

"If I do not want to show you my face, does it make sense that I would reveal my name?"

"I thought you were hiding your face because you're 'ugly.'"

"And I thought we both agreed that was a lie."

"Touché."

They continued down the silent, dark hallway. Maria stumbled behind him as they drew closer to the lobby, so he reached behind and took Maria's wrist, guiding it to the wall.

This was unfortunately where they had to part. Rhys knew Maria would be safe in (ugh) Archer Kinsey's presence, and as much as it killed him to leave her, he had to before the lights turned on. It would be a while until they could meet again, but next time, he believed he would finally be able to introduce himself.

It didn't matter if she didn't remember him now. She would, one day. And until then, Rhys would continue to protect her from the shadows.

Glossary

Astaroth: A powerful demon known for practicing blood magic. Astaroth was once imprisoned in a time prison, but due to certain events, was released. He has a cult following in the mortal realm.

Beastblood: Non-humanoid creatures originating in the Veil. They are often associated with animalistic traits and remain within the Veil, usually unable to get to the mortal realm on their own. Some examples of Beastbloods include lycans, chimera, and dragons.

Elves: Truebloods with a distinctive appearance characterized by elongated ears. They possess the innate ability to distinguish truth from lies. In addition, Elves can wield elemental magic, enabling them to control and manipulate natural elements such as air, water, fire, or earth.

Fae: Winged truebloods who inhabit a continent alongside the elves, with whom they are in constant conflict. Fae are known for their trickery and manipulation, and they have elemental magic. They are physically incapable of lying and must always speak the truth, which often leads them to use clever wordplay and misdirection instead.

Infinity Hallway: A corridor used by time agents to travel through time. It contains multiple doorways, each leading to a different point in history or the future. However, the hallway can be dangerous to humans and may cause madness or disorientation to those who stay for extended periods.

Linguist's Orb: A fae device capable of instantly translating any language. It was created because Fae speak many different mutually unintelligible dialects.

Magician: The offspring of two shadowborn. Generally, magic weakens as the generations are mixed with human genes. Magicians can perform spells, although their abilities are not as potent as those of shadowborn. They cannot open rifts like their shadowborn counterparts.

Mortal Realm: The realm where humans and non-magical creatures live. It is separate from the Veil and lacks the magical properties and creatures that exist in other realms.

Psychic: The child of two magicians. While they cannot perform spells, psychics possess limited abilities and are born with a connection to the Veil. They are unable to open rifts, however.

Rift: A magical portal between realms that can be opened by swinging a blade through open air and concentrating on the desired destination. This ability comes easily to most shadowborn, and allows them to travel between the Veil and the mortal realm.

Ruby Council: The governing body of trueblood demons in the Veil. They hold significant political power and are responsible for maintaining order and enforcing laws among demonkind. One of the most powerful and wealthy members of the Ruby Council is Neil Abbott. As a member of the council, he wields a great deal of influence and is respected by many in the demon community.

Shadowborn: A hybrid born from the union of a human and a trueblood, possessing traits from both species. They are considered half-bloods and are often seen as shadows of their trueblood parents. Shadowborn have the ability to open rifts between the mortal realm and the Veil, and are stronger, faster, and more durable than humans. They can also perform magic, with some being born with rare and powerful abilities. Generally, the child of two shadowborn will either be a shadowborn or a magician.

Time Agent: A highly trained agent responsible for maintaining the timeline and ensuring that all events occur as they are supposed to. Time Agents use the Infinity Hallway, a special place that enables them to travel through time and space. They must be well-versed in historical events and possess advanced technology to prevent paradoxes and other disruptions to the timeline.

Time Prison: A highly-secure supernatural prison designed to hold dangerous beings. It's a place where inmates are isolated from the rest of the world and thrown in a different time period, making it nearly impossible for them to escape.

Trueblood: A magical humanoid being originating from the Veil. Truebloods identify themselves with human-categorized monsters such as angels, demons, vampires, shifters, and more. They are not affiliated with any religion. Truebloods can only open rifts from the Veil to the mortal realm but cannot close a rift if they are in the mortal realm. They migrated to the mortal realm during the 1800s. Truebloods possess magical abilities and often hold positions of power and influence in the Veil and mortal realm.

Veil: A mystical realm imbued with magic that is filled with unpredictable and often dangerous forces. It is the birthplace of all truebloods and beastbloods, and it is separated from the mortal realm by a thin barrier that can be traversed by opening a rift.

Wisdom Tree: A sentient and omniscient tree located in the Veil, guarded by three fierce warriors. Although the tree was once thought to be a mere rumor, the grove in which it resides is not difficult to find. However, once you leave the grove, your memories of the tree are erased, making it difficult to recall any information or knowledge gained from the tree.

About the Author

Samantha Gao is a New Adult author with a passion for all things fantasy and paranormal romance. Her writing is fueled by her love for paranormal romance, and she enjoys creating compelling characters that readers can relate to and root for. After graduating from college with a degree in a completely different field, Sam decided to pursue her life-long dream of becoming a writer.

When she's not busy crafting stories that will transport readers to another world, Sam enjoys watching Asian dramas (with subtitles, of course!), listening to music, and indulging in her weakness for chocolate.

Sign up for her newsletter here: subscribepage.io/SamGao

facebook.com/whitemoonlightpress

instagram.com/whitemoonlightpress

amazon.com/author/samgao

bookbub.com/profile/sam-gao

goodreads.com/samgao